The Nostradamus Inheritance

First published in Great Britain
in 1985 by Poplar Press Ltd,
13 Burlington Lodge Studios,
Rigault Road, London SW6 4JJ

Reprinted 1985

ISBN 0 907657 08 7

British Library Cataloguing in Publication Data

Leonard, Raymond.
The Nostradamus Inheritance
I. Title–Nostradamus
823'914[f]
PR6062.E71

Printed in Great Britain by
Redwood Burn Limited
Trowbridge, Wiltshire

The Nostradamus Inheritance

RAYMOND LEONARD

POPLAR PRESS LTD
LONDON

PROLOGUE
In the Beginning

Although the summers were usually blisteringly hot in Salon, on this day a raging thunderstorm accompanied the procession as it approached the cemetery. Through his tears, Chavigny could make out the oxen, searching for footholds in what had been a dusty track only minutes earlier. Chavigny forced his gaze into the water-filled grave, passively awaiting its charge; his eyes focussed on a giant bullfrog, trying to escape the trap from which its blind leap had condemned it. As he watched the frog's vain attempts at freedom, the man took comfort in the knowledge that while his Master's name was chiselled on the tombstone, the mire would never claim his body.

Momentarily, a smile crossed his face at the thought of the dignitaries, trudging respectfully behind an anonymous wretch in a coffin; how could the pauper have dreamt the eminent role he was destined to play in death. But the smile left Chavigny's face when he realised how much he envied the pauper the right to play the Master!

The procession halted, and the coffin was manhandled to its final resting place with what little dignity the conditions allowed. Even the fact that the dignitaries were standing ankle deep in mud, somehow testified to the importance of the occasion. As the priest stubbornly chanted the service across his rain-soaked Bible, Chavigny found himself recalling his first memories, on the disease-infested streets of Paris.

His parents had perished in the plague and he had been as close to death as any five year old could be. Then the Master painstakingly nursed him back to health, before tutoring him for the task he had now inherited, the task that weighed so heavily on this dreadful day.

Chavigny started to shiver at the thought of the vile things which lay ahead. That very night, the enbalming fluid had to be applied to his Master's cold body, before beginning the long journey to the North. And when this final service was completed, Chavigny was destined for a life of poverty as he tried to further the epic task that the Master had started. But much worse than the poverty, was the burden of living out his life with the curse of knowledge, a curse that would be passed on to his son, as yet seven years unborn.

Chavigny mourned as he made his way home from the graveyard. He mourned for his Master, he mourned for himself, but mostly he mourned for distant mankind. With each clinging step, the sky grew ever darker and the rain cascaded down like tears; but was the grief from God, or might the Devil be weeping for a lost disciple?

CHAPTER 1

The tranquility which pervaded Omaha State University bore testimony that the rush of term time had been replaced by the leisurely pace of the summer break. Any academics still on campus had migrated to the Faculty Lounge where they could browse through their journals in air-conditioned coolness.

Seated in an old leather armchair under the portrait of a past Dean was Professor Frank Cooper, his rangy, six foot three frame bent into a posture of deep concentration. Frowning and stroking his nose, he hunched over the book lying open on his lap. Only the occasional, mumbled comment or scribbled note marked the passage of the morning.

'You *still* here, Frank?' Peter North's voice rasped. The Professor lurched upright and his book jolted onto the polished floor, much to the annoyance of the other people in the room.

He wasn't pleased to see Dr. North. In the Professor's experience, only two kinds of 'animales academici' exist; whereas the first retain their love of discovery until the grave, the second resemble a moderately proficient filing system, which wouldn't recognise an original idea if one had the misfortune to enter their heads. The Professor firmly labelled Dr. North as an academic of the second kind.

The newcomer picked up the book from the floor and read its title aloud, '*The Prophecies of Nostradamus*. What's this Frank?' he grinned, 'I didn't know you were into Astrology—I thought Archaeology was your game.'

'It is.'

'Then why in God's name are you reading what some charlatan

wrote centuries ago?'

The Professor gave a non-committal shrug, 'I have my reasons.'

Dr. North laughed out loud, 'You'll be telling me next that you check your horoscope!'

Patiently the Professor shook his head, 'I don't subscribe to horoscopes, but some of the things I've been reading take a lot of explaining.'

Dr. North raised a mocking eyebrow, 'Like what?'

'Like Nostradamus predicting that London would be destroyed by fire in 1666.'

To the Professor's dismay, Dr. North slumped down in the armchair beside him. 'I can see you're really getting hooked on this astrology crap.'

'Wasn't it you who said that a genuine academic keeps an open mind?'

Dr. North changed the subject, 'Anyway, what will you be doing this summer, Frank, digging more burrows in Egypt?'

'No, I've had enough of the desert for a while.'

'Don't tell me you've sold your spade? I know you too well for that.'

'Not sold, only greased. I won't be needing it in Paris with Ian.' The Professor rose to his feet.

'Paris. You lucky dog.' Dr. North's voice overtook the Professor as he was leaving the Lounge, 'Hey, didn't Nostradamus come from Paris?'

The Professor waited until the door had swung shut behind him before muttering, 'No, but he might be buried there!'

As he strolled home through the leafy suburbs, the Professor wondered what Dr. North would have said if he'd known the whole story, 'Boy, would that have convinced him I was going crazy. An academic of my years should know better than to take this kind of letter seriously.' Yet, in the three months since the letter dropped into the mailbox, he had thought of nothing else. 'I must be mad to give up my place on Hammond's Expedition, to go on a wild goose chase to Paris.'

And to make matters worse, he knew precisely what Ann would have said about the letter—'Forget it, Frank, it's probably one of your students with a practical joke. . . Concentrate on writing your books.' But then Ann had always been the practical one, she had even joked that being English and being practical were mutually inclusive.

Now the sight of the rambling, 19th century house at the end of the street brought more memories flooding back. After all, he had used half the money from Ann's life policy to buy the place, a new 'home' for himself and Ian. And now he was eating into the rest of his capital to rush after what might only be a stupid hoax. He shook his head as he walked up to the front door. The Professor made a point of never using credit cards, wearing a watch or carrying keys; so he rang the bell and waited. 'Hi, Brenda, is Ian in?'

The woman gave the brass doorknob a quick polish with her sleeve, 'Ian's always in when normal people are at work, Sir, you know that,' she answered, with the trace of an accent betraying her Irish ancestry. 'He got up early today, eleven o'clock. Said you left him some books to read. You'll find him in the study.'

Brenda was no substitute for Ann in the Professor's eyes but then she wasn't meant to be. The rooms were always spotless, her cooking was good and, best of all, she kept herself to herself. Besides, having an attractive woman around the place gave the house the superficial resemblance of home. Back at the University, Peter North had probingly joked that Brenda looked too good-looking to be wasted as a housekeeper. Yet she had had the job for four years, and there hadn't been a single complaint on either side. Maybe it was because Brenda's age was midway between his own and Ian's that the three of them got on so well; but as a substitute for Ann, that would be asking too much of any woman.

When the Professor entered the study, the only clue to his son's presence was the toe of a sneaker, jutting up from behind a heap of books. Seeing his father's face peering over the pile, Ian diplomatically eased his feet off the desk, 'Hi, Dad, have you got a cure for tired eyes?'

The Professor smiled, 'So you've started to read the books. What do you make of them?'

Ian tossed the book he'd been reading onto the pile, 'Well, until I started working through these books, I'd always thought that astrology was bunk, a sort of prehistoric astronomy.'

'And after reading the books?'

Ian laughed, 'Now I *know* it's bunk. Besides, who cares about the future anyway?'

Ian looked mischievously at his father, 'There's something heavy going down, right? C'mon, you can tell me what it is.'

The Professor hesitated uncomfortably, 'We've never had secrets before, Ian, but I can't let you in on anything until next week. Trust me.'

'You're the guy who pays the bills,' answered Ian, running a comb through his hair. He noticed the book his father was carrying, 'More Nostradamus! You're really sold on astrology then?'

Trying to appear non-committal, the Professor replied, 'Let's say that I've got an open mind, but all these books need reading before our trip to Europe.'

Ian opened his eyes wide, 'All of them?'

The Professor nodded, 'Especially the ones on Nostradamus.'

As the Professor closed the study door, he reflected on the problems that his son had faced since the death of Ann. Ian was barely seventeen when a patrolman, fresh out of police academy, rang the doorbell to report the hit-and-run. The duty sergeant had instructed the patrolman to tell Professor Cooper of the tragedy, so when Ian said his father was out, the man cooked up some story about a parking violation and left.

Determined to prove his initiative, however, and avoid another ten mile round trip, the patrolman finally returned to the Cooper house and told Ian of his mother's death. If the Professor hadn't arrived home early that afternoon, both Ann and Ian would have been lost to him within the space of three hours. As it was, Ian still carried scars on both his wrists.

Fearing that his son would attempt suicide a second time, the Professor had kept a close watch on him. After a few weeks' desolation, however, Ian renewed his studies and threw himself into campus life, joining the college soccer team and assuming a wildly gregarious life style. This image, coupled with his solid, six foot frame and flowing blond hair, had earned him the label of 'Tarzan' from his team mates.

At twenty-three, he graduated in Astronomy from Omaha State University; unfortunately, America was in deep recession and jobs for astronomers weren't easy to come by. So now, at age twenty-four, Ian slept mornings, played racquet ball in the afternoons and stayed out most of the night. Yet, for all his wild image, Ian possessed the same Achilles heels as his father: an inability to talk openly of Ann. At Ian's insistence, there were no pictures of his mother in the Cooper house, nothing existed to rekindle the sorrow of seven years before.

Once in his room, the Professor smiled at the sight of the oddments on his bed. Although he was the veteran of many archaeological expeditions, the preparations had never been this easy. For this trip, all he needed was a flashlight, a knitting needle, four briefcases, a painter's brush and an old raincoat. As he packed this array of trivia into a suitcase, he thought how the objects seemed more appropriate to a garage sale than an archaeological dig. But he wasn't complaining about the simplicity of the project. While alot of energy had been dissipated in finding backers for his past expeditions, this one was coming out of the thirty thousand dollars still left from Ann's life policy. If the letter turned out to be a hoax, the fewer people who knew about it the better.

One week later, as the QE2 was preparing to sail for Southampton, Ian and the Professor strode briskly up the gangplank. Professor Cooper was wearing a sombre grey suit, while Ian's leather jacket presented a perfect match to his decaying blue jeans and sneakers. The Officer at the top of the gangplank scarcely bothered to check the Professor's ticket; however, he followed a more formal procedure for his son.

'Hey man,' declared Ian to the Officer, 'why the third degree?'

The Officer smiled politely, 'It's nothing personal, sir, but you do resemble a Viking who's looking for a pop concert!'

After showing their reservation tickets to a steward, the man led the Professor and Ian through the crowds on the deck and down into the ship's interior. They passed several avenues of shops before the steward stopped outside 'Transatlantic Class' Cabin 26, Deck 3. Once the steward had left, the Professor sank, with an audible sigh, into an armchair, 'This sure beats flying.'

'But it isn't as quick,' quipped Ian.

'Listen, Ian. Ever since this boat was launched, I've promised myself that one day I'd sail in her; now I'm doing it! Besides, this summer's "dig" has waited four hundred years to be found, so what difference will another week make?'

Ian flung his travel bag into the corner, 'Don't stop now, tell me more about the "dig".' To Ian's annoyance, his father remained silent. 'So, you're still staying clammed up?'

The Professor nodded, 'Once we're at sea, I'll tell you everything, though in truth, there isn't much to tell.'

Ian eased off his sneakers, 'This gets more mysterious by the minute!'

The men's conversation was interrupted by cheering through the open porthole from the well-wishers on the quayside; this was closely followed by three shrill blasts from the ship's siren. The Professor and Ian rushed topside.

Imperceptably at first, the liner began her three-thousand-mile voyage. Soon, the flotilla of tugs was returning to New York harbour as the great ship steamed for the horizon at twenty knots.

Ian turned to his father, 'Now that we're on our way, will you *please* tell me what this is all about?'

'Patience, Ian, you'll soon know as much as I do. But you tell me something first, what did you think of Nostradamus?'

Ian looked seriously at his father, 'To be perfectly honest, Dad, his effect on me has been nothing short of negligible.' Noticing the disappointment on his father's face at his flippancy, Ian said, 'C'mon, Dad, it's all garbage, it's got to be, nobody can predict the future.'

'I only wish I could agree with you, God knows I've tried to convince myself, but so many predictions have come true that I can't believe it's only coincidence.'

Later, back down in their cabin, Ian lay back with his hands behind his head. 'Okay, so if Nostradamus is so hot, why hasn't he predicted any of the good things that have happened since the sixteenth century, like the end of slavery, penicillin or the Beach Boys! Jesus Christ, this guy makes Hamlet look like an optimist. Anyway, how would you describe the old fake?'

The Professor thought hard before answering, 'Fascinating, weird and frightening.'

Ian laughed, 'Those are strong words. What's so fascinating, weird and frightening about Nostradamus?'

'Fascinating; because Nostradamus predicted a bookful of things which have really happened. Weird; because I can't come up with a way that the future can be predicted.'

'And frightening?' asked Ian impatiently.

'Frightening, because if Nostradamus has been right so far, I don't like his thoughts for the future.'

The Professor pulled out a pipe from inside his jacket pocket and poked inside it with a small penknife. After knocking the charcoal into an ashtray, he filled the pipe with tobacco, lit it and reclined back in the armchair. Still he said nothing. Ian's patience was at breaking point when the Professor noticed his son's frustration, 'Fifteen more minutes, Ian, and I'll tell you everything—then you'll have me committed to an asylum for senile academics.' Fourteen long minutes later, there was a polite knock on the door; it was the steward with their luggage. When they were alone again, the Professor said, 'The brochure guaranteed our luggage within an hour of sailing. It was right on time.'

The Professor lifted his suitcase onto the bed and unpacked contents into a neat pile. He motioned to Ian, 'I wouldn't want you to think that I was a professional smuggler, but sometimes an archaeologist needs to get a ''sensitive'' article through customs.'

Quizzically, Ian raised an eyebrow but said nothing.

'It's years since I've done anything like this, Ian, so it seemed advisable to try a dummy run.' The Professor turned the case upside down and shook it theatrically, 'Empty, right?'

Ian screwed up his face, 'What is this, Dad, some kind of magic act? Of course the case is empty.'

Exhibiting a mischievous grin which had been absent for three months, the Professor opened a hidden compartment and took out an envelope, 'Brenda's been working on the case for weeks. Good, don't you think?'

Ian shrugged, 'Okay, so I'm impressed, but why go to all this trouble?'

The Professor handed Ian the envelope, 'When you've read the letter, you'll know why.'

After noting that there was no postmark, Ian withdraw the letter and began to read.

> Dear Professor Cooper,
>
> My identity must remain a secret, therefore you can only take the contents of this letter on trust. However, if you wish to make the most momentous discovery of this age, follow my instructions precisely. I realise that as a scientist, you will ridicule astrology, yet rather than use the medium of a letter to explain the base upon which this only 'true science' is constructed, I will ask but a single question, 'Do you recall the lions in Trafalgar Square?'
>
> Now we pass on to the reason for my letter. Michel of Notre Dame, the man known to you as Nostradamus, is not buried at St. Laurent but is entombed within Notre Dame Cathedral.
>
> Accompanied by your son, you will travel to Paris and enter the Great Church. At the end of the central nave, on the right, you will find an arch, through which exists another chapel with nine pews. You are to stand on the third pew at exactly noon on the second day of July (the anniversary of Nostradamus's death). Facing the outer window, and with your arms raised in the sign of the crucifix, the shadow of your clenched fists will fall on two brown stones in the chapel wall. When pressure is simultaneously applied to these stones, a door that has been hidden for centuries, will open.
>
> You will pass through this door and enter the true resting place of Nostradamus. Within the tomb are but two objects, the first is the coffin of Nostradamus, which must not be

> lated. The second is a wooden truck. You will remove the tents of the trunk and take them to a place of safe keeping America. The trunk's contents have not been seen for over four centuries, so guard them well and say nothing!

Ian gazed at the letter in disbelief, 'This is some kind of gag right?' The Professor gently shook his head. 'I don't believe it' gasped Ian, 'We're going on a four thousand mile wild goose chase because someone sent you a phony letter? I'll bet that one of your students is still laughing at us from the quayside!'

The Professor took the letter from Ian, 'There's one factor you don't know, and that's where I met your mother when I was an exchange student, way back in 1960, the same spot that I proposed to her a year later. It was right beside one of the lions in Trafalgar Square.'

Ian hesitated several moments before saying, 'Okay, so I don't claim any answers about the lions but it must be coincidence. Fortune-tellers play on that kind of stuff.'

The Professor frowned, 'It would be one hell of a coincidence, no one, except me, knew where I proposed, so how did the mysterious letter writer find out?' Ian's silence testified that he didn't want to discuss Trafalgar Square anymore, so his father said, 'Okay, maybe the letter is a fake, but I've thought of nothing else since it dropped through the mail box. Nostradamus was even on my mind when I jumped that red light three weeks ago.'

Ian hadn't seen his father in this sort of state before, so he finally smiled and said, 'Personally, I think this is just your mid-life crisis, but you're paying for the trip so if you say the letter's genuine, it's genuine. How do you want us to play this?'

Placing a grateful hand on Ian's shoulder, the Professor said, 'We use this voyage to learn everything we can about Nostradamus, especially his prophecies for the future.'

For the next three days, the men endlessly discussed how Nostradamus could have charted world history into the centuries beyond his death. Listen to the 25th prophecy, Ian,' said his father as the QE2 began the fourth day of the crossing, '"WILD BEASTS, FILLED WITH REVENGE, WILL CROSS THE RIVERS AND ENTER GERMANY. THE BATTLEFIELD WILL BE WAGED AGAINST THE PLAGUE OF GERMANY WHO KNOWS NO LAW. HISTER'S END WILL COME IN A CAGE OF IRON AND GRANITE." That prophecy can't be dismissed as coincidence, Ian. The wild beasts were the Russian Bear, the British

Lion and the American Eagle. Even the cage of iron and granite is a perfect description of the bunker where Hitler died!'

Ian's voice seemed to lack its normal bite as he quipped, 'Nostradamus might have been a great prophet but he was a lousy speller, HITLER is spelt with an "L".'

Turning to another page, the Professor said, 'Okay, if you want to laugh that one off, what about this, "IN THE YEAR 1600 PLUS THREE TIMES TWENTY AND SIX, THE CITY OF LONDON WILL FALL TO A GREAT FIRE. AS THE JUST DIE WITH THE UNJUST, NOT EVEN TEMPLES WILL WITHSTAND THE FLAMES."'

Ian remained unimpressed, 'Coincidence, pure coincidence. The reason why predictions seem to be so accurate is that guys like you "sift" them. I mean, who's going to make a big deal about a prophecy that didn't come true? It's the same with historical figures, they either become saints or lousy creeps. Albert Schweitzer might have abandoned his sweet old mother to go get a suntan in Africa, and maybe Hitler grew roses but who's going to remember that?'

Ian gazed at the passing waters of the Atlantic through the porthole, 'Okay, I admit that some of Nostradamus's predictions have come true, but there's still one problem that won't go away.'

'Oh, and what's that?' asked the Professor.

'Well, let's say that it was written down in black and white that you were scheduled to go up on deck in fifteen minutes and get blown over the side. Now with that knowledge, you'd deliberately flip providence and stay down here, right?' Turning from the porthole, Ian gave a wink, 'Q.E.D!' he declared, 'the future can't be predicted.'

The Professor smiled, 'Very neat, but only at first sight. You're making the assumption that free will exists, but what if we are just puppets, going through the pre-ordained motions that destiny has mapped out for us? Maybe that's what Shakespeare meant when he said "All the world's a stage and all its men and women merely players."'

Putting his head in his hands, the Professor added nervously, 'That's what really frightens me, sometimes it seems that mankind is like a pre-programmed pack of lemmings, racing towards the cliff edge.'

Ian reached out and put his hand on his father's shoulder, 'Let's agree to forget all this prediction stuff, at least for the rest of the cruise. We haven't taken a vacation together in years, so let's soak up the sun and relax. This guy Nostradamus will turn out to be as big a phony as the creep who sent you the letter, just wait and see.'

For the remainder of the voyage, while the Professor listened to the morning news of a deteriorating world situation, Ian stayed firmly in bed. These sleeping arrangements were reversed at night, with Ian trying not to disturb his father when he returned to the cabin in the early hours. The gesture was wasted, however, because the Professor found sleep impossible.

Two days later, when the men were on deck watching the ship approach the quayside at Southampton, Ian quipped, 'One way or the other, we'll soon know. It's June 28th, only four days to go. What do we do next?'

The Professor glanced at his son, 'First we go look at the lions in Trafalgar Square, just for old times sake, then we fly to Paris and take a fast train to Salon. If the history books are right, Nostradamus is buried at the Church of St. Laurent.'

Ian laughed, 'Why not? We may as well see the place where the guy *is* buried, before we go to where he *isn't*.'

'Still sceptical?'

'You bet, but at least I'm getting a free vacation!'

Although it was early afternoon when the man arrived at the medieval churchyard, already the trees were casting menacing shadows across the gravestones. But even in the gathering gloom they experienced no difficulty in finding the grave of Nostradamus. It was surrounded by a cosmopolitan collection of devotees, who repeatedly lit up the headstone with camera flashes.

'It seems that you're not the only man who's hooked on Nostradamus,' said Ian, 'and one thing's for sure, those guys don't think the grave's empty.'

The Professor shrugged, 'Those guys didn't get a letter. Anyway, let's get out of this place. I've seen enough. Tomorrow we get our first look at the cathedral.'

Neither man was sorry to leave the cemetery. Even at the middle of summer, several hours had to pass before the chill of the churchyard had left their bones.

The following morning, the two men left their hotel near the Eiffel Tower and hailed a cab for Notre Dame. After braving the traumas of the Paris rush hour, the cab halted with a screech. 'We are at the cathedral, monsieur.'

Leaving the cab to rejoin the rampaging traffic, Ian and the Professor stood gazing upward at the magnificent Gothic cathedral.

'A guy could get a crick in his neck doing this,' joked Ian, after some minutes. 'C'mon, let's go inside before I get vertigo, or see the Hunchback in the bell tower!'

At a slow pace, the Professor followed Ian towards the open doors of the cathedral. Ian turned round, 'C'mon, Dad, get the lead out of your socks, this isn't the "last mile".' Once they were together again, the two men passed beneath the central entrance arch.

Touching his son's arm the Professor whispered, 'I don't know if you believe in omens but this is the door of the Last Judgement.'

The contrast between the humid, bustling Paris outside, and the candlelit medieval tranquility inside, defied description. 'I didn't dream it'd be so big.' gasped Ian in an uncharacteristically reverent tone, 'Even if the letter is a hoax, it's worth the trip just to see this place. Man, have you ever smelt anything so old and acrid before, and will you listen to that choir chanting. This is some church.'

Although neither man claimed strong religious convictions, the cathedral was casting the same spell on them as it had on countless thousands since its construction, eight centuries before. Finally, when they had adjusted to their surroundings, Ian whispered, 'This is the first time I've been in a real cathedral. I though it'd be like an oversized church, but this is way-out, the guys who built this place sure believed in something.'

The Professor nodded, 'I guess you're right. Its a real act of faith to dig the foundations for a church that won't be finished until you've been dead for three centuries. Maybe that's why Notre Dame is France to most Frenchmen. Did you know that Napoleon crowned himself Emperor here?'

Gripping his father's arm, Ian said, 'Let's save the history lesson for later, Dad, it's time to do what we came for, but don't be too disappointed when there's no little chapel to the right of the nave.'

'Disappointed?—I'll be delighted!'

The Professor followed Ian down the central nave, past the clusters of tourists who were silently admiring different features of the great church. At the trancept of the cathedral, the Professor halted in mid-step. There, between the sparkling northern and southern rose windows, stood a chapel to the right of the chancel! In the flickering light of the cathedral's countless candles, a name could just be made out—'Chapel of St. Denis'. Beyond the chapel, a curved archway formed the entrance to a narrow passage. An icy shiver ran the length of the Professor's spine as he stared spellbound down the passage. Now a primeval instinct told him not to proceed a step further, but it was already too late, Ian had disappeared into the darkness beyond the archway.

Forcing his feet to take a single step at a time, the Professor followed the route his son had taken. After edging along a dimly lit passage for what seemed an endless journey, but in reality was no more than ten paces, the Professor emerged into the all-enveloping brightness of another small chapel.

In the chapel, a woman was about to photograph the altar, but thinking the Professor was an official, she quickly slipped the camera into her pocket and left to rejoin her tour party. The Professor's heart pounded with a mixture of dread and excitement in the fear that only a wall now stood between him and the tomb of Nostradamus.

'Whoever set up this hoax gets top marks for detail.' Ian's echoing voice broke the Professor's trance.

'Hoax?'

Ian nodded, 'I still think the story is too far out to be real, but I've got to hand it to the hoaxer, he's really done his homework. I've counted the pews, there's nine on either side, exactly like the letter said. And look at that wall!'

Several hundred brown stones were randomly incorporated in the chapel wall; and if the letter were genuine the Professor knew that pressing just two of those stones could open the tomb. Fingering the stones, the Professor asked, 'You still think it's a hoax?' Ian nodded. 'In that case, let's try an old treasure hunter's trick for finding secret doors.'

Ian opened his eyes wide as his father withdrew a knitting needle from inside his coat. 'Okay Ian, first we need to guess where my shadow will fall tomorrow.'

Ian glanced at the sunlight streaming through the chapel window, then he pointed to a section of wall facing the third pew. 'Seems right,' agreed the Professor, 'so let's see if this needle will pass between any of the stones.'

After the initial probings had met with no success, the Professor started to wonder if it really was a hoax after all. Ian took hold of the Professor's arm, 'C'mon Dad, let's split before we're discovered.'

Ian's grip made the Professor drop the needle. While he was on his knees retrieving the needle, the Professor tried a final jab, barely two feet above the ground. Without warning, the needle scraped between two of the slabs, and then another two! In a matter of minutes, the cracks between thirteen stones had been penetrated.

Ian's face went white, 'Oh Christ, it's true! There's a door, a goddammed door!'

'Keep your voice down,' muttered the Professor, 'God knows what's waiting for us on the other side so it's more critical than ever to maintain secrecy. Let's get back to the hotel and plan for tomorrow.'

Leaving the cathedral through the central door, the two men found themselves back in the warm Paris sunshine. 'It's easy to lose sight of what we're doing,' whispered the Professor. 'Tomorrow we plan to rob a tomb and then leave France with some valuable artifact.'

Ian laughed out loud, 'And I always thought it was me who was the wild man in the family.'

The Professor forced a smile, 'You could call tomorrow a hazard of the profession. It's a dilemma that any archaeologist could face. I've often wondered what I'd do in this situation, now I know.'

When Ian walked towards a parked cab, the Professor called him back, 'Let's not catch a cab, I've always hankered for a trip along the Seine; besides, anything must be safer than another cab ride.'

From his seat on the open-deck launch, Ian noticed that 'La Prefecture de Police and Le Palais de Justice' shared the island with the cathedral. He pointed his hand, 'You do realise that if we screw up tomorrow, we'll be visiting those other two buildings.'

'A confidence boost is just what I need right now.'

Soon the launch was pulling into the landing stage beyond the Eiffel Tower. During the short walk to the hotel, the Professor kept a watchful eye on Ian; he had not seen his son this excited since the family visited Disneyland, twelve years ago. Ian kicked a can, 'This is unbelievable. Everything's exactly the way the letter said it would be. And if the letter's been right so far, you know what that means?'

His father nodded, 'It means that one of us is going where no man has been for four hundred years.'

Ian screwed his face, 'One of us?'

'That's exactly right, one man goes in the tomb, the other stays outside.' Taking a nickel from his pocket, the Professor winked as he flipped it in the air, 'Heads or tails?'

CHAPTER 2

Back in their hotel room, the two men discussed the morning's events. 'Well, it sure isn't a hoax,' declared the Professor, 'unless the guy behind it built a tomb under the cathedral.'

'It's genuine, okay,' conceded Ian, 'but that only leaves us with a bigger mystery. Why hasn't the letter writer entered the tomb himself?'

With a troubled voice, the Professor answered, 'Ever since the letter arrived, I've asked the same question.'

'And?'

'I haven't come up with an answer, so let's concentrate on tomorrow.' The Professor looked out of the window, 'I wasn't serious about you entering the tomb. As leader of the expedition, it's my duty to go inside.'

Ian leapt off the bed where he'd been lounging, 'Christ, dad, this isn't an expedition, so don't go pulling rank on me.'

The Professor shook his head, 'It's an expedition to me, and as leader I'm going inside.'

Ian waved his hands in desperation, 'B...but you don't know what you'll find. Maybe the place is booby-trapped. Besides, I'm fitter than you, I should go in while you wait outside.'

The Professor said firmly, 'If it's booby-trapped, I'll know what to look for,' then with a fatherly smile, he added, 'anyway, whose damn letter started all this in the first place?' Ian was about to continue the argument, when his father raised his hand, 'I've been an archaeologist for twenty years, dreaming of exactly this situation, so I'm going in and that's final.'

When Ian was young, his father had patiently discussed science with him for hours; however, when the Professor finally tired of listening to some irrelevant argument, he'd give his son a certain look which meant that the conversation was finished. This was exactly the look that Ian was now receiving. 'Okay Ian. Having settled on who goes inside the tomb, let's talk about the trunk.'

Ian added, 'And the coffin?'

The Professor shook his head, 'We're not Burke and Hare, the coffin is no concern of ours, it's the trunk we want.'

Ian sat back down on the bed. 'That's right, how the hell are we going to get a great trunk out of the cathedral without being seen? I'll bet it's even too big to go down that narrow passageway.'

The Professor smiled, 'That part's easy, we leave the trunk but steal its contents.'

Ian raised an eyebrow, 'Something tells me that you've done this before. I'm starting to see a whole new dimension to you.'

The Professor laughed, 'Believe me, Ian, whatever I've done in the past was strictly small-time, compared to robbing Notre Dame Cathedral!'

That night, while trying to snatch some sleep before the big event, the Professor reflected on his career as an archaeologist. At high school, he had toyed with being a lawyer or doctor, until a summer study trip took his class to the Museum of Antiquities in Cairo. There, dominating the display of treasures from Tutankhamun's tomb, was the golden mask of the Pharoah. From the moment that the young Frank Cooper saw the mask, he had but one ambition in life, to unearth a similar find. After all these years, he might just be on the verge of doing so.

Ian couldn't sleep either, but his thoughts were different. The whole affair was turning into the crazy sort of adventure that you only read about in books, except this was for real. But he was very concerned about his father's safety in the tomb. He still had trouble thinking about the death of his mother, and now his father was putting his life on the line.

Ian's watch was showing 11.50 a.m. on Wednesday July 2nd, as father and son, each carrying two briefcases, entered Notre Dame Cathedral. Having briskly made their way to the chapel, they breathed a sigh of relief on finding it empty.

Ian glanced at his watch, 'Just three minutes to go.'

'Have you got the chalk ready?'

Ian opened his hand, to reveal a sweaty stub of chalk.

Loosening his collar, the Professor said, 'I'll stand in front of the third pew while you give me the countdown.'

The sunshine, streaming though the stained-glass window, cast the Professor in a dazzling quilt of colours, Ian stated, 'One minute to go.' Next he whispered, 'Thirty seconds left.' With the countdown standing at seventeen seconds, the Professor's shadow suddenly disappeared. 'Shit, the sun's gone behind a cloud!'

'Language—remember where we are.'

Ian looked blank, 'B...but what should we do?'

'Continue counting.' When the count had fallen to five seconds, the Professor stood on the third pew, looked directly into the overcast window and raised his arms in the sign of the cross.

As Ian said 'ZERO', blinding light streamed through the window, and the Professor cast a perfect crucifix on the wall. Beneath each clenched fist was a large brown stone! The sheer imagery of the scene mesmerised Ian and he just stood there, open mouthed.

'Quick,' yelled the Professor, 'mark the stones before the light goes out again.'

Still in a daze, Ian shuffled to the wall and chalked the two stones with a cross. An instant later, another cloud plunged the chapel back into gloom, but it didn't matter, the task was complete.

The men gazed at the chalk marks on the wall, until a high-pitched shriek shattered their concentration. An old woman was standing transfixed in the archway. From the anger in her face, it was obvious that she'd witnessed the whole scene. Her little chapel was being desecrated by 'etrangers' and as a Catholic, it was her duty to defend it.

Wildly brandishing her knurled stick, and screeching abuse in a sharp Parisian accent, the woman advanced to do battle with the defilers. For an instant, neither man knew what to do, until the old woman caught the Professor a glancing blow on the forearm.

'Let's go, Ian. Unless we make a fast exit, this is going to be our Waterloo!' Swiftly, the men performed a pincer movement around their attacker, staying well clear of the flashing stick, before making a rapid retreat under the archway. Even as they dashed back into the body of the Cathedral, the angry shrieks of the old woman still echoed after them.

It was approaching two in the afternoon before the Professor thought it safe to re-enter the Cathedral. Even then, he still worked on the premise that the authorities might be looking for two men, so he told Ian to wait outside for ten minutes. When the Professor nervously eased his head out of the passageway, there was no sign of the old woman. The chapel was deserted. After Ian had rejoined his father, the Professor said, 'Okay, let's get the tomb open before we're discovered again.' Feverishly, the men searched the wall for the chalk marks but they had completely vanished!

'That's it then,' said Ian dejectedly, 'they must have scrubbed the stones clean. Finding the right two now would be harder than getting a ticket for a "Coasters" concert. This is the end of our wild goose chase so let's get the hell out of here.'

The Professor didn't move, 'I never thought you'd quit so easily, Ian. There must be something we can do.' Silently, the Professor gazed at the rows of identical brown stones, then he said, 'It's a long shot but you may have solved our problem.'

Ian stepped back, 'Me? How?'

'Well, these walls look as if they haven't seen water for centuries, so if the stones were scrubbed clean, they should be a different shade from the others.' The two men stared where their memories told them the stones should be.

'Here's one,' exclaimed Ian in jubilation.

'And here's the other,' said his father. Spaced about six feet apart, two stones looked distinctly cleaner than the rest.

Ian reached out and touched one, 'Hey, I'm impressed by the reasoning, dad, this one's still damp.'

'Make sure that no one's coming this way, 'instructed the Professor, 'we don't want to be caught in the act again.'

Ian grinned, 'Quit worrying, I've already covered that base. You know those signs inside the entrance to the Cathedral, where the arch is under repair, I guessed that one of them read "Falling Masonry", or something dry like that, so I moved it to block the passageway.'

The Professor smiled, 'Good thinking Ian, but check it out anyway.'

Ian took a furtive glance down the passageway, 'We're okay, the sign's still in position.'

The Professor pointed at one of the stones, 'No point in waiting; on the count of three, you heave on that one while I do the same to this. Ready?' Ian nodded. 'One, two three, push.'

The men pushed the brown stones as hard as they could but the inertia of centuries resisted their efforts. Then a dull rumble seemed to come from beneath their feet, until a crack suddenly appeared in the wall, about two feet up from the floor. The crack grew larger until the door they'd identified the previous day jerked back noisily into the wall, revealing a low gaping chasm that looked cold, black and uninviting.

'I guess we've found the Devil's coal chute,' gasped Ian.

The Professor forced a smile, 'Don't worry, it had to go underground or someone would have calculated that part of the cathedral was missing.'

'But how come it's that slit shape?'

Bravely, the Professor answered, 'How else could Nostradamus' coffin be slid down sideways?'

Ian gripped his father's arm, 'Having looked down that chute, this sure isn't the place for heroics, won't you change your mind and let me go?'

The Professor shook his head, 'I appreciate the offer but the tab's got my name on it.'

Ian grew more agitated, 'But anything could go wrong, what if the door can't be opened from the inside?'

The Professor smiled, 'Then I've got problems.' Opening one of the briefcases, he pulled out the old raincoat and put it on. Then, after throwing the four briefcases down the chute, he lay on the floor, winked at Ian and said, 'See you in half an hour.'

With a final gulp of air, the Professor slithered down the chute after the briefcases. Although he'd presented a brave face to Ian, he harboured no illusions of the risk he was taking. Traps were uncomfortably common in such situations. The chute might lead to a subterranean well and he would end his life amongst the skeletons of others who had launched themselves into that stale atmosphere. Therefore, it was with considerable relief that the Professor landed heavily on a slab floor at the bottom of the chute.

An instant later, however, the slab started to sink under his weight. Simultaneously, the comforting shaft of light from the chapel began to disappear until finally, with a thunderous noise, the trap door slammed shut, plunging the Professor into an all-consuming blackness. Yet as he lay there motionless on the damp floor, he took comfort in the thought that if the door could be closed from the inside, maybe it could also be opened.

The Professor tried to stand up, only to bang his head against the ceiling. He jabbed his hand into the raincoat pocket and pulled out the torch. After fumbling with it in the dark, he succeeded in pressing the switch forward, only to be momentarily blinded by the bright beam. Slowly, he adjusted to his surroundings.

He was in a low, square room, about four feet high and ten between walls, with the only entrance being the one by which he'd come. A lever, connected through pulleys to an oak beam, protruded from the wall near the chute, with the beam itself being securely clamped to the stones which formed the doorway back into the chapel. In the light of his torch, the Professor noted that the lever operated the chute door.

With the problem of leaving the tomb solved, the Professor shone his torch around the room with an increased confidence. Apart from himself, and the scattered briefcases near the base of the chute, only two other objects existed. Resting in one corner of the tomb was a gold embossed coffin. In the opposing corner a large trunk occupied a recessed niche.

For a moment, the Professor wondered why, if the trunk's contents belonged to Nostradamus, the coffin had been separated from the trunk by the maximum distance possible? He brushed this question aside as the euphoria of success swelled up inside him. With the passing of each second, the Professor grew ever more convinced that he was the first person in the tomb since it was sealed, over four hundred years ago. This was the situation he had dreamed of a thousand times, discovering an unrobbed tomb.

Suddenly, a less pleasant thought struck him, was it unrobbed? Maybe the trunk had already given up its contents, to some long-dead tomb robber? The Professor crawled across the tomb and shone his torch over the coffin.

It was standing on a large slab, with barely a hand's gap between the top of its lid and the low roof. 'There's no way I could open that', he muttered, 'which is exactly why it was placed that way.' He reached out and touched the coffin, it was stone, with heavy gold inlays decorating the sides. Losing interest in the coffin, the Professor directed his torch at the old trunk and like a miner working a narrow seam, he inched his way across the tomb.

Although the journey was scarcely ten feet, by the time the Professor reached the trunk, he had grazed both knees. Oblivious to the pain, he touched the lid, it was wood, probably oak, strengthened by two cast iron stiffners. Even in the scant light, there could be no doubt regarding the quality of the trunk's construction. It had been built to last for eternity.

Shielding his eyes, he blew away the accumulated dust of centuries, his torch picked out an inscription but he couldn't read it. The Professor reached inside his jacket, took the painter's brush and delicately removed the dust from the chiselled letters. The light of his torch revealed the inscription—'Michel de Notre Dame'.

The last element of doubt was removed. This was the trunk of Nostradamus! For a few seconds, the Professor just squatted there, savouring the exhileration of victory. Then he saw the lock.

Nostradamus' trunk had been sealed with a heavy metal lock. The locksmiths of the sixteeth century being masters of their trade, getting into the trunk wouldn't be easy.

Yet he had to do something, already twenty minutes of the half hour agreed with Ian was gone. He reached out to examine the lock; to his amazement, it came off in his hand. The lock hadn't been fastened. Perhaps Nostradamus' followers had forgotten to lock the trunk, or deliberately left it open? Either way, the only factor of importance was that he could open the lid. Then another possibility engulfed him. Was the lock open because the trunk was empty? Had a previous visitor placed the lock back in position as a bizarre joke on anyone who might follow him into the tomb?

The Professor realised that he could kneel there for eternity, trying to guess what, if anything, was in the trunk, but there was only one way to find out. He snatched a breath of musty air, gripped the torch between his teeth and placed both hands firmly on the lid. With all his strength, he heaved the lid. With an ear-piercing screech, the rusty hinges moved and the lid came up in his hands. At last he knew how Howard Carter felt when he entered Tutankhamun's tomb. But did the trunk contain a priceless treasure or was it empty?

The excitement was unbearable as, still with the torch clenched between his teeth, he peered over the lid. The trunk's dimensions were deceptively large for the sparseness of its contents, but what the hell did that matter, everything appeared to be undisturbed, just the way that Nostradamus' followers had left it, in 1566.

One corner of the trunk was occupied by a large gold casket, whose gems sparkled in the light of the torch. In the opposing corner, a collection of manuscripts had been stacked so neatly that they could have been placed there the day before. An envelope rested on top of the manuscripts and on the envelope, a simple crucifix delicately twinkled.

The Professor picked up the casket and tried to open its lid, but it was securely locked. For a moment, he thought of forcing the casket, but the watch he'd borrowed from Ian showed that it was already 2:52. Time was starting to run out.

Quickly, he placed the casket in one briefcase and the letter, manuscripts and crucifix in another; realising that he didn't need the last two briefcases, he tossed them into the trunk and snapped the lock into position. The Professor smiled, thinking of some future archaeologist discovering the briefcases.

When he directed his torch onto the watch, it was 2:58. Two

minutes more and Ian would signal it was safe to climb back into the chapel. With one hand on the lever, he switched off the torch and waited silently in the inky darkness. Soon, a bleep from the watch signalled 3:00 p.m., but no knock came. The minutes seemed endless. He turned the torch on his watch: 3:15. The Professor continued to crouch in the darkness, pleadingly awaiting the signal from his son.

Suddenly, the scene being enacted in the Chapel above assumed crystal clarity in his mind. The old woman must have returned and identified Ian. Now a gendarme waited in the chapel for the Professor to reappear. Maybe the world's press were there, waiting with cameras to interview him, like Lazarus rising from the dead!

The Professor had already convinced himself that the best policy was to climb back into the chapel and face the consequences, when two sharp knocks echoed round the tomb; it was the signal from Ian! He pulled on the lever for all his life was worth. At first nothing happened, then he sensed movement. The lever descended with gathering speed until the door jerked open with a loud crack, filling the tomb with blinding light. The route back to the chapel was gaping open.

The Professor took hold of the two briefcases and heaved them through the opening, then he climbed up the chute after them. As soon as he was standing safely beside his son in the chapel, he ripped off the raincoat and flung it down the hatch. 'Quickly, Ian, let's seal the entrance.'

The men pressed the two brown stones, which now protruded several inches out of the wall. After the door had slammed shut, the Professor wiped his brow and asked, 'Why were you late with the signal?'

Ian shrugged apologetically, 'Some crazy Italians couldn't decipher French, so they climbed over the sign and took a million pictures in the chapel. Man, was I relieved when they finally left.' Ian noticed the rips on the knees of his father's trousers, 'Are you okay?'

The Professor nodded reassuringly, 'I'm fine, but the sooner we're out of this place the better.' He tossed his son a briefcase.

'Where are the other two cases?'

'Didn't need them.'

'And what's in these?' quizzed Ian excitedly.

'Let's get back to the hotel and find out.'

With vice-like grips on their briefcase handles, the two men walked steadily through the cathedral. The excitement of the occasion forced a long forgotten memory to form in Ian's mind. His mother had taken him Christmas shopping when he was eight and, like most boys, he'd wanted her to buy him a toy revolver. But she, as a lifelong pacifist, had refused. So, after making sure that the assistant wasn't looking, Ian had slipped the gun in his jacket pocket.

As they'd been leaving the store, he'd felt exactly the same combination of fear and elation that he was experiencing now, as if 'unseen eyes' were methodically burning two holes in the back of his head. He grinned as he remembered that after arriving home with the gun, he was so scared, he sneaked into the garden and buried it. The gun was probably still there to this day.

The guilty feeling had lasted Ian the length of the nave, but as they re-emerged through the entrance arch into the Paris sunshine, it vanished.

Firmly holding their briefcases, the two men mingled with the crowds on the left bank of the Seine. After passing two gendarmes outside a waterside cafe, the Professor touched Ian's arm, 'According to my old tutor at Oxford, the French are the most nationalistic people on God's Earth. You don't need to be clairvoyant to guess our fate if they find we've robbed their beloved Cathedral.'

Within an hour of leaving Notre Dame, they regained the sanctuary of their hotel room. 'Mission accomplished,' declared Ian in triumph.

'Yes,' agreed his father, 'but we don't know what we've achieved.'

Ian nodded impatiently, 'We will as soon as you've opened the briefcases.' The Professor hesitated, so Ian asked, 'C'mon Dad, what's wrong?'

The Professor stared at the two cases, 'All my life I've dreamt of this moment but now my instincts are to throw these cases straight in the river!'

Ian opened his eyes wide, 'You can't be serious! After all the trouble we've gone to...'

The Professor fingered one of the cases, 'I guess you're right. Anyway, you're an equal partner in this enterprise, open your case first.'

Whatever reservations the Professor had, Ian didn't share them. With an excited grin he blew the remaining dust from the case, 'Here goes!' He unfastened the leather restraining straps, pressed the lock, lifted the flap and looked inside.

The Professor's sense of foreboding lifted as Ian removed the casket from the briefcase. Although the casket had looked valuable inside the tomb, only now could its true splendour be appreciated.

'Wow,' gasped Ian, 'I wonder how much we could get for that. It's got more jewels than Cartier's.'

Ian tried to open the casket but it was firmly locked. 'What do we do?'

'Before we resort to forcing it, let's see what's in my case.' Having opened the second briefcase, the Professor stacked the manuscripts on the bed then, almost as a reflex action, he turned the briefcase upside down and shook it. Out dropped the crucifix.

Ian picked up the crucifix and examined it; a smile creased his face, 'You know what? This isn't an ordinary crucifix, it's a key and I can guess what lock it opens.'

Ian placed the stem of the crucifix into the casket's lock and delicately turned it clockwise. A faint click signalled that the casket was open. Ian began to lift the lid but then he snapped it shut again and handed the casket to his father, 'If you've been hooked on this for twenty years, who am I to burst your bubble?'

It was with heartpounding excitement that the Professor opened the casket and peered inside. To his surprise, the casket contained nothing more than a compact cylindrical object, cocooned in a velvet-lined resting place. 'What is it?'

Ian took hold of the casket, 'I know what it looks like,' he said disbelievingly, 'but it just can't be. . .' Ian picked up the object and started to examine it, 'Well I'll be damned, it's not possible!'

'What's not possible?'

Ian looked his father full in the face, 'Do you know what this thing is?' The Professor shook his head. 'You're not going to believe it.'

For once, it was the Professor who was at the limit of his patience, 'Stop prolonging the mystery, tell me what it is.'

'It's a telescope! Kind of crude, but a telecope all the same.'

'And why's that impossible?'

Ian looked up, 'Why? Simply because Nostradamus had been dead for fifty years before Galileo came up with the telescope.' Ian gave the telescope to his father, 'It's your expedition, try it out.'

The Professor walked to the window and focussed the telescope, 'It *is* a telescope,' he exclaimed. 'The image isn't good but I can see people on the Eiffel Tower.'

Ian threw his arms up, 'This is where I flip out! What's a telescope doing in Nostradamus's tomb? It's like finding an empty

Coke bottle in the Great Pyramid! The telescope just shouldn't be there, unless someone planted it later.'

The Professor shook his head, 'That's not the answer, Nostradamus's name is engraved on it. And if the value of the casket is anything to go by, this telescope was his number one possession.'

Ian remained silent, then he said, 'In that case, it looks like Nostradamus and not Galileo invented the telescope, and kept it a secret.'

The Professor turned the telescope over in his hands, 'I can't imagine any real scientist inventing something as important as the telescope and keeping it a secret.'

Ian shrugged, 'Why not? After Newton invented calculus, the guy kept it a secret for twenty years while he used it to solve every other problem in science. It was only when Leibniz looked like he might get all the laurels for coming up with calculus on his own that Newton came clean.' Ian's gaze came to rest on the documents, 'Maybe one of those gives a lead?'

The Professor placed the telescope back in its casket and picked up a manuscript. Having given the first page a cursory glance, he dropped it back on the bed. 'It's in Latin.'

Ian shrugged, 'That figures. Nostradamus was a medical man.'

The Professor managed a smile, 'It may "figure" but it isn't too helpful. How's your Latin?'

Ian laughed, 'Non-existent, and yours?'

The Professor frowned, 'That's the problem—I forgot my Latin years ago.'

'That's great,' exclaimed Ian, 'neither of us can read what we've found. So now what do we do?'

The Professor sat on the edge of his bed, 'It's uncanny, almost supernatural, the way we're following the sequence set out for us in the letter. Now we're exactly where the writer of the letter said we'd be, ready to take everything back to America.'

CHAPTER 3

The dread of being branded a criminal was uppermost in the Professor's mind during the flight back to America. Although he had tried to boost Ian's confidence by pretending that smuggling was a sub-branch of archaeology, in truth, this was his first premeditated crime since taking a Chevy for a joyride as a teenager! But no problems had been met at De Gaulle airport: just a distinguished academic and his son returning from a vacation. The official at the entrance gate had even smiled and enquired in good English if anything eventful had happened in Paris?

Upon their arival back in Omaha, the two men didn't even dare glance over their shoulders until they were clear of the airport and safely lodged in the back of a cab. 'Where to?' asked the driver.

'Omaha Central Library,' replied the Professor. As the cab sped along the freeway, the Professor's heart started to lose some of its pounding, 'Wouldn't want to go through that again,' he whispered, 'if we'd been caught, there would have been hell to pay.'

Ian grinned, 'But we weren't, so quit worrying.'

Soon the cab drew up outside the library. The Professor settled the fare and then kept a steady eye on the vehicle until it was clear out of sight, 'Perhaps I'm being unnecessarily cautious, but taking a cab home from the airport would have been too easy to trace.'

Ian couldn't help laughing as he said, 'You've seen too many spy movies, but I guess we don't lose by being careful. C'mon, let's have a coffee before phoning another cab to get us home.'

The grandfather clock was chiming three when the man heaved their suitcases onto the writing desk in the study. 'Welcome home, Sir, and you too, Ian,' said Brenda fussily, 'You both look tired from the journey. I'll make some coffee.'

Ian took hold of Brenda's arm, 'First things first!' He handed the woman a small, neatly wrapped parcel. 'I wasn't sure what to buy, but all pretty girls like perfume.'

Brenda blushed a little, 'Oh you are a charmer and that's for sure. I'll bet you've bought one of these for all the girls you know.'

Ian hesitated, then with his best, roguish grin, he turned his flight bag upside down over the table. Out dropped eight, identically-wrapped, parcels!

While the coffee was being prepared, the Professor used the opportunity to stack Nostradamus' manuscripts in the bookcase, 'They're as safe there as anywhere.'

Ian nodded, 'And the casket?'

The Professor shrugged, 'Since we covered it in that soluble paint, it doesn't look valuable anymore. Even a thief wouldn't give it a second glance now, so what's wrong with leaving it in the middle of the desk?'

That evening, while Brenda was at a movie, the men discussed their next move. Ian said, 'Priority number one is to get the manuscripts translated, agreed?'

The Professor nodded, 'The question is how?'

Ian leaned back in his chair, 'I've been giving that some thought; how's this for an answer. Unemployment's high, I can testify to that, so there's got to be students searching for vacation jobs. Why not place an ad for a translator?'

The Professor shook his head, 'What would it read? Man wanted to translate stolen documents?'

Ian looked upset. 'I can see the dangers too, Dad, but can you think of anything better?'

The Professor thought for a while, then he said, 'I know a dozen experts on Latin but we can't involve any of them without telling everything.'

Ian smiled, 'That's settled then, an ad it is?'

Hesitantly, the Professor nodded his head, 'But we'll have to be damned careful about security.'

The card which appeared on the Bulletin Board in the Students' Lounge carried a simple message:

VACATION JOB

Person required to translate manuscripts from
Latin into English.
Telephone Professor Frank Cooper, 374-2632.

It was late afternoon when the phone rang in the Cooper study and a pleasant female voice said, 'I'd like to speak to Professor Cooper.'...

'This is the Professor, can I help you?'

'Has the job of translating the documents been taken?'

'No.'

'Then I'd like to be considered.'

'Are you good at Latin?'

'You're dealing with a modest girl here, Professor, but I've been studying it for around five years. Last semester I received an A grade.'

'That sounds impressive, when can we meet?'

'I don't want anyone beating me to your place, give me the address and I'll drive right over.'

Fifteen minutes later, the Professor opened the door to an attractive woman in her early twenties. She had shoulder length blonde hair and was wearing a simple white blouse and black skirt. The woman was twiddling a pair of spectacles in one hand and brandishing the ad in the other, she smiled, 'I came up with the sure fire method of being first in line for the job. I stole the ad!'

The Professor laughed. 'That's one way to stay ahead of the field.'

The woman politely shook the Professor's hand. 'My name's Mary Molina and I need a vacation job before my final year at med-school.'

The Professor pointed to the open door, 'No point talking on the doorstep, you'd better come inside where it's private.'

Many hesitated, 'Is there another woman in the house?'

The Professor scratched his head, 'Woman? Well, there's Brenda, our housekeeper, why do you ask?'

'Could I see her?'

'See Brenda? Okay, but I can't think why.' The Professor went inside, ten seconds later he returned with Brenda Perkins.

Mary looked both pleased and relieved, 'It was nothing personal, Professor. But we get some "iffy" ads on our bulletin board and a good Catholic girl can't be too careful.' She smiled.

After briefly discussing how the national austerity drive was filling the med-school with suicides who had left their corpses to science, the Professor asked Mary to describe her background. 'Well, my home town's New York, if you can still call the big apple a town. My mother's a dressmaker and my father's a policeman.'

The Professor's heart started to pound again. He knew it hadn't been a good idea to advertise for a translator. 'A policeman, you say?'

Mary's face broke into a mischievous smile, 'Well, not like a real policeman who walks a beat and swings a billy club. My Dad's a pathologist. Spends his time doing autopsies on murder victims and say's he's the only guy who'll never be out of a job.'

With a sigh of relief, the Professor said, 'I guess he's right, please continue.'

Mary shrugged, 'There isn't much more to tell. I've three brothers and four sisters, I'm studying medicine and, like I said on the phone, I need a vacation job to pay the rent.'

The study door swung open, and Ian entered the room. He was unshaven and still in pyjamas. When he saw the woman seated in the armchair, his jaw dropped open, then he said, 'Mary? What are you doing here?'

Mary said nothing. The Professor broke the icy silence by saying, 'I take it that you know each other?'

Still embarrassed, Ian nodded, 'We had a few dates when I was at the University.'

The Professor noted how this reply triggered a look on Mary's face which indicated something beyond 'a few dates'.

'What are you doing here now?' asked Ian politely.

'I'm applying for a job with your father,' answered Mary coldly, 'I assume that the Professor is your father?'

Ian nodded, then he said, 'Now I get it. You've come about the ad. I know that you're a talented woman but can you translate 16th century Latin?'

'Latin's Latin,' she answered curtly, 'it doesn't change with time, that's why it's called the eternal language. I like reading the Bible in its Latin form.'

Ian laughed out loud, 'You must be kidding.'

Mary gave Ian an icy stare, 'Why, for reading the Bible or reading it in Latin?'

To diffuse the confrontation, the Professor said, 'The manuscripts we need translated are highly confidential, so we'll need your word that everything will remain secret.'

Mary looked up, 'Sounds melodramatic.'

'I suppose it does,' conceded the Professor, 'but in the academic world, everyone wants to be first to publish a new theory. I'm sure you understand?'

Mary didn't look convinced, 'It's hard to imagine how a sixteenth century document could have any secret value now.

Anyway, we've not discussed money yet!'

The Professor laughed. 'That's what I like, a practical woman. Okay, what's the going rate for translations?'

Mary pulled the ad from her bag, 'I checked before leaving the University, six dollars an hour?' she said hopefully.

'Agreed.'

'That was quick. I expected some haggling over speed before settling for four dollars. The work is that important?' The Professor nodded. 'In that case, I need the money, you need the translation, so we've got ourselves a deal. You have my word that I'll not reveal a single comma of what I find.'

Mary held out her hand to shake on the deal but the Professor hesitated. Ian broke the deadlock by saying, 'Believe me, Dad, if there's one person in the whole world who I'd guarantee to keep their word, it's Mary.'

With a smile, the Professor took Mary's hand, 'In that case, we've got a deal. Welcome to the Nostradamus Project, Mary.' Ian crossed to the bureau and took out a bottle of wine and three glasses. While Ian poured the wine, the Professor winked at Mary, 'So you'd have settled for four dollars? Ann always said that I was never much of a businessman.'

When they were midway through their second glass, the Professor remarked how Molina seemed an unusual name and he asked Mary where her family had come from. 'A little fishing village in Ireland called Mal Bay,' she replied.

The Professor raised an eyebrow, Molina doesn't sound Irish.'

'It is and it isn't,' said Mary, 'Three years ago, my father went back to Mal to trace our ancesty. It seems there was a sailor called Molina with the Spanish Armada. Some of the Spanish fleet escaped Drake and sailed along the west coast of Ireland, then a storm blew one of the ships onto the rocks near Mal Bay. Manuel Molina managed to swim ashore. Church records show that he married an Irish girl, Kathy Flinn. It was the descendants of Manuel and Kathy who emigrated here during the potato famine of the last century.'

When the wine glasses were empty, Ian said, 'Why not ask Mary to translate the letter?'

The Professor walked to the bookcase and returned with a manilla envelope, 'Okay Mary,' he joked, 'I've set my watch, start earning your six dollars.'

Mary looked at the writing on the envelope, 'This reads, "Greetings to my friends in the New World".'

Ian glanced at his father, 'As usual, the old boy's right on target; Nostradamus has even elevated us to being his friends.'

Mary dropped the letter, 'Nostradamus! Are you saying that this letter was written by Nostradamus?'

The Professor nodded.

'*The* Nostradamus?'

'The real McCoy,' said Ian.

Mary sat down, 'I was really enjoying this afternoon, you know? I thought you guys were for real, then you ask me to translate a letter written by Nostradamus. This is where I make my exit!'

'Mary,' said the Professor, 'we're genuine and so is the letter. You've translated the envelope, now read the contents.'

Mary gave a non-commital shrug before withdrawing the yellowed parchment from its envelope. 'Well, it's dated July 1st, 1566 and was written at some place called Salon in France.'

Ian drummed his fingers, 'We'd managed to get that far ourselves, tell us something new.'

Mary took careful hold of the parchment and began to read.

> Greetings to the readers of this letter, some four centuries hence. Forgive me for not referring to each of you by name, but time is short and already the chill of my last night approaches. Knowing that I shall not see the dawn, I have privately confessed my sins to my good friend and disciple, Chavigny.
>
> Soon, my tired old carcass will be transported to Paris, where it will be entombed within a secret vault in the great Cathedral, a vault constructed for me by my patron, Queen Catherine herself. My grave in the churchyard of the Cordeliers is destined to be occupied by a pauper who, unknown to himself, will also expire this very night. I have seen that the pauper's grave will be defiled in the year 1700, therefore a metal plate is to be placed in his coffin, bearing the single inscription '1700'. This act of prophecy may appear to be nothing more than the stubborn pride of an old man, but what better way is there to convince you of the validity of this letter?

Mary stopped reading and twiddled her glasses. 'Is that it,' asked Ian, 'the whole of the letter?'

Mary shook her head, 'That's only the first paragraph, Latin's an efficient language.'

The Professor poured another glass of wine, 'Then please continue,' he urged.

'Okay,' said Mary, 'but I still think this is a put on.'

A sturdy trunk, containing my 'enlarger' and astrological records, is already lodged in the tomb beneath the Cathedral. A duplicate set of these documents is held by Chavigny, who has been tutored in what must be done after my death. None but Chavigny knows of these arrangements, not even my beloved wife will be told. Now I shall recount how the manuscripts came into existence.

In my youth as a medical student at Avignon, I used a single lens to enlarge specimens of nature. Then I wondered on the effect of placing a lens at each end of a hollow reed. To my surprise, distant objects now appeared closer.

My enlarger revealed a planet beyond the orbit of Saturn, which in the vanity of youth, I named Nostra. Nostra journeys the Sun as I, and I alone of my age, know the Earth also does. After years of failure, I finally completed the Herculean task of re-writing the theorems of astrology, so that the planet Nostra was incorporated.

Now a remarkable thing occurred. I discovered that the accuracy of my projections had so improved that future events could be foretold with almost godlike precision. But I have not lived in enlightened times and my own fate would not have required calculation if I had revealed that the Earth was not the centre of creation! Yet by disguising each prophecy within an amusing riddle, my life has run its natural course and the stake has not claimed me.

I have seen that astrology, in the primitive form of my youth, still exists in your day, but take my oath that compared to the elegance of my equations, your astrology is nothing more than witches' tea leaves.

The trunk contains a complete library of my theorems. They are your inheritance, for your age needs them like none before. I bequeath you the culmination of my knowledge.

Yet a deathbed is not the place for vanity; this letter must conclude with a warning. The documents in your possession are as much a curse as a blessing, as much a burden as an advantage. I pray that the proximity of the Cathedral, and the crucifix placed on the manuscripts, will remove the vestiges of evil. But take care.

Finally, a confession. For a reason I have been unable to acertain, one prediction in ten is not fulfilled. I have my own speculations on the source of the error, but perhaps it is the Almighty Himself, saving a poor human from the curse of infallibility. Therefore, with my last breath, I will pray that when the die is cast, the events witnessed for your time do not come to pass.

God be with you,
Michel of Notre Dame

The occupants of the study stared blankly at the letter, still delicately held between Mary's finger and thumb. Finally, Ian broke the silence, 'That was one hell of a letter!'

Mary shook her head, 'It was much more than that. If it's genuine, only God knows what Nostradamus has predicted for humanity.'

Ian took the letter and slipped it back in its envelope, 'It's genuine all right,' he said with conviction.

'What makes you so sure?' demanded Mary.

'Because when Nostradamus' grave was opened up by robbers in 1700, they ran like hell at the sight of a grinning skeleton, holding a metal plate with the date ''1700'' engraved on it!'

Again the room went silent, then the Professor said, 'Before discussing the letter, you'd better let Mary in on the whole story. There's no percentage in trying to keep secrets now.'

For the next hour, as Ian recounted the trip to Notre Dame, Mary scribbled notes of the salient points. When the story was finally over, she looked critically at her note pad, 'The things you've told me beat any fiction that I've read. But assuming it isn't a hoax, either yours or someone else's, there are more questions than answers.'

The Professor nodded his agreement, 'Try us with your questions.' he invited.

'Well,' said Mary, 'for a start, we don't know who sent the letter saying where Nostradamus was buried, or the reason it came to you and not someone else. And why was the letter posted now, after a lapse of four centuries? Then there's the riddle of what stopped the letter writer going into the tomb himself.'

The Professor smiled, 'That was a good resumé, Mary. Now I'll tell you what we do know. First, you can forget about a hoax, I've had the parchment carbon-dated and it's definitely mid-sixteenth century. Besides, the casket's worth a fortune and there's the problem of the secret tomb.'

Mary nodded, 'Okay, the hoax is receding, unless it's you two behind it.'

The Professor shook his head dismissively before continuing, 'Secondly, we can be pretty near certain that Nostradamus was a genius of the first order. He invented the telescrope fifty years ahead of its time, and knew that the Earth orbits the Sun. Then, there's the worrying fact that the history books record how most of the events he predicted have now happened.'

Ian interrupted to say, 'And don't forget to add that

Nostradamus' theories on astrology were more advanced than any of his time.'

The Professor corrected Ian, 'Of any time, I'll bet.'

'Okay,' said Ian, 'so the guy was a genius, the big question now is, what happens next?'

Mary looked at the Professor, 'It's your show,' she said politely, 'but there seems to be two lines of investigation.' By a wave of his hand, the Professor indicated for Mary to continue. 'Well, while I'm translating the manuscripts, why don't you two go visit an astrologer and see what can be found about Nostradamus.'

'Sounds a good plan,' agreed the Professor, 'any suggestions where to find a good astrologer?'

Mary thought hard for a few seconds, then she said, 'Hugo Lawrence tops most people's list, why not try him?'

Ian said, 'We'll do just that. Lawrence is the only astrologer that I've any respect for. Man, some of his predictions make your flesh creep! Looking at Mary, he asked, 'How long will the translating job take?'

Mary scrutinized the manuscripts, 'Working day and night, all summer I guess.'

Ian thought for a few seconds then he smiled and said, 'Why not save yourself some rent by moving in here with us, we've got more rooms than the Y.M.C.A.'

Mary smiled. 'This may come as a surprise but I've never stayed at the Y.M.C.A. But my dormitory *is* closing for the summer so strictly as a *working arrangement* it would be pretty convenient.' she said, looking pointedly at Ian. ''And cheaper, of course.'' She glanced at the manuscripts, 'It's less than three hours since I saw that ad, yet now I couldn't walk away from this if I wanted to.'

'None of us could,' muttered the Professor.

It was 8.15 that evening, with Mary already well into the first manuscript, when Ian entered the study. Mary took off her spectacles and leaned back in the swivel chair, 'I often wondered if we'd meet again,' she said, 'but who'd have dreamt it'd be like this?'

'I've missed you.'

Mary looked bitterly away from Ian's gaze, 'That's crap, Ian, and you know it. I waited a full hour outside the cinema that night, three times I was propositioned by perverts who didn't deserve to be regarded as human, the worst damn hour of my whole life, and afterwards, nothing! Not a call, not one call in two years. And you say you've missed me!'

As Mary fought back her tears, Ian said, 'It was the hardest decision I've ever made. I can still see you standing there in the distance. But you always paid for everything and I was turning up again without a nickel in my pocket. It was a conflict between pride and love, and I guess pride won.'

Mary gave Ian a contemptuous stare. 'Look, does someone write this stuff for you or can it be made up as you go along?' she snapped angrily. 'I've seen you around, and "pride" hasn't stopped you making it with half the girls on campus so let's not fool around, okay? Remember that nickname you used to kid me with?'

Ian looked blank so Mary said, 'You've even forgotten that you used to call me the "Virgin Mary". You didn't turn up that night because you'd found greener pastures and you didn't have the guts to tell me!'

Ian was about to continue his protest, when his father chose that moment to enter the study. After Mary had quickly put on her spectacles to hide her eyes, everyone, including the Professor, pretended that nothing had happened. 'I've managed to book an appointment with Hugo Lawrence,' said the Professor, 'He's somewhere in the Middle East at the moment, all hush hush stuff, but his secretary says that he always finds time to see "academics". We're in his diary for August 27th.'

Although the appointment with Dr. Lawrence had seemed a long way off, soon August was almost gone and Ian and the Professor were in New York. 'These astrologers know how to live right,' whispered Ian, as an attractive secretary directed the men to a lavish waiting room.

'Dr. Lawrence will be right with you,' she said sexily, giving Ian a smile which lingered some seconds longer than protocol demanded.

After a brief delay, the carved oak doors to the main office opened and a distinguished, middle-aged man appeared. The man's short, black beard seemed in keeping with his white polo sweater and gold scorpion medallion. With an assertive self-confidence, he simultaneously thrust out his hand and spoke in a deep, resonating voice, 'Good afternoon, gentlemen, I am Hugo Lawrence, let's go to my office.'

The visitors followed Dr. Lawrence into the sort of office which Ian had thought only appeared on the cover of *Time* magazine but didn't exist in reality. Dr. Lawrence lodged himself at a desk, designed to overawe anyone seated in front of it. Behind the doctor, a plate glass window gave a panoramic view of the New York skyline, while a hi-fi system soothingly completed the scene. A grin crossed Ian's face as he noted how there wasn't a crystal ball in sight!

Dr. Lawrence noticed Ian's expression, 'I guess this seems a little ostentatious to "academics",' he boomed, 'but when you're advising heads of state on how to invest their billions, you've got to look the part.'

Lowering his voice, he asked, 'Now, what can I do for you gentlemen?'

The Professor laughed, 'That's a strange question for a man with your reputation.'

Dr. Lawrence smiled mischievously, 'My dear Professor, the fancy nameplate outside this suite says that I'm an astrologer, not a mind reader!'

Conceding the point, the Professor said, 'Exactly so, and that's what we'd like to talk to you about. We're writing a book on the history of prediction, with a whole chapter devoted to yourself as the world's foremost living astrologer.'

Hugo Lawrence beamed broadly and sat a little higher in his chair, 'You flatter me, gentlemen.'

'Not at all,' insisted the Professor, 'your record speaks for itself. The assassination of Kennedy, the Six Days War, predicting that Jimmy Carter would be President when he has still a southern senator, even the two disasters with the Space Shuttle . . .'

'I suppose that I have had my little successes, but if you know so much about me already, how can I help?'

The Professor took out a notebook, 'We'd like your opinion of someone else.'

'Someone else,' said Dr. Lawrence somewhat deflatedly, 'who?'

'Nostradamus, just how good was he?' said Ian.

Dr. Lawrence gave his visitors a wide grin, 'Gentlemen, you've come to the right place to talk about Nostradamus. I've written several books on the man.' He waved his hand at a well-stocked bookcase. 'After you've left, I'll have my secretary pack you off a set of my books, and because of the nice things you've said about me, I'll let you have them at cost.'

That's very generous of you,' smiled the Professor, 'Now, as the world's number one living astrologer, how do you rate Nostradamus?'

Dr. Lawrence raised his eyebrows well up his forehead, 'He was the best, the very best.' He leaned forward, almost as if he was about to say something conspiratorial, 'You may have gathered that I'm not a modest man, you can't afford to be in this profession, but I've got to hold my hands up to Nostradamus. Keep it to yourselves, but I'm not in his league, no one is. I've spent years trying to figure out how he made his predictions.'

'And?' asked the Professor.

'And I'm no wiser now than when I started. If I make a forecast, only a couple of years into the future, it takes months to check out the calculations and even then I keep my fingers crossed tight where no one can see them. How the blazes Nostradamus saw First World War dogfights sure beats me, unless the guy had a pact with the Devil!'

Uneasily, the Professor said, 'Can I ask a personal question, doctor?'

Dr. Lawrence smiled professionally, 'Why certainly, but I won't guarantee an answer.'

'Okay, then,' probed the Professor, 'assuming that we are speaking generally, are you an optimist or pessimist about the future?'

The pronounced delay before Dr. Lawrence replied, left no doubt that the question had touched a raw nerve. The Professor glimpsed something in the eyes of the astrologer which he'd hoped wouldn't be there. Finally, Dr. Lawrence said, 'I wish to God I could say an optimist.'

'But you can't. Why?'

Toying with his gold scorpion, Dr. Lawrence answered, 'I told you that I was an admirer of Nostradamus and he sure wasn't an optimist for our age. Let me give you some advice, Professor. If you want to sleep at night, don't try to decipher what Nostradamus predicts for us. I did, and I've had nightmares ever since.'

Ian thought he saw Dr. Lawrence press something beneath the desk, simultaneously there was a faint buzz in the outer office. Soon, Dr. Lawrence's secretary appeared, almost gliding through the door carrying a tray of coffee. While Ian was helping the woman distribute the coffee cups, Dr. Lawrence said, 'I'd rather not discuss the future any more if you don't mind, Professor, it's a pleasant day so why spoil it.' Then, almost as an unguarded afterthought, he added, 'My wife and I have chosen not to have children, draw whatever conclusions you wish from that.'

For the rest of the meeting, the three men talked philosphically about the implications of prediction. Finally, as they were leaving the office, Dr. Lawrence said, 'Best of luck with the book,

Professor, but don't wait too long in getting it published!'

On their flight back to Omaha, the men discussed the meeting with the astrologer. 'What did you make of Hugo Lawrence?' asked the Professor.

Ian grinned, 'Not what I'd expected. I thought he'd have a pointed hat and stars on his coat!'

The Professor managed a smile, 'Don't forget that he's a trained scientist, Ian. I did a bit of background reading, he's got a real doctorate in mathematics from Cal. Tech.'

Ian took his gaze off the air hostess's slim figure, 'One thing's for sure, the guy knew more than he was willing to say. And when an astrologer doesn't want to discuss the future, it can't be a good sign.' Ian adjusted his seat to a reclining position, 'The way that Lawrence idolised Nostradamus gave me the shivers. Even after four centuries, the old fakir is still way ahead of the field.'

The Professor adjusted his own seat, 'Don't joke, Ian, I don't like the way things are going.'

Ian opened his eyes, 'Joke? This whole affair is just like the White Queen's race in *Alice in Wonderland*. You have to run as fast as you can just to stay where you are, and much faster if you want to get anywhere.'

CHAPTER 4

When they landed back in Omaha, the Professor noticed how the leaves had lost their lush green shine and some now displayed an autumn gold. Yet summer still clung warmly to this late August day as Ian and his father arrived home. 'Hi there everybody,' shouted Ian, noisily bursting through the front door, 'Slay the fatted calf, the prodigals have returned!'

With less exuberance, the Professor said, 'I'm going to freshen up; why don't you ask Brenda to fix some coffee.'

Ian laughed, 'Coffee? I'll take a beer. Boy am I thirsty!'

Mary was sleeping in an armchair when Ian entered the study. Stacked neatly beside the woman were two sets of manuscripts, and resting on top of each was an open Bible. Ian touched Mary lightly on the shoulder. The woman screamed and then flung her arms around Ian, almost pulling him off his feet.

'Er...Mary, that's quite a welcome home but you're breaking my neck!' He noticed that Mary was trembling, 'Hey, are you okay? You're shaking like a leaf.'

Still clutching Ian tightly, Mary stammered, 'I ... I just had the worst nightmare of my life.'

'Do you want to talk about it?'

'Sure I want to talk about it, only that's the weird thing, there's nothing to talk about ...'

'How so?' quizzed Ian.

Mary pushed herself away from his embrace, 'It's really frightening you know. A second ago I was absolutely terrified, now I can't remember why.'

Ian gave Mary a comforting smile, 'From the size of those notes, you've been working too damn hard! And what's with the Bibles?'

Mary looked blankly where Ian was pointing, 'This gets worse, I don't remember leaving those two Bibles out!'

Still holding Mary's hands, Ian changed the subject, 'You know, I'm really sorry about what happened between us.'

Mary stared sadly at Ian but said nothing. Ian persisted, 'If we're going to work together, we've got to forget the past.'

When Mary still said nothing, Ian walked over and picked up a vase of flowers, 'Listen, if you don't say something nice, I'm going to tip this water all over my head!' Methodically, Ian counted up to five, before suddenly up-turning the vase over his head.

With impeccable timing, the Professor chose this moment to walk into the study; giving his son a bewildered stare, he said, 'I know you're thirsty, but this is ridiculous!'

When everyone had finished laughing, the Professor noted with satisfaction how Mary and Ian seemed much more relaxed together.

'How did you two get on with Dr. Lawrence?' asked Mary.

'That's easily summarised,' answered Ian, 'One, Hugo Lawrence rates Nostradamus as the "numero uno" genius of all time. Two, the guy's terrified of the future. And three, astrology is still trailing centuries behind the manuscripts we've inherited.'

'It figures,' said Mary cryptically, and looked at the others, 'Now I'll up-date you with my work. I finished the last translation this afternoon.'

Giving Mary's hand an affectionate squeeze, Ian said, 'That's probably what triggered your nightmare.'

The Professor looked concerned, 'Sorry to hear about the nightmare but Ian's probably right, it was the relief of completing such a huge task. Anyway, tell us your main conclusions.'

Ian laughed, 'Don't be so formal, Dad. You sound like you're conducting a Ph.D. examination.'

Apologetically the Professor said, 'I'm sorry Mary, it's just the style I've picked up during the last twenty years.'

'Don't apologise, I'm starting to feel like one of the family. Anyway, there are three conclusions. The first two are predictable, but the third. . .'

Ian squeezed Mary's hand tighter, 'C'mon, don't build up the suspense, it's high enough already!'

In a soft voice, Mary said, 'The first conclusion is in line with what Hugo Lawrence told you, Nostradamus' astrology is in a different league to anyone else's.' She pointed her hand towards the three-inch pile of typed notes, 'That's the astrology of Nostradamus, all five hundred pages of it! So even with the translations, it would send someone nuts trying to make a single prediction.

'Yet for all its sophistication, the man knew his theories weren't perfect. Which leads me to the second conclusion. Nostradamus guessed correctly that there were planets which his little telescope couldn't see, and these were causing one prediction in ten to be wrong.' Mary went ominously silent.

'And what's your third conclusion?' demanded Ian impatiently.

Mary looked down at the carpet, 'It's what I feared from the beginning...' Noticing that Mary had started to tremble again, Ian affectionately placed his arm around her, which seemed to give her the strength to continue.

'My third conclusion,' she said in a scarcely audible voice, 'is that Nostradamus knew his work was evil! Oh sure, the early manuscripts are euphoric but that was when he thought it was a gift from God. Later, after seeing the horrors of the future, the man changed his mind. Towards the end, he was certain that the equations came from the Devil himself.'

Mary pointed at the manuscripts, 'See that one with the charred edge? Nostradamus threw it on the fire after prophesying the death of a friend. Then some irresistible force made him plunge his hand into the fiames to save it.'

'Did he say why his work was evil?' asked the Professor.

'No,' answered Mary, 'but he kept warning about completing the circle.'

Ian raised an eyebrow, 'Completing the circle? Sounds like witchcraft to me.'

Mary shook her head, 'During the last month I've come to know Nostradamus pretty well, and for all his astrology, the guy was religious. He was writing about prophecy when he said that completing the circle was the ultimate danger.'

Ian shrugged, 'In that case, why didn't the man tell us what it meant?'

'All his manuscripts are like that,' answered Mary, 'packed full of riddles and rhymes.'

Noting the apprehension in Mary's voice, the Professor said, 'No wonder you had a nightmare after being locked up with these manuscripts for weeks.'

Mary nodded, 'I've got to admit that I've not been sleeping too well, but everything should be okay now that the work's finished.'

Ian looked at Mary, 'Finished? We've inherited a mountain of theorems that are so way out that they're impossible to use; we've got to avoid completing the circle, even though we don't know what it means, and both Hugo Lawrence and Nostradamus can't bear to face the future. Finished? The show's only just starting, the question is, what do we do next?'

The Professor looked at Ian, 'C'mon Ian, you're an astronomer, what do you do with a long equation?'

Ian's face broke out into a triumphant grin, 'Now I get it, put everything we've got onto a computer?'

The Professor nodded, 'A big computer will give more predictions in a second than Nostradamus could dream of in a lifetime.'

'I hate to be a party pooper,' said Mary, 'but before a computer can give answers, it needs to be programmed. I've examined the equations and take my word, they're really heavy. It would need a grade "A" mathematician just to understand them, let along write a programme.'

Ian shrugged, 'We found ourselves a grade "A" translator, now we'll dig out a mathematician.'

The Professor eased back in his chair, 'And how do you reckon we're going to do that? We were lucky to find Mary but we can't place another ad on the Bulletin board, asking Einstein to please step forward.'

Ian laughed, 'Sometimes you sound more like me than I do! Anyway, now it's you who's not thinking like a scientist. We just look through the science journals until we find our man.'

'Or woman, you sexist!' added Mary.

The next morning, the three people submerged themselves in the Mathematics and Computing section of the University library. It was approaching eleven when Ian's gaze locked onto an article in an obscure journal. He beckoned the others across, 'This could be just the guy we're looking for.'

The Professor picked up the copy of *The International Journal of Scientific Prediction*, 'At least the title sounds right,' he said, retreating to a place where they could talk freely, 'now let's see what you've unearthed.' The journal was folded open at a paper written by Doctor Bronwen Jones, entitled 'Predicting the Future by Catastrophe Simulation'.

Looking at the complex equations, the Professor said, 'If I wasn't supposed to be an expert on hieroglyphics, I'd say it looks like hieroglyphics to me! You'd better explain what it's about.'

Ian took hold of the journal, 'Well, this guy Jones is saying that if you had a big enough computer, the future could be predicted by catastrophe theory. But don't be fooled, Dad, the title might sound great but without a set of programmes, it's all moonshine.' Ian paused before adding, 'Now if we got our act together with this guy Jones?'

'Let's not rush into things, Ian,' insisted the Professor, 'we don't know anything about this "Bronwen Jones".'

Ian looked upset, 'Hey, do you think I'm nuts or something? I wasn't suggesting that we burst into his office and yell out the whole story. We've got to play this guy cool. Feed out a bit of bait as if we were after a young trout, then see if he nibbles?' Ian noticed that Mary was smiling, 'What's so funny?' he demanded.

'It's just that Bronwen's a Welsh name.'

'I know that.'

Mary laughed out loud, 'A Welsh name for a *woman*!'

Ian's face went blank, then he grinned, 'I should have known that no guy would be dumb enough to be called "Bronwen"! Anyway, the plan's the same, phone her and say that you're sold on her work and want to know if it can be applied to the past as well as the future.'

Although the Professor didn't look convinced, eventually he said, 'I guess it could work, how do we get in touch with her?'

Mary looked at the article, 'According to this, she's a Reader in Mathematics at some place called University College, Cardiff.'

It was 12:05 p.m. in Cardiff, when a rasping woman's voice said, 'University College, can I help you?'

'I'd like to speak to Dr. Bronwen Jones, Department of Mathematics.'

'One moment, sir, the extension's ringing.'

A few seconds elapsed, then an even raspier Welsh voice said, 'Jones here.'

'Good morning, Doctor.'

'It's afternoon.'

'Not in Omaha. My name's Frank Cooper.'

'This call must be costing you a fortune, Frank Cooper, so what can I do for you?'

'I've just read your paper on predicting the future.'

'Are you a mathematician?'

'No, an archaeologist.'

'Seems a funny subject for an archaeologist to be interested in but I suppose it takes all sorts. Anyway, what do you think of it?'

'Fascinating, but is it possible?'

'Sure, if you've a big enough computer and the programmes to go with it, but we don't so it was just a philosophical abstraction.' Hardly pausing for breath, the Welsh woman declared, 'Now, I wouldn't want you to think me abrupt, but I'm in the middle of a discussion with a student, so could you get to the point?'

'Certainly, Doctor. Your work could be relevant to a project I'm running. Any objection to myself and two colleagues visiting you?'

'None, always willing to discuss my work, even with an archaeologist. I'm flying to Australia next month but if our chat can wait until January, I'll be in the States myself.'

'How about tomorrow?'

For a few seconds, the phone in Cardiff went silent, then an incredulous Dr. Jones said, 'Did I get you wrong? I thought you were in Omaha?'

'Wc are, but flying standby would get us to London by late afternoon, American time.'

'You make it sound important but if it's got anything to do with the military, don't bother coming, I'm an out and out pacifist.'

'No, the military isn't involved, now tell me how to find you.'

The flight from America proved uneventful, except for the grin on the taxi driver's face at Heathrow Airport when Ian winked and calmly said, 'Cardiff!' They were able to sleep during the train journey and arrived at the university by ten o'clock. The Professor knocked politely on Dr. Jones' office door, to be greeted by a booming Welsh voice, 'C'mon in, it's open.'

Somewhat meekly, the three Americans entered Dr. Jones' domain. During their transatlantic telephone conversation, the Professor had formed a preconception of what Dr. Jones would be like. He'd expected to meet a woman in her mid-forties, of matron-like stature and with a 'say what you mean' approach to life. To his surprise, he wasn't far wrong.

After the Professor had introduced his colleagues, Dr. Jones said, 'If the security man wasn't a distant cousin, I'd have been thrown out of this building two hours ago. You're booked in at the Caerphilly Arms, nothing extravagant mind but it's got a bar which stays open, so what are we doing here?'

Although the term 'hotel' flattered the Caerphilly Arms, being little more than a Welsh pub which took in paying guests, there was a welcoming atmosphere about the place, with the ram's head above the bar giving the establishment character. After completing the formalities at the booking desk, the Americans joined Dr.

Jones at a table in the small bar.

The woman put down her whisky, 'This is all very mysterious. Since your phone call I've been trying to guess what's so secret that it couldn't be discussed over the phone.'

The Professor smiled reassuringly, 'I appreciate that it isn't normal to get invited to a midnight meeting with three strangers. However, before answering your question, I'd like to ask you some.' Dr. Jones shrugged. 'Okay' said the Professor, 'question number one; can the future be predicted?'

Dr. Jones nodded, 'That paper of mine proves it can, but not by mortal man.'

The Professor looked at the Welsh woman, 'Why?'

'Why, because we haven't a big enough computer.'

'Say we had the computer,' interrupted Ian.

'Then we wouldn't know what equations to feed it.'

Ian poured himself a whisky, 'And what if three travellers from a distant land handed you the equations?'

For the first time since they'd met, the woman smiled, 'There's nothing like starting a meeting with a joke.' She looked at the faces round the table, 'You can't be serious? Surely you're not saying that you've developed a set of equations which describe the future?'

Ian grinned, 'And if we are saying just that?'

The woman screwed up her face, 'Then I'd say that you lot didn't come here by airplane after all; you must be escapees from an asylum!'

For some seconds, an eerie silence descended on the little bar in the Caerphilly Arms then Bronwen said, 'Anyway, even if some fairy godmother gave you the equations, name a computer which would take them?'

The Professor reached for his pipe, 'How about the TITAN complex in Omaha?'

Bronwen's face flared red, 'TITAN's owned by the military, you told me that your visit didn't involve the military.'

The Professor smiled, 'There are two TITANs and I just happen to have a time sharing arrangment on the prototype in the University.'

Methodically, Dr. Jones opened her handbag, took out a small cigar and lit it, 'Let's get this right. You're saying that you can predict the future?'

In a hushed voice, the Professor answered, 'You're one step ahead of us. We *may* have a set of equations which could predict the future, but until they're programmed, who knows? That's why we're here, we need someone to put the equations on TITAN, what do you say?'

The woman leaned back and drew on her cigar, 'I say that I'd need to know a hell of a lot more before getting involved in such a hairbrained project.'

'Such as?' asked Ian.

'Such as the name of the genius who gave you the equations?'

Putting down his drink, the Professor said, 'I'll need your word that everything you hear will be kept secret. If not then we'll get right back on our plane and go home.'

Dr. Jones replenished her whisky glass, 'You swear it's got nothing to do with the military?'

'Not as far as we know,' reassured the Professor, 'at least not directly.'

Dr. Jones waved her hand, 'Okay you've got my word, now what's all the mystery?'

The Professor looked at Mary, 'I reckon that Dr. Jones is more likely to believe you.'

Hesitantly, Mary said, 'I suppose you've heard of Nostradamus?'

'Nostradamus? Wasn't he that fortune teller from the Middle Ages.'

Mary nodded, 'Yes, except he was an astrologer.'

'Same thing,' said the Welsh woman contemptuously, 'it's a load of rubbish.'

Mary shook her head, 'That's just what I said two months ago but not any more.'

Dr. Jones stubbed out her cigar in the ashtray, 'I thought you three were scientists.'

'We are,' answered Mary curtly.

'You can't be, no scientist worthy of the name subscribes to astrology.'

'Why?' asked Mary.

Dr. Jones waved her arms in a wild arc, almost catching Ian's nose, 'How could anyone predict the future by plotting the positions of the planets?'

Ian edged himself out of the woman's reach before saying, 'That's what we'd hoped you'd be able to tell us.'

Dr. Jones threw up her hands, 'Now just wait a minute, don't say that this meeting's about astrology?' She looked at the faces round the table, 'Well I'll be buggered, it *is* about astrology.

Reputable scientists shouldn't get involved in such mumbo-jumbo!'

The Professor started to bristle, this time *he* poured a whisky before saying, 'And what's the first commandment of a 'reputable scientist?'

'You tell me,' snapped Bronwen, 'it's your pantomime.'

Forcefully, the Professor said, 'An open mind, just that!'

This remark visibly hurt the Welsh woman and she paused, as if counting to ten, before saying, 'All right, I'll open my mind to astrology but I'll apply the second commandment to the crap you're going to tell me!'

'And what's the second commandment?' asked the Professor.

'A critical mind.'

Both scientists glared at each other, before simultaneously bursting out laughing.

'That makes it one set all,' quipped Ian.

Bronwen passively sipped her whisky while Ian told the story of the letter, the tomb, the manuscripts and the translations. When the tale was complete, the Welsh woman smiled, 'It'd make a great script for a film, hope the ending's good?'

Ian looked disappointed, 'I guess you still don't believe us?'

Bronwen reached out and ruffled Ian's hair, 'You've all got honest faces, so I'll accept that you think it's true, but it's a story that even my Great-Uncle Thomas wouldn't be taken in by. You're obviously the victims of a remarkably elaborate hoax.'

The Professor raised an eyebrow, 'What makes you so sure?'

Condescendingly, Bronwen answered, 'Whoever sent your letter had to know that the other letter in the tomb was addressed to you. The only way they could've known that is by placing it there themselves!' Bronwen poured herself yet another whisky and waited for a reply.

'You're not being fair, Doctor,' protested the Professor, 'the letter wasn't addressed to me directly, only to "my friends in the New World."'

Bronwen grinned, 'Same thing. Even a dumbo would have been suspicious if it had been written in blue biro and addressed to "Professor Cooper".'

Mary intervened, 'Of course, you might be right, maybe the letter is a hoax, but dare we ignore the other possibilities?'

Bronwen put down her glass, 'What possibilities?'

'First the easy one,' said Mary, 'the manuscripts did belong to Nostradamus and some distant descendant of Chavigny who knew what was in the tomb sent the letter.'

Bronwen shrugged, 'That wouldn't prove Nostradamus could foretell the future.'

'True,' conceded Mary, 'or that he couldn't?'

Bronwen scratched her head, 'Can't disprove a negative so what's the second possibility?'

Mary smiled, 'Everything's genuine. Nostradamus really could predict the future and we've inherited his equations. Of course we won't know for certain until we find someone to put them on a computer.'

Bronwen picked up the whisky bottle, saw it was empty and theatrically dropped it in the waste basket, 'Can't think where all that whisky's gone.'

Ian stood up, 'I'll get another'

'Get two,' said Bronwen, 'I don't like to drink alone!'

Turning her attention to the Professor, Bronwen said, 'These manuscripts you keep talking about, have you get one with you?' The Professor pointed to his briefcase. 'Okay,' said Bronwen, 'not that I believe a word mind, but it might be amusing to see the equations.'

The Professor opened his briefcase and handed Bronwen a translation. The woman waved her hand at the bar, 'You three amuse yourselves while I wade through this gobbledegook.'

Obediently, the Americans moved to the bar, leaving Bronwen, the manuscript and one whisky bottle at the table. The barman had long since departed for his bed before Bronwen finally rejoined the others.

'Well?' asked Mary.

Bronwen screwed up her face in a non-committal smile, 'Well, if this manuscript is genuine, its writer invented calculus a hundred years before Newton!'

Ian shrugged, 'Why not? The guy invented the telescope fifty years before Galileo.'

Bronwen waved Ian quiet, 'It doesn't stop with calculus, the manuscript is full of probability theory and even something which doesn't exist yet, Nostradamus calls it "calculated chance".'

Ian opened his eyes wide, 'You said "Nostradamus calls it", does that mean you back the manuscript as genuine?'

Bronwen shook her head, 'That's too big a leap. All it means is that I'm not laughing it off as a fake anymore. But this girl is staying firmly on the fence until I've done some simulation runs back at the University. So if you'll excuse me. I'll start them now.'

Ian blinked, 'Don't you mean "first thing in the morning"?'

Bronwen gave Ian an indignant glance, 'When I say now, I mean now! I told you that my cousin was the security guard, so I'll see you all at my office at nine. Sleep well, I've got work to do. Goodnight.' With that, Bronwen rammed the manuscript under her arm, dropped the spare whisky bottle into her pocket and left.

Over breakfast, the Americans discussed the events of the previous night. 'That Dr. Jones just isn't for real,' said Ian, 'and was it a good idea to leave her with the manuscript?'

The Professor dropped a sugar lump into his coffee, 'I didn't notice you volunteering to Indian wrestle to get it back?'

Mary burst into a giggle. 'It wasn't that funny,' said Ian.

'I'm laughing at something else,' said Mary.

'Like what?' demanded Ian.

'It's not very charitable,' she said guiltily, 'but I've just remembered how you described poor Dr. Jones.' Ian looked blank. 'You remember,' insisted Mary, 'a young trout, that's what you said.'

Ian grinned, 'Well, at least I got the fish right.'

The Professor didn't laugh, 'You two are not being very Christian. My guess is that there's a different person under that craggy Welsh exterior to the one we met last night.'

Ian looked at his watch, 'It's eight thirty and somehow I don't think we should be late.'

The voice of the Welsh barman-cum-waiter, carried across the small dining room, 'Your taxi's outside, sir.'

After a brief journey through the damp streets of Cardiff, the Americans arrived at Bronwen's office. Mary's polite knock was answered by the Welsh woman's window-rattling voice, 'Come on in, the door's open!' Inside the office, the atmosphere comprised stale cigar smoke, with an half empty whisky bottle standing defiantly amongst a collection of dirty glasses and crumpled paper. Bronwen was crouched near the window, typing instructions into a computer terminal. The Professor coughed politely.

Instead of turning to greet her visitors, Bronwen commanded, 'Sit down, just waiting for a printout on lunar eclipses.' Without protest, the Americans patiently waited while the printer hummed out a wad of results, which Bronwen excitedly tore off and scrutinised on a table near the window.

After some minutes, the Welsh woman swivelled round and attempted a smile, but the smoke from her cigar made her eyes squint and the gesture was lost. If it was possible, Bronwen Jones looked even more bedraggled than she had the night before.

'Morning,' grunted Bronwen in a voice which made it impossible to distinguish if this was a greeting or merely an observation, 'hope you all slept well.'

'We did,' replied the Professor. 'What have you found out during the night?'

Bronwen laughed, 'That's what I like, cut out the small talk and get straight to the point. What have I found? Well, it isn't a hoax, that's for sure. I've tested one theory after another and they all hold up.'

Bronwen jabbed her hand towards a portrait of Sir Isaac Newton on the wall, 'Up to now, that man has been top of my list of geniuses, but if this really is the work of Nostradamus, Newton's relegated to being a first year undergraduate. The manuscripts include matrix manipulation, celestial mechanics and numerical integration, none of which were thought of until Nostradamus had been dead for centuries.'

Ian grinned, 'Oh behalf of the inmates, 'it's swell to welcome you to the asylum. Now where does this leave us?'

Bronwen ran her fingers through her wiry, yellow hair, 'Leave us? It leaves me believing every damned word of your story. That still doesn't prove the future can be predicted, mind you, only that the manuscripts are the work of a brilliant brain. Until everything's on the computer, we'll not know if the man behind this charade was as dotty as me for getting mixed up in this.'

The Professor smiled, 'You'll do it then?'

Tossing her cigar butt into the ashtray, Bronwen answered, 'Just try to stop me!'

She picked up the whisky bottle and waved it invitingly at her visitors who, in turn, declined the offer. After pouring herself a drink, Bronwen walked across to the window, 'For eleven, dreary years I've looked at the same, miserable view. This place owes me a sabbatical, so from today I'm on it.'

'Won't that make you unpopular with the University authorities?' asked Mary.

'Stick the University authorities, I know how to deal with their sort,' snorted Bronwen. 'I do what I think is right, always have done, always will do. Now I think it's right to join your team.' Then, almost as a minor afterthought, she said, 'I'll fly back to America with you. You have a big house?'

The Professor nodded.

'Spare room?'

Again the Professor nodded.

Bronwen smiled, 'That's settled then, I'll stay at your house, right?' The Professor smiled, 'You'll be most welcome.'

Bronwen crossed to a cabinet and respectfully picked up a ceramic rugby ball, 'I always travel light, so, apart from clothes, this is the only thing I'll be bringing. Pontypool gave it my father after he scored five tries in a cup final.'

Self-consciously, Bronwen polished the ball on her sleeve, 'If you people find that I do a lot of yelling and running about, don't let it get you down. That's just the way I work. Can't give a leopard new tricks, or something like that . . .'

The Professor held out his hand, 'Welcome to the Nostradamus Project, Doctor, we're glad to have you on the team.'

Bronwen grasped the hand and smiled a deep genuine smile, 'We'll be working closely from now on, and my socialist upbringing makes me hate crap titles like Doctor or Professor. My name's Bronwen, call me Bron. What shall I call each of you?'

Within hours of their return to Omaha, Bronwen Jones assumed command of the Nostradamus team, the Cooper household and every other resource that might prove to be of use. The study became her private office and the nerve centre for the project. At Bronwen's instructions, the Professor diverted all the funds at his disposal, and some which weren't, to 'Project Nostradamus'.

Soon, a direct link was established between TITAN and the office in which Bronwen worked sixteen hours a day, seven days a week. The other members of the team were drafted as the Welsh woman's research assistants and each morning they would dutifully line up to be told their tasks for the day.

Although Mary was growing ever more worried about the wisdom of the work, inspired by Bronwen's infectious enthusiasm, she somehow managed to combine her medical studies with being a part of the Nostradamus team.

As the weeks passed, the Professor grew ever more overawed by the sustained drive of the Welsh woman. Late one evening, while Bronwen was working in the 'office' as usual, the Professor said to Ian, 'That woman just isn't human, she only works and sleeps. Ten like her could move a mountain on cigars and whisky!'

Ian started to laugh.

'What's so funny?' asked his father.

'You've just triggered a conversation I had with Bron yesterday. I told her that whisky would be the death of her, and you know what she said? 'If it is then sprinkle some on my grave!'

The Professor smiled. 'That's Bronwen all right.'

Ian raised his hand, 'Quiet, Dad,' he insisted, 'I haven't reached the funny part yet. When I was leaving the "office", Bron shouted after me, 'With whisky at ten dollars a bottle, make sure it's passed through your kidneys before you do the sprinkling!'

It was early October when the books arrived from Hugo Lawrence. 'Stick them in my room, Frank,' insisted Bronwen, 'I'll read them in my spare time.'

Two weeks elapsed before Bronwen called the Professor into the study, 'I've looked at some of those damn books and I don't like what I've read.'

Apprehensively, the Professor asked, 'Like what?'

Bronwen attempted to get a brush through her hair as she said, 'Well, like an Irish priest called Saint Malachy, way back in 1143, predicting how many Popes there'd be before the end of the world?'

'And?'

Bronwen gave up trying to get the brush through her hair and flung it into a corner, 'And the last one's batting now.'

The Professor sat down, 'I thought you didn't believe in prophecy.'

Bronwen waved him to shut up, 'A woman can change her mind, can't she? Especially if she's just read Morgan Robertson's vision of the sinking of the Titanic. The image was so damn vivid that he wrote a book about it in 1898, called "The Wreck of the Titan". Robertson got everything right, including writing that it was the maiden voyage of the "Unsinkable Titan". He gave its length, weight, number of passengers, the shortage of lifeboats, the exact place where it hit the iceberg, its speed at impact, the month of April and even that it had three propellers and went down nose first!'

The Professor shuffled uneasily, 'That makes the lions in Trafalgar Square seem third rate.'

Bronwen looked puzzled, 'Lions in Trafalgar Square? I don't get you, Frank.'

The Professor shook his head, 'It isn't important, Bron, except that if you're selling prophecy, you're preaching to the converted.'

At 7 a.m. on the morning of December 23rd, when the three Americans assembled to be detailed their duties, Bronwen proudly announced, 'We're almost there, by Friday we should be running the programme.'

At first, the others didn't know how to react, then Mary said apprehensively, 'I didn't realise we were so close.'

Bronwen smiled, 'Do you know why we've made such good progress?'

Mary shook her head.

'Because collectively, we're cleverer than Nostradamus. The old man was an expert on astrology, medicine, mathematics and archaeology. By some way-out coincidence, this exactly matches our own talents.'

Bronwen turned her attention to the Professor, 'We've a decision to make, do you want a printout of the predictions or can I rig up an audio link with TITAN?'

'What's the difference?' asked the Professor.

'Well, Frank, instead of typing in our questions, we could speak to TITAN and listen to its answers.'

Mary sank into a chair, 'That's creepy', she said softly, 'the voice of Nostradamus bridging the centuries.'

Bronwen raised an eyebrow, 'I never saw it like that,' she confessed, 'but I suppose you're right.'

After a momentary silence, the Professor said, 'Let me get this clear; the computer can talk?'

Bronwen grinned, 'Yes, Frank, but it can't think. Now what do you say?'

With a shrug, the Professor said, 'Okay, we're committed to the project so let's go for the verbal system.'

Bronwen winked, 'That's what I guessed you'd say, Frank, so here's a list of instruments we'll need.'

As the Professor took the list, he said, 'A person could get to feel that they were being manipulated around here.'

Bronwen smiled mischievously, 'I can't think who by? Now run along and get the equipment, I've got work to do.'

On Christmas Day, Brenda prepared an excellent dinner but Bronwen didn't join the celebrations, 'Can't waste valuable hours on some pagan feast,' she shouted through the locked study door when Ian invited her to join them. It was at such times that the Professor feared that Bronwen's dedication to the project was turning into an obsession.

Christmas Day came and went without Bronwen making an appearance outside the study, then Friday arrived. When the team lined up to be detailed their tasks, true to her forecast, Bronwen calmly declared that the programme was complete. Pointing her finger at an audio system, hanging from a four inch nail on the wall, the Welsh woman said, 'Sorry about the plaster, Frank, but that little speaker is waiting to talk.'

Bronwen calmly lit a cigar before saying to the Professor, 'I gave you the job of deciding how to test the system, what ideas have you come up with?'

As if he was a freshman being interrogated by a senior academic, the Professor answered, 'Set the datum to Nostradamus' death, call this "year zero", then let the programme run on and see how close it comes to getting history right.'

Bronwen slapped the Professor on the back, 'Not bad, Frank, you'll need to be more precise but it'll do for starters. Now everybody cross their fingers, the subroutines couldn't be tested separately so they either work together or it's back to the drawing board. Here goes.'

As Bronwen reached to activate the system, Mary jabbed out her hand and covered the switch. 'What the hell do you think you're doing?' snapped Bronwen angrily, 'get off that damn switch!'

Mary shook her head, 'Sure, we've all put a ton of work into the project, especially you Bron, but my instinct yells stop, destroy the programme, burn the manuscripts and forget that any of this happened!'

The other members of the team looked blankly at Mary, then Bronwen snapped, 'Does your instinct tell you why we should quit now?'

Mary shook her head, 'I just know that the work is evil, don't you sense it yourself?'

Bronwen glared at the woman, 'No, I don't, but then I haven't got your religious hangups.'

In desperation, both women looked at the Professor for his decision on how to resolve the first major conflict since the project started. 'Let's agree a compromise,' he said calmly, 'I guess that we can't do any harm by just checking history, so I propose we run the programme up to the present day. That way we'll know if the programme works, if it does then we stop and vote on whether to let it run on into the future.'

The Professor looked in turn at each member of the team, when no dissent to the plan was voiced, he said, 'Okay, let's get started.'

CHAPTER 5

The grandfather clock had just finished chiming when Bronwen declared—'Okay, Frank, the system's operational, say something to add your voice pattern to TITAN's recognition library.'

The Professor hesitated, 'I should say something special, like Armstrong on the Moon but my mind's a blank.'

Bronwen shrugged, 'What you just said was fine. The system's ready when you are.'

Only now did Professor Cooper realise just how profusely his hands were sweating. The same foreboding which had gripped Mary had now descended on him. Quelling his doubts, the Professor instructed, 'TITAN, recount important events since 1560.'

The audio system hung passively on the wall while, some miles away, TITAN performed the innumerable calculations needed to give an answer. First the Professor's speech was reduced into its constituent parts. Vowel and consonant sounds were sorted and analysed and the essential meaning of the sentence was determined. This rationalised question was then passed to the computer's logic generation package. Finally, the answer was converted back into English, with the entire process occupying less than one second. TITAN's synthesised voice echoed into existence, 'Clarify what constitutes an important event.'

Leaping out of her chair in jubilation, Bronwen yelled 'It's working! It's working!'

'Then why is it being tight on answers?' asked Ian.

'That's simple,' answered Bronwen. 'What your father regards as important, TITAN might dismiss as trivial. Even though the packages are able to sort out what you really mean from what you actually ask, computers still can't make a value judgement.'

'Okay,' conceded the Professor, 'then tell me what to do?'

With an excited grin, Bronwen said, 'It's simple, Frank, just tell it what you mean by important.'

Hesitantly, the Professor said, 'An important event is a major war, the birth of a world figure or anything which significantly changes the history of America or England.'

'Sounds a bit chauvinistic,' laughed Bronwen, 'but it'll do for starters.' Bronwen handed Ian a sheet, 'Here's a "potted" version of world history. When TITAN starts giving answers, see if it gets any right.'

From the back of the room, Mary asked nervously, 'How long will the calculations take?'

'Less time than it took Nostradamus to dip his quill,' answered Bronwen, proudly, 'but there might be a delay through timesharing.'

'I wasn't impressed with TITAN's voice,' said Ian, It sounds inhuman.'

'We could have had male, female or neutral,' quipped Bronwen. 'I chose neutral to avoid TITAN developing a "cult follo ...",'

The Welsh woman was interrupted in midword by TITAN, 'I am ready to output.'

Glancing at the Professor, Bronwen saw that he was again hesitating, 'For Christ's sake, Frank, if you don't tell it to begin, I will!'

In a barely audible voice, the Professor said, 'Please begin.'

> The year fifteen hundred and sixty-four will herald the birth of a supreme writer; this will be counter-balanced by the death of a master artist.

After searching his list, Ian said excitedly, 'TITAN's smack on the mark, Shakespeare was born and Michelangelo died!'

Bronwen waved her hand, 'Don't run up any flags yet, Nostradamus still had two years to live in 1564. Move further on in time, Frank.'

'Please continue, TITAN.'

> The base of time will be changed in the year 1582. Future pronouncements relate to the new base.

'Don't bother looking that one up,' said Bronwen, 'Pope Gregory introduced his calendar in 1582.'

Glancing up from his notes, Ian noticed that Mary was trembling. 'What's wrong?'

'It's the way TITAN speaks,' she stammered, 'it's really eerie.'

Bronwen shrugged casually, 'The voice and phraseology are a bit strange perhaps.'

'Strange?' said Ian, 'With the disembodied voice and all, it even sounds as if Nostradamus is choosing the words.'

Bronwen smiled, 'In a way I suppose he is but don't let a man who's been dead for centuries frighten you.'

All conversation now ceased as TITAN's predictions began to emerge at a faster rate than Ian could tick them off.

> 1588 will see England emerge victorious from a great sea battle with Spain.
>
> During year 1620, the religious fathers will sail to the Americas.

After some minutes, and a dozen predictions later, the Professor said, 'TITAN, please stop.' He turned to Ian, 'How many are right so far?'

Ian looked puzzled, 'How many? Everything's correct.'

In an uncharacteristically emotional voice, Bronwen said, 'It's bloody incredible. If I hadn't written the programme myself, I'd suspect fraud.' She fumbled a cigar from her pocket, and gestured to the Professor to let the programme continue.

> 1649 will witness the King of England losing his head, with a Republic being his replacement.
>
> During the year 1652, the English dictator will be poisoned in London.

'Hold it right there,' said the Professor. 'If TITAN's referring to Oliver Cromwell then he wasn't murdered in 1652, in fact he died of old age.'

Mary breathed a sigh of relief, 'That's the first mistake, and I've never been so glad to see an error in my life.'

Ian scrawled a big X on his list, almost puncturing the paper in the process, 'I don't get it? How come TITAN got that one wrong?'

Oblivious to the others, Bronwen exclaimed, 'Bugger it. I thought this might happen, but this is not the time for inquests, let's keep going.'

> A king will rule England once more and he will grant a charter to a company of learned philosophers.

> The year 1666 will witness an English mathematician explaining the motion of the heavens, whilst his capital burns.

'That's Newton,' said the Professor.

Bronwen nodded, 'Except that Nostradamus knew the laws of motion before Newton was born.'

Biting his pencil, Ian said, 'This thing's got me beat. Why doesn't a bum prediction throw the whole of history out after that point?'

'The programme doesn't build on previous events,' answered Bronwen dismissively. 'Each prediction is a unique solution to the governing equations and isn't influenced by anything before or after.'

Ian smiled, 'You mean like last year's weather not affecting next year's forecast?'

Bronwen shrugged, 'Yeah, something like that.'

'Ian may understand what you're talking about,' conceded the Professor, 'but I sure don't. I would have guessed that history was like a tall building, and removing some bricks at the base would affect everything higher up?'

'Don't they teach you "soft scientists" anything?' chided Bronwen. 'Okay, Frank, let me spell it out. When the programme makes a prediction, it doesn't calculate it from previous events, only from the relative positions of the planets at that instant. If you were a gambling man, you'd understand what I mean. Say you had studied the form and come up with five "winners" for tomorrow's races, then just because the first one loses, that doesn't screw up the rest of the races.'

'Hey, Bronwen,' said Ian with a sly smile, 'you've just given me a great idea for making a few bucks!'

Although Mary gave Ian a disparaging glance, Bronwen laughed and ruffled his hair, 'Ian, you're a lad after my own heart.'

'We haven't heard much about America yet,' interrupted the Professor.

'That figures,' teased Bronwen, 'why should TITAN concern itself with a minor British colony?'

'In that case,' said the Professor, 'let's move on to 1776.' TITAN obeyed.

1776. A great nation is born across the mighty ocean.

1789. Whilst the Americas appoint their first President, a peasants' revolt erupts in France.

1815. A victory at Waterloo leaves Britain standing supreme.

1826. The mighty ocean is vanquished by a ship without a sail.

1837. The great Queen ascends the British throne.

1854. Britain and France unite against the Tsar of all the Russias.

1859. An English philosopher blasphemes with regard to the origin of life.'

'Stop it there, Frank,' insisted Bronwen, 'assuming that TITAN was talking about Charles Darwin, why did it call the theory of evolution blasphemous?'

Ian shrugged, 'Maybe Nostradamus' religious beliefs are behind the choice of words?'

Quietly yet positively, Mary said, 'There is another possibility. Perhaps Darwin's theories are blasphemous and the programme knows it.'

Bronwen looked blankly at the ceiling. 'You can't be serious?' she laughed. 'With your medical background you should know better.'

'I may not be right,' conceded Mary, 'but believe me, I am serious.'

Bronwen flexed her shoulders, 'Who knows what to believe anymore, so let's get on with it, Frank.'

1901. With the death of its Queen, the Great Empire passes its zenith.

1903. An American conquers the skies.

1914. The world begins its first holocaust.

1918. A transitory peace prevails.

1926. A revolution of the Left occurs in Britain.

1927. The British Monarchy is restored.

'Hold it there, Dad,' said Ian, 'I haven't any record of a revolution in Britain in 1926.'

Bronwen nodded, 'But there was the general strike and my father helped organise it, God rest him.'

The Professor shook his head, 'There's one hell of a difference between a strike and a revolution.'

'A single bullet?' suggested Bronwen, raising an eyebrow, 'But let's not argue now, Frank, tell TITAN to get on with its predictions.'

1933. The anti-Christ leads Germany.

1939. The second holocaust begins.

1945. A mushroom cloud heralds the final transitory peace.

A death-like shiver ran along each spine. 'Transitory?' repeated Bronwen in a low voice, 'I don't like the word transitory.'

'For God's sake, stop the thing now,' pleaded Mary, 'can't you all see that this is the work of the Devil?'

Bronwen dismissed Mary's plea, 'Bullshit'.

Unperturbed, TITAN continued its pronoucements,

1949. The ultimate alliances are forged and the battle lines drawn.

1962. Two projectiles are exchanged between East and West, at a price of four million dead.

After TITAN had been abruptly halted, Ian said, 'Now that sure isn't on my list, thank God.'

'God had nothing to do with it,' snapped Bronwen, 'the world was on a hair trigger and pure dumb luck pulled us through. I can still remember the night, fleets of British and American bombers in the air over Swansea, all with their targets mapped out in Russia. At least I had the good sense to get blind drunk.'

'Bronwen's right,' agreed the Professor, 'if the Russian missile ships hadn't turned back from Cuba, it would have meant war.'

'But by the grace of God, it didn't happen,' pleaded Mary, 'so why does that thing say it did?'

When everyone looked at Bronwen for an answer, she said provocatively, 'I know where the cock-up is, but let's press on, Frank.'

> 1967. A brief but decisive war erupts between two heathen nations in the Holy Land.
>
> 1968. The warrior president of France is assassinated.

'Wrong again,' said Ian, 'I saw the movie on T.V. and the ''Jackal'' didn't get de Gaulle.'

Bronwen nodded, 'And if I'm right, the errors will get worse as we approach the present.'

Giving Bronwen a long stare, the Professor stated, 'Do you want to tell us why?'

'Of course I do, we're a team, but later, Frank, later.'

> 1968. The man whose namesake was a heretic, preaches Universal Brotherhood and is assassinated.

'That was Martin Luther King,' said Mary.

> 1979. A false prophet returns to Persia.
>
> 1980. Russia extends her empire to the east. For three days, great armies, beyond those dreamed of in antiquity, lock in combat over the plains of Germany before a fragile peace is proclaimed.
>
> 1982. Britain defeats an unfamiliar enemy in the Southern Ocean.
>
> 1984. Gold medals dazzle the West, but Russia turns her back to them.

'Stop TITAN!' commanded the Professor.

'Christ, Frank, why have you stopped this time?' snapped Bronwen.

'Because we're getting too close to the present. If the next prophesy jumps a few years, we'll be into the future.'

Bronwen scowled angrily, 'But the whole damn point of the programme is to see the future. Who gives a bugger about the past?'

Firmly shaking his head, the Professor stated, 'Don't start yelling, Bronwen, I said you'd get your vote, but first let's examine the predictions that TITAN has got wrong.'

Ian looked at his scribbled notes, 'Well, there wasn't a revolution in Britain in 1926; no nuclear missiles were fired in 1962; General de Gaulle didn't get assassinated and instead of going to war with Russia over Afghanistan, we just skipped the Moscow Olympics.'

Staring at Bronwen, the Professor said, 'Okay, you predicted that the errors would get worse, and they have, let's hear why.'

Bronwen began to dust her ceramic rugby ball with her sleeve, 'I won't claim credit for the theory, Frank. Nostradamus guessed the same thing centuries ago, but this is what's happening. The equations are based on six planets plus the Earth, but we know that there are nine planets. Now the relative influence of each planet is determined by the "inverse square law" which, for your benefit, Frank, means that the outer planets usually have little effect because they're so far away. But what if every planet stretched out in a line on the same side of the Sun?'

Raising his hands in protest, the Professor said, 'Okay, I'm no mathematical genius, but common sense says that such a line up is virtually impossible?'

Ian shook his head, 'The odds are way-out, dad, but the first conjunctions started in '76 and they go on until 1993. The old guy teaching us cosmology said that the line-up wouldn't happen again during the entire life of the Universe.'

After trying to come to terms with the idea that the solar system had been winding down to an 'impossible' conjunction for four billion years, the Professor said, 'If I've got you right, the equations give errors because of the outer planets?'

Bronwen grimaced, 'I'm saying a whole lot more than that, Frank. The planets shouldn't line up at all during the entire life of the solar system but, sure as hell, they're going to! Now if that isn't a sign of something big then you tell me what is?'

Mary looked apprehensively at the speaker on the wall, 'No wonder Nostradamus feared for our future, and he only knew that seven planets were coming into line. Let's rip out the link to TITAN and leave our fate with God.'

Bronwen glared angrily, 'You're missing the whole damn point. Nostradamus *saw* what's waiting out there and we've got to do the same. Alright, what's heading our way may not be good, but it sure won't get any better because we refuse to see it.'

Looking at each of his colleagues in turn, the Professor said,

'Since the project started, we've known that sooner or later, this point would be reached. The future's hanging on that bent nail, waiting to be told but do we want to hear it?'

Impatiently, Bronwen snapped, 'You're wasting time again, Frank. If you insist on a vote, let's have it.'

Controlling his temper, the Professor said, 'Don't worry, Bron, you'll get your vote soon enough, but first everyone has the right to speak. How about you going first!'

Bronwen reflected before saying, 'I vote that we run the programme and stick the consequences. If Nostradamus was right and our fate is in the stars then it can't be changed, so what difference does it make to know it? However, if we *can* change the future, seeing what shit's coming our way might give us the chance to duck in time.'

Bronwen raised her hands to heaven, 'Don't get me wrong, I'm more frightened of the future than the three of you put together! The world's run by power-mad idiots; how civilisation's got this far sure beats me. Yet even believing this, I still want to see the future. Why? Because I go along with the old Welsh proverb which says 'To be forewarned is to be forearmed.'

The Professor indicated to Mary that it was her turn to speak. 'There are a thousand reasons for destroying the programme,' she said softly, 'but I'll give only one. Who is the greatest authority on Nostradamus? Not me, not even Bronwen, but Nostradamus himself. And what did Nostradamus think about the equations? I'll tell you, he thought they were the work of the Devil. Remember the crucifix on top of his manuscript. Need anything more be said? Let's destroy the programme and burn the manuscripts while we still can. Leave the future in God's hands.'

Looking at Ian, the Professor said, 'That makes it one vote each, which way do you go?'

Ian took hold of Mary's hand, 'Honest to God Mary, I wish I could go along with you but I can't. Nostradamus may have had hangups about his equations but he sure went to some trouble to get them to us. That can only mean that whatever's waiting for us in the future must be a whole lot worse than any danger from using the programme. Therefore I vote that we cross our fingers and let the programme run on into the future.'

Bronwen gave Ian a bearhug, 'That makes two votes for the programme, one against,' she exclaimed triumphantly, 'which way do you go, Frank?'

The Professor gazed out of the study window as he said, 'When the letter came, I wanted to throw it on the fire but I couldn't, some invisible force seemed to be stopping me. I know it sounds crazy, but I'm convinced that a time bomb's been ticking away in Nostradamus' tomb for centuries, and now it's ready to go off. The arguments are too evenly balanced for my vote to be based on logic, but a gut feeling tells me that the programme is evil. I vote *no*.'

Bronwen, amazed, spun round on her chair, 'You disappoint me, Frank, gut feelings without evidence have no place in science.'

'It gives us a problem though,' said Ian, 'do we toss a coin at two votes all?'

Bronwen went silent then she startled the others by exclaiming, 'What a load of idiots. It doesn't matter how we decide. Toss a coin, roll the dice, it just doesn't matter . . .'

Ian looked blankly at Bronwen, 'I didn't understand a word of that.'

Bronwen waved her hands in the air, 'Don't you see what I'm getting at?' she declared. 'We don't know our decision yet but the programme does!'

When the others still said nothing, Bronwen said in exasperation, 'TITAN can generate random numbers, right? I'm going to ask for a single digit number, if it's nought to four then we go along with Mary and destroy the programme; but if it's five to nine we run on into the future. Any objections?'

Looking at the confused faces of her colleagues, Bronwen said, 'I'll assume your silence means that you agree. Ian you take hold of this hammer and if TITAN gives the wrong answer, smash the speaker into little pieces.' Looking up at the speaker, Bronwen said confidently, 'Okay, you glorified slide rule, give me a single digit number.'

'NINE.'

As TITAN's synthesised voice echoed in the room, a more familiar voice said 'You four have been working in here for hours so I thought you might like some coffee.' The occupants of the room were startled to see a smiling Brenda Perkins, standing in the open doorway.

'Th. . .thanks, Brenda,' said the Professor, 'put the tray on the table and we'll have it later.'

Once Brenda was safely out of the room Bronwen said, 'Stick the coffee! Run the programme now.'

The Professor did nothing. 'Hell, Frank, what are you waiting for? Run the damn programme!'

When the Professor still did nothing, Bronwen yelled, 'Do you want a re-run; best out of three, is that it? It won't make a scrap of difference but okay. Mary, you ask for a number.'

Mary shook her head.

'Christ!' exclaimed Bronwen, 'this is getting us nowhere fast. Ian, you ask it for a number, please?'

Ian complied. 'NINE,' answered TITAN.

Bronwen beamed, 'Now you, Frank,' she insisted.

'Okay TITAN, give me a single digit number,' commanded the Professor.

'NINE'.

Bronwen smiled broadly, 'You can toss the hammer away, Ian, if we stand here till eternity, we'll still get the same random number.' Turning to the Professor she said, 'Face facts, Frank, it's been written that we run the programme, so for Christ's sake, get on with it.'

The Professor tried to give Mary a reassuring smile but it was lost because her eyes were closed in prayer, then he said, 'TITAN, please continue giving the history of nation states up to and *beyond* the present.'

For a few, brief seconds, the members of the Nostradamus team gazed at the silent speaker on the wall, then the slight electronic buzz which preceded speech was heard, finally, TITAN's voice again filled the study.

> 1985. War erupts in the Southern Americas.
> 1986. Strife and conflict in the lands of the Bible.
> 19—. End of programme.

The listeners looked blankly at each other, praying that their ears had played a terrifying trick. 'Ple...please repeat your last statement,' said the Professor.

'19— End of programme.'

'B...but I told you to tell us the future.'

'Correction, Professor,' declared TITAN. 'You asked for the history of nation states.'

'T...then why have you stopped at 19—?'

'Because 19— is the year in which nation states cease to exist.'

Except for the faint electronic hiss, the room fell silent, yet still the occupants sat gazing at the speaker, willing TITAN to crackle into existence and declare that it had made a ghastly error. When this did not happen, Bronwen calmly turned off the terminal and sank back in her chair.

'Does that last message mean what I think it means?' asked Ian.

Bronwen nodded, 'The stupid, power-hungry bastards are finally going to succeed in blowing themselves and the rest of us to hell.'

Looking fixedly at Bronwen, the Professor said, 'You voted for running the programme so you tell us where we go from here?'

Bronwen stood up. 'I know where I go, Frank, straight to your booze cabinet for a stiff drink.'

After silence had again descended on the room, Ian said, 'Why assume the worst, order TITAN to spill out the facts.'

Squinting her eyes, Bronwen said, 'I'm not sure that I want to know the "facts". Anyway, without all nine planets, there's bound to be uncertainty, but maybe we can find when the bubble bursts by running a monthly check?'

Bronwen looked at Mary's tearstained face, 'Do you want to go out of the room before we re-run the programme?' she asked kindly.

Mary shook her head.

After activating the terminal, Bronwen said, 'Okay, TITAN, evaluate 19—again but this time go in monthly steps until nation states cease to exist, is that clear?'

'Yes.'

January — Nation States
February — Nation States
March — Nation States
April — Nation States

With a one minute delay between pronouncements, TITAN's cold voice continued to echo round the study.

May — Nation States
June — Nation States
July — Nation States

'So far so good,' said Ian, brandishing his crossed fingers, 'maybe it was a programming bug after all.'

August — Nation States
September — No Nation States

This statement again brought a deathly silence to the room. 'TITAN, state the exact date in August when nation states cease to exist,' demanded Bronwen.

'The programme is not sufficiently refined to answer your question,' echoed the metallic reply, 'but before September.'

'Okay,' said Bronwen, 'then tell us why nation states cease to exist.'

'During August, the Earth undergoes a nuclear and biological holocaust,' stated TITAN without emotion.

Bronwen threw up her arms, 'I knew it! I knew it!' she spluttered wildly, 'those idiots are going to blow us to pieces!'

'TITAN just can't be saying that every last person will be destroyed,' pleaded Mary, 'only that nation states will cease to function properly?'

'I pray to God that you're right,' said the Professor, 'TITAN, how many people will be alive in the United States in September 19—?'

The speaker assumed a brief silence while TITAN performed countless calculations, then it coldly replied, 'ZERO.'

The Professor had to strain every sinew to resist ripping the speaker off the wall and throwing it through the closed window, yet he forced himself to ask, 'What will be the population of Russia and Europe in September?'

After a delay of two minutes, TITAN gave the answers, 'Russia—ZERO, Europe—ZERO.'

Ian twisted his face in disbelief, 'The whole Earth just can't be dead,' he pleaded, 'check on Australia and Africa.'

When the Professor gathered the nerve to put these questions to TITAN, the reply was the same, 'Australia—ZERO, Africa—ZERO.'

Bronwen refilled her glass, 'That's it then,' she said philosophically, 'the world's going to end in August!'

Opening the study window, the Professor took a long deep breath, then he turned and faced the others, 'If Nostradamus witnessed the holocaust four centuries ago, it explains why he feared for our time.'

Ian nodded, 'It also explains why Hugo Lawrence can't sleep at night, he must have seen it too.'

'He has,' declared Bronwen.

The Professor looked quizzically at the woman, 'How come you know what Hugo Lawrence has seen?'

Bronwen shrugged, 'It's no great mystery, Frank. Remember those books he sent you? Well his secretary packed his personal copy on Nostradamus by mistake. Anyway, when I opened the book, out dropped a handwritten sheet giving his detailed translation of the prophecies.'

'And?'

'Give or take a bit, they fit what we've just heard, Frank.' Bronwen rummaged through the filing cabinet until she came across a pink sheet, 'I wanted to spare you this, but now, what the hell.'

Bronwen read out, '"WHEN FORTY YEARS HAVE ELAPSED BEYOND HUMANITY'S SECOND CATACLYSM, THE GREATEST HORROR APPROACHES, HERALDED BY A BRIGHTNESS IN THE HEAVENS, WAR, FAMINE AND DISEASE WILL FALL FROM THE SKY." That was prophecy 46, Frank, now I'll read 29. "THE DAY OF JUDGEMENT IS AT HAND WHEN A FISH IS RELEASED WHICH TRAVELS OVER LAND AND SEA" And if you hate that one, wait till you hear 87. "FALLING FROM THE SKIES, EARTHSHAKING FIRE WILL LAY WASTE THE MIGHTY NEW CITY. EVEN THOSE TAKING REFUGE WILL FIND NO RESPITE."'

Bronwen emptied her glass before continuing, 'Hugo Lawrence seems to think that the next prediction belongs with the others but he doesn't make it clear if it's the first or last. Anyway, here's how he translates Nostradamus' fifth prophecy. "BOTH WEAPONS AND ORDERS ARE ENCLOSED IN A FISH. THE GREAT ONE TRAVELS FAR BUT RETURNS TO WHENCE HE CAME."'

'Before we get hung up on more prophecies,' declared Ian, 'let's exhaust the alternatives about the one that TITAN came up with.'

Bronwen looked tolerantly at Ian, 'From where I'm standing, the alternatives are thin on the ground.'

'There is one alternative, a big beautiful one!'

Bronwen shrugged, 'Okay Ian, you've got the stage, what have we missed?'

'Simply that none of this happens anyway. We know that Nostradamus' equations are fallible, you told us yourself that the errors could go way out while the planets are in conjunction.'

Thumping his fist in jubilation, the Professor exclaimed, 'Ian's right! The programme was wrong about a missile exchange over Cuba and half a dozen other things, so why must it be right about the end of the world?'

Bronwen picked up her rugby ball, 'Okay, Frank, it's a straw to clutch at, but don't forget that the programme's got two World Wars to its credit and, if you want my guess, it's hell bent on a hat trick.'

The silence that descended on the study proved to be even more unbearable than talking about the holocaust. 'So,' snapped Bronwen, 'are we going to sit on our backsides and let four billion people die or do we do something about it?'

Easing his feet off the desk, Ian said, 'Sitting tight with our fingers crossed may be the way to play this. Changing the face of destiny could be real dangerous.'

'Don't give me any of that destiny crap. You may be ready to roll over and die but I'm not.'

'Calm down, Bron,' said the Professor, 'What Ian meant is can we interfere with the future, and if we can, then dare we try to change it?'

Bronwen leaned back in her chair, 'Those are different questions, Frank. Can we change the future? Of course we can. If we'd known that the First World War was going to be triggered by the death of an Archduke, we could have killed the assassin.'

'Your second question's more difficult. Dare we change the future? I spent a lot of time thinking about that when writing the programme. Say we'd prevented the Second World War in '39 then maybe Germany would have developed the bomb in the forties and destroyed everybody in the fifties? Ian's right, trying to change the future is real dangerous, but what could be more dangerous than everyone on Earth being killed?'

The others remained passively silent.

'So,' she said contemptuously, 'are you all going to console yourselves that the programme could be wrong, and if it isn't then bang, no world, or are we going to do something positive?'

'We must do something,' said the Professor, finally, 'but God knows what.'

'I know what as well as God,' snapped Bronwen.

'There's no need for blasphemy,' said Mary.

Bronwen gave Mary a fleeting smile to show she was pleased that the woman had sufficiently recovered to argue, then she ignored the remark. 'There are two things we do,' declared Bronwen. 'First I'll include the outer planets into the equations, that'll eliminate any doubt about the holocaust.'

The Professor didn't look convinced, 'Can you do that in time?'

'I don't know, Frank,' admitted Bronwen, 'Nostradamus was a genius but he didn't have TITAN. I'll try to add one planet at a time and see what happens.'

Putting his hand on Bronwen's shoulder, the Professor said, 'If anyone can do it, it's you.'

Bronwen smiled, 'Thanks for the vote of confidence, Frank, but I've never thought of myself as a genius. Anyway, here's the second thing we do. Only the people in this room know what's coming and we're not in a position to stop it, so let's contact someone with a few more resources.'

'Come on, Bron,' coaxed Ian, 'tell us who we contact?'

Without displaying any emotion, Bronwen answered, 'Possibly the man who's scheduled to press the button in August, your President.'

Shuffling his feet uneasily, the Professor said, 'I don't like it. If ever there was a self-fulfilling prophecy, this is it. God knows what we'll trigger by seeing the President.'

Bronwen laughed in annoyance, 'Have you forgotten what will be triggered if we don't?'

Holding up his hands, the Professor said, 'Okay, even if I agreed to your plan, how in tarnation are we going to see the President?'

'We're not, Frank, you are.'

The Professor poured himself a whisky, 'You've omitted telling me how I'm supposed to get in to see the President.'

Bronwen waved her hand dismissively, 'I wish you wouldn't keep bothering me with details, Frank. You're a respected citizen who lives in a so-called democracy; go to the White House and demand to see the President.'

'Just like that! I turn up, unannounced and demand to see the President?'

'No, Frank,' said Bronwen patiently, 'not just like that. You say that you've got vital information concerning national security and you won't tell it to anyone but the President himself. After all, Frank, every damn word is true and that's for sure!'

CHAPTER 6

A crisp January morning greeted the Professor and Ian when they stepped off the plane at Washington. After the brief formalities of a taxi to the hotel, the men set off walking for the White House. 'I can't believe this is really happening,' muttered the Professor, 'another half mile and we'll be outside the gates, then what do I do?'

Ian smiled reassuringly, 'Just follow Bron's instructions; walk right up to the Duty Sergeant and demand to see the President. This isn't the Kremlin, the worst they can do is say no.'

'Which is just what will happen. I didn't even vote for the man.'

Ian laughed, 'That's the spirit Dad, but why not lie a bit, tell them you were strong in the campaign which got the guy elected. Anyway, Bron's right, we haven't any alternatives. If you write in for an appointment and wait till your number comes up, everybody will be dead. Besides, what would you say in the letter?'

It was the first time that either man had been to the Capitol, so when the White House came into view, the Professor thought how it reminded him of an American version of the Taj Mahal, set amidst a green carpet. As they absorbed the shimmering view, Ian said, 'It's hard to relate this scene to what it will look like in August after the Russians score a direct hit.'

The Professor bowed his head, 'I wish you hadn't said that. For a few seconds, I'd managed to forget Nostradamus and the reason for being here, now it's come flooding back.'

Ian placed his hand on his father's shoulder, 'Sorry Dad. Now it's better that we don't go any closer together, I'll meet you for lunch as arranged. Good luck!'

Soon Ian was absorbed amongst the tourists visiting the Capitol, leaving the Professor walking alone towards the White House. 'There's no going back now,' he told himself as he addressed the sentry on the gates, 'My name's Frank Cooper. I'm a Professor at Omaha State University and I'd like to see the President on a matter of national security.'

The guard looked embarrassed. In the four months he'd been assigned to the White House, this situation hadn't arisen. Sure, it had been covered in training, like what to do in the event of a nuclear attack, but nobody expects it to happen. Keeping his head rigidly forward, he glanced at the tall, lean man who'd spoken to him. The guy seemed prosperous, even important. Maybe this was some kind of secret initiative test that they didn't tell you about, and he was overdue a promotion, better treat the man seriously.

'If you'll excuse me, sir...I mean Professor,' said the guard politely, 'I'll need to phone for advice.' The guard went over to a sentry box at the railing fence and picked up a phone. After a whispered conversation he returned and said, 'Wait here Sir, someone's coming to deal with you.'

Ten minutes later, a corpulent figure appeared on the White House lawn, moving towards the gate where the guard was standing. As the figure came nearer, the Professor made out a middle-aged man in an expensive, banker-style suit and dark glasses. The man gave the impression that he would have been more at home in a film about the Mafia than as an aide at the White House. He opened the gate and engaged in a quiet conversation with the guard, who pointed in the direction of the Professor. The man pulled off his mirror sunglasses and twiddled them dextrously as he coldly eyed the person who wanted to gain entry to the White House. Finally, he walked across, 'You the guy who wants to see the President?' The Professor nodded.

'Name?'

'Frank Cooper.'

With an expressionless face, the man asked, 'You got identification?' Professor Cooper reached inside his pocket, pulled out an ID card and handed it to the man. 'Professor of Archaeology? The guard says you want to see the President about national security, is that correct?' The Professor nodded. 'In that case, my name's Clive Glenn, I'm an aide to the President. Please follow me.'

Clive Glenn escorted the Professor to a small, side entrance into the White House and gave the door three, sharp knocks. The door opened, to reveal the relative darkness of a White House corridor. The Professor had to stoop to avoid hitting his head on the doorframe as he followed Clive Glenn inside. Out of vision, next to the door, another guard stood sentry. 'We'll have to take the precaution of searching you before passing beyond this point, Professor.'

During the search, the guard was visibly disappointed when a 'hidden gun' turned out to be nothing more dangerous than the Professor's pipe. 'He's clean,' conceded the guard grudgingly.

'Okay,' said Clive Glenn, 'let's go to my office.'

The two men walked through a maze of descending corridors, before finally halting outside a door marked 'Security'. Clive Glenn took out the biggest bunch of keys that the Professor had ever seen, selected one and opened the door. The office they entered was sparse, damp and bore an uncomfortably close resemblance to a cell, with the only concession to natural light coming from a grille near the top of one wall. Beyond doubt, it was not the sort of room that the Professor had thought could exist in the White House.

Lodging himself behind a battered steel desk, Clive Glenn noticed the expression on his guest's face, 'Sorry about the surroundings, Professor. The plush offices always go to the big spenders, with "Security" getting what's left.'

Clive Glenn directed his hand towards a spindly wooden chair, 'Pull that over while we talk.' When they were facing each other across the metal desk, the man leaned forward and said, 'Now what's this about wanting to see the President?'

Calmly, the Professor answered, 'Just that, I need to see the President on a matter of utmost importance.'

Clive Glenn attempted a friendly smile. 'You said national security was involved.' The Professor nodded. 'Okay, I handle security for the President, you can tell me what it's about.'

The Professor shook his head firmly, 'I'm sorry, but what I've got to say is for the President's ears alone.'

Clive Glenn shrugged his shoulders, sat back on the hind legs of his chair and pulled out a packet of cigarettes. He offered a cigarette to his guest, which was declined, before lighting one himself.

While Clive Glenn gently blew smoke rings into the air, the Professor realised that the man was deciding whether to adopt a hard or soft approach. After what seemed an eternity, yet was no longer than the time it took to smoke the cigarette, Clive Glenn spoke 'Look, Professor, you must realise what a busy man the President is, even heads of state can't be sure of seeing him. Now if you could give me some indication of why you want to see the President, maybe there'd be a chance.'

Again the Professor shook his head before speaking, 'All I can say is that the security of the nation is at stake.'

Clive Glenn raised an eyebrow, 'And you won't disclose anything beyond that?'

'No.'

The man smiled patiently, 'Try and see my point of view, Professor. You'd never believe the number of cranks and weirdos who line up to see the President. Now I'm not saying that you're a crank, but if you won't say what this is all about, how can I be sure?'

The Professor placed his palms on the metal desk, 'I fully appreciate your problem, but nothing's changed. I want to see the President and no-one else will do.'

Clive Glenn gave a disappointed shrug. 'This conversation is leading exactly nowhere; so I'll tell you what we do. Take my card, go home and chew over what we've said then come back at two tomorrow and we'll take it from there, okay?'

After the Professor had nodded his agreement, Clive Glenn rang a bell on his desk. The door opened and a soldier carrying a rifle entered the room, 'Please escort the Professor from the White House.'

Over lunch with Ian, the Professor described the morning's events at the White House, 'I got further than expected, but there's not a country on Earth where you could see the head man without saying what it was about.'

'I guess so,' said Ian, 'but where do we go from here?'

The Professor shook his head, 'God knows, but I don't look forward to spending tomorrow in another eyeball confrontation across a tin desk.'

Ian took a big bite out of a doughnut, then he said, 'This trip was Bron's idea, you'd better phone her and say what's happened.'

As the men talked, neither noticed the tall, balding man in his mid-fifties who was seated alone at the bar. The man had positioned himself in such a way that the bar mirror gave an uninterrupted view of the Professor's table.

The phone in the Cooper house was answered by Bronwen, 'That you, Frank?'

'Yeah, Bron.'

'How'd you get on at the White House?'

'I didn't, they wouldn't let me see the President unless I said what it was about.'

'And you didn't?'

'No.'

'Good.'

'Why good?'

'Because I've come up with a foolproof plan to get you in.'

'I hope it's better than your last one,' said the Professor dryly.

'It is. Now quit worrying, Frank, and listen carefully. While you and Ian have been having a holiday in Washington, I've found a new use for the Nostradamus programme, individual horoscopes. I've just finished running one on that President of yours and now I know more about his past than his mother does.'

'Anything interesting?'

Bronwen laughed, 'He wouldn't be a politician if there wasn't something "interesting" in his past.'

'Okay, what did you find?'

'Well, it ain't no Watergate, Frank, but the President won't sleep until you've told him how you know about a couple of "sensitives". Have you a pen and paper handy?' The Professor said that he had. 'Okay, Frank, now write down exactly what I'm going to tell you...'

The following afternoon, the Professor strode confidently towards the White House, with the letter describing the "sensitives" lodged firmly in his pocket. 'Hello again, Professor,' said Clive Glenn as he was escorted into the subterranean office. 'Perhaps this time you'll tell me everything?'

The Professor shook his head, 'Fraid not.'

Clive Glenn sat back disappointed, 'They told me that there'd be days like this. C'mon Professor, give a guy a break, I'm just trying to do my job you know?'

The Professor smiled, 'Don't panic, I've found a way round our problem.'

Clive Glenn didn't look convinced as he said, 'Glad to hear it, because I sure haven't.' Then he grinned and added, 'Tell me your solution, Professor, and I'll see how many marks it gets.'

As the Professor reached inside his jacket pocket, a worried look flashed across Clive Glenn's face. 'It isn't a gun,' said the Professor quickly, 'remember I was frisked before coming in here.'

Clive Glenn breathed a sigh of relief, then he said, 'How'd a college Professor know a word like frisked?'

With a shrug, the Professor answered, 'I watch television.'

Both men laughed before Clive Glenn said, 'Okay, so what's in your damn pocket?'

The Professor pulled out the letter, 'This is strictly for the President. You'd better believe that when he's read the letter, it's the President who'll insist on seeing me.'

Clive Glenn held his hand out for the letter. 'Sorry,' said the Professor, 'first I'll need your oath that no one, and I mean no one but the President will read it.'

The man shook his head, 'That solution gets zero out of ten, Professor.'

He slumped back in his chair, 'Why?'

'Why? Because it's not the way we do things round here. You know what our number one security job is?' Blankly the Professor shook his head. 'Keeping the President alive so that he can make the big decisions.'

The Professor held up his hands, 'And what's that got to do with my letter?'

Clive Glenn eased back in his chair, 'Do you know how many letters the President gets each day?' The Professor managed a non-commital shrug. 'Two thousand! Now you must admit, Professor, that no man alive could read that many.'

In protest, the Professor said, 'I'm not giving you two thousand letters, just one.'

Clive Glenn reached for a cigarette, 'And give me one good reason why your letter should climb to the top of the heap? We've checked you out, Professor. You've got a good academic reputation but that's all. There's N.A.T.O. commanders who don't get their correspondence read personally.'

In desperation, the Professor said, 'Can't you even try with the letter?'

Clive Glenn thought for a while, then he said. 'I trust you Professor, and that means the letter could be important. But the best I can do is take it to the Director of the C.I.A. and let him decide; what do you say?'

The Professor nodded reluctantly, 'I guess it's trust on both sides.'

Clive Glenn gave a friendly smile, 'Okay Professor, I'll bust a gut trying, but a snowball's got more chance of surviving in hell than this letter has of reaching the President!'

The next day Frank telephoned and was put straight through to Clive Glenn. 'Everything's been cleared. I expected the bureaucracy to scream like spiked pigs but instead the letter went straight from the Director of the C.I.A. to the President himself. Either this is your lucky day, Professor, or you've got friends in extremely high places.'

In what had decidedly become a more reverential tone, Clive Glenn said, 'Maybe the letter got through because the guy who runs the "agency" used to be a Professor himself? Richard Stroud was brought in from Harvard two years ago to polish up the image of the C.I.A. after the fiasco in Latin America. It was Mr. Stroud who personally smoothed your passage to the President's office, but I guess you might already know that? Anyway, he wants to see you before you meet the President at four o'clock.'

The Professor was soon being escorted into a plush waiting room, where a middle-age secretary kept a watchful eye on him while continuing her typing. Soon a soft buzzer sounded and the secretary told the Professor that he could go in. Almost before he had entered the lavishly furnished office, he was warmly greeted by a small, immaculately groomed man in his mid-forties. The man had neatly cut black hair and was wearing an expensive three piece suit; unlike Clive Glenn, there was no obtrusive bulge under the breast pocket. 'Nice to meet you Professor,' said the man extending his hand in greeting, 'My name's Richard Stroud.'

Although the Professor hesitated marginally before taking the hand, it turned out to be a firm, friendly handshake. 'I assume you've read my letter?' said the Professor.

Stroud looked wounded, 'Not at all, you said it was for the President's eyes only, so I personally gave him the letter, unopened.'

Noticing the suspicious expression on the Professor's face, Richard Stroud said, 'Don't believe eveything you hear about the C.I.A. We're not monsters, just ordinary citizens trying to make the country a decent place for people like you. I admit that sometimes we have to use...unpleasant methods, but only when there is absolutely no alternative and even then, with extreme reluctance.'

Hesitantly, the Professor said, 'I don't doubt your word, but I still can't understand why you've made it so easy for me to see the President of the United States?'

Stroud smiled, 'I like you, Professor. You're polite yet direct and to the point. Let's call your meeting with the President a public relations exercise in open government. The media claim that government is remote from the ordinary man and that the individual is lost in the sheer weight of bureaucracy, so it's nice to be able to demonstrate to at least one person that it simply isn't true.'

Professor Cooper was confused, this was the last type of interview he'd expected with the Director of the C.I.A. Yet Stroud kept on talking with an easy friendly confidence.

'Take a look at this,' Stroud said, holding out a framed photograph of an elderly man in a Russian uniform. 'That's Peter Nicholovich, the Head of the K.G.B. To the media, we're deadly rivals but his job is the same as mine: to keep everything ticking over nicely in the interests of both our countries. Nobody wants drastic events to happen, so we don't. . . rock the boat.'

Stroud leaned forward in his chair, 'Take my word, Professor, we are reasonable people and the world's a whole lot safer now than when you and I were kids.' Stroud gave a friendly point at the clock, 'Anyway Professor, the President is scheduled to see you at four and we don't want to keep him waiting. It's been a pleasure talking to you, maybe we'll meet again, who knows, but I hope you feel reassured about the activities of your Government.'

Clive Glenn was waiting outside Richard Stroud's office. 'Come on Professor, time's running out, it's already 3:17, lucky I had you security checked this morning. However, it'll be necessary to search you.'

The Professor raised an eyebrow, 'I've already been searched.'

Clive Glenn shook his head, 'That search doesn't rate. You're going to meet the President of the U.S. of A. and it's our job to guarantee that you're not a walking bomb. Soon you'll know what a *real* search means.' After calling in the guard, Clive Glenn said, 'Take the Professor to the Search Room, then if he's clear, escort him to the President.'

At precisely 4:00 p.m., the Professor was shown into the Oval Office. Seated looking out of the window, was the President of the United States. The President was a big man, both in physique and achievement, with more votes being cast his way than for any man previously. And even during the worst depression to hit America since the thirties, the polls still showed him way ahead of any rival. To most Americans, this man epitomised the American dream, God-fearing, straight-talking and richly successful.

As the Professor stood self-consciously in the doorway, trying to decide what protocol demanded he do next, the President swivelled round in his chair and gave his visitor the sort of smile which should be reserved for a lifelong friend. 'Sit down, Professor,' he said in a firm, welcoming voice. 'I've just read your little note for the tenth time since it arrived. You've sure got me beat, how in blazes did you find out about the Israeli reactor or, better still, my trip to China in '86?'

The Professor sat down in front of the desk, 'I know a lot more than that about you, Mr. President.' The President raised one eyebrow. With a grin, the Professor said, 'For example, I know that your mother called you her Little Cowboy.'

The President went quiet for a few seconds before he smiled and said, 'That's quite remarkable, I made my mother stop calling me that when I was five. Until you reminded me, I'd even forgotten about it myself, so how could you know?'

The Professor shook his head dismissively, 'What I know about your past was only the passport into this office, Mr. President. I've come to talk about the future and that isn't at all good.'

The President settled back in his chair, 'I've heard a lot of bad things in my time, Professor, I doubt if anything you can tell me will be worse.' The President put his feet on the corner of the desk, 'Don't be put off by my eyes being shut, it helps me concentrate. Now let's hear your story.'

Hesitantly, the Professor asked, 'Do you believe in astrology, Mr. President?'

'Nope!'

'Then my job's ten times harder, but here goes.'

To the occasional 'hmm' or nod of the President's head, the Professor recounted the complete saga, from the mysterious letter to the coming holocaust. When he'd finished, the President's eyes remained firmly closed. Although the Professor had tried to anticipate the range of reactions that the President might adopt, this hadn't been one of them.

As the minutes continued to elapse, the Professor started to wonder if the President really was asleep? When he was at the height of confusion with regard to what to do next, the President opened his eyes, 'I've heard a bookcase full of strange stories in my time, Professor, but yours takes the prize! Now let me tell you something; a lot of men have faced me across a lot of tables over the years but when it finally came down to it, they all had the same reason for seeing me. To get something! So I'll ask you a straight question, Professor, what's your angle?'

Without flinching, the Professor replied, 'I'll give you a straight answer, Mr. President. To save the world.'

The President looked annoyed, 'So you're sticking by your story that some crazy astrologer, four hundred years ago, saw the end of the world coming about now.'

'Not "about now", Mr. President, it's more precise than that.'

'Oh, you've got a date?'

The Professor nodded.

'Then don't keep it to yourself.'

'August.'

When the Professor said, 'August,' the President's expression suddenly changed. 'Aug...August, did you say? In seven months time?'

Clumsily, the President poured two glasses of water from the decanter and pushed one to the Professor before starting to gulp the other, 'You'd better tell me your story again, slowly right from the beginning.'

This time the President made notes, every so often stopping the flow of events to check that he'd got a fact right. When the tale was again completed, the President sat nervously nibbling the end of his pencil, scrutinising every word he'd written.

After some minutes, he finally said, 'Supposing, just supposing, I take your story seriously, then it leaves me with a lot of gaps...' He looked Professor Cooper square in the eye, 'Who sent you the letter which triggered all this?'

The Professor shrugged politely, 'I wish I knew, but I don't.'

The President leaned forward, 'You can't even make a guess?'

The Professor shook his head.

'Okay let's try a new tack. Has your programme come up with a single event which wasn't known already?'

With a distinct note of confusion in his voice, the Professor said, 'It's predicted the holocaust.'

The President held up his hands, 'That hasn't happened yet, pray God it doesn't.' Pouring himself another glass of water, he said, 'Do you see what I'm getting at? You could have been set up for all of this. If the equations are based on the Earth's known history, it wouldn't be surprising if the computer got things right. After all, Professor, any idiot can predict the result of last night's big fight this morning.'

The Professor started to protest, 'B...but what about the predictions which turned out to be wrong?'

'Let's say that could have been put there to achieve exactly the effect they have achieved.'

The Professor found himself with conflicting emotions. What the President said could be true, how he prayed it was, yet a deeper instinct told him that the programme was genuine. Then he remembered the tests at the University. 'We had the parchment carbon-dated, Mr. President.'

'So what? I can obtain genuine parchment from any age you name, but it sure doesn't prove that the writing's genuine.'

The Professor leaned back in his chair, 'So you think it's all a sophisticated Russian plot?'

The President screwed up his face, 'I'm not saying anything for certain, but until your programme predicts something new, something big, then our Russian friends come out top of my list. Believe me Professor, even Stroud couldn't start to guess some of the things we've set up to confuse Moscow!'

The President eased back in his chair, 'Let's not jump to any conclusions, one way or the other, what we're talking about is too damn important. I'd only be playing at being President if I closed my eyes to the possibility that the programme is for real.' The President reflected before saying, 'If the programme's genuine, everything comes down to just two questions. Will it happen, and can we do anything about it?'

After a pause, the Professor replied, 'I don't want to sound like a politician, Mr. President, but there aren't any straight answers. Will it happen? If the programme's genuine, even allowing for the conjunction of the planets, the odds are that it will. Can anything be done about it? Can mortals change the hand of destiny? I don't know, but if anyone can stop the holocaust, it's you.'

The President managed a slight smile, 'You over-estimate the powers of my office, Professor, if you think that destiny comes under this administration.'

The President reflected on his words before saying, 'Talking of destiny, Professor, are you a religious man?'

With a note of surprise, the Professor answered, 'Religious? I can take it or leave it.'

'You're not a Catholic?'

'No, Mr. President, why do you ask?'

'No reason, just covering all the bases.'

While the Professor was trying to decide if the last question had any hidden significance, the President asked another, 'From what you've told me, the programme might get an event wrong but never the date. If there's going to be a holocaust, it must be during August?'

The Professor nodded, 'It's August or not at all.'

The President reclined into the leather upholstery of his chair,

'I'll summarise the position, Professor. I still think it's a Russian plot to frighten the hell out of us, but I could be wrong. The easiest way to prove out the programme is to predict something big, like a natural disaster. So here's what I want you to do; scan the next few months for something unpleasant coming our way; when you find it, come and tell me, okay? While you're doing that, I'll get a few lifeboats launched, just in case the damn programme really works.'

The President stood up, thus indicating that the meeting was over, 'I'll leave orders that if you want to see me, day or night, you're to be given top priority.'

As the Professor was closing the door to the Oval Office, he noticed that the President had picked up the photograph of his three daughters from his desk. The expression on the man's face said it all: Professor Cooper had lost count of the times he'd had the same thoughts about Ian during the past week.

While he was being escorted through the White House, back to the entrance through which he'd arrived, the Professor tried to make some sort of sense from his meeting with the President. Why had the date of the holocaust produced such a devastating effect on the man? It was almost as if the President had already heard 'August' from another pair of lips, a pair of lips of some importance? Yet what did it matter, the only important fact was that the President had finally taken him seriously. The Professor's mind was so engrossed in these thoughts that he didn't notice the tall balding man, the same one who'd been in the bar the previous day following him back to the hotel.

In the hotel lobby, the Professor was excitedly greeted by Ian, 'Before spilling out your news, Dad, I'll tell you mine. A thief went through every suite on our floor! Can you picture the scene, everything tipped into a heap on the carpet? The cops think he was searching for something special.'

The Professor raised an eyebrow, 'Why do they say that?'

'Why? Because the guy in the next room to us is a banker, there was five grand in his case but the thief ignored it!'

'Did he get anything from us?'

Ian laughed, 'Two pairs of socks and a handkerchief don't make much of a target for a guy who's immune to five grand, that's the beauty of travelling light.'

The Professor smiled, 'Guess so, but it makes you wonder what the thief really wanted.'

Ian shrugged, 'Anyway, that's my news, now it's your turn. Did you get to see the President?'

The Professor nodded, 'But the meeting's left me more confused than when we arrived. The sooner we get back to Omaha and run that damn programme again the better.'

'How'd you get on with the President?' Bronwen's voice greeted the men through the open study door as they entered the house. The Professor followed Ian into the smoke filled study, to find Bronwen, cigar in month, in a familiar crouch over the computer terminal.

'Can I open a window before telling you what happened?' asked the Professor.

'If you must,' muttered Bronwen, 'but you know I can't think clearly in fresh air.' With a gentle swirl, the cigar smoke slowly started to drift through the open window. However, with the room only half clear, Bronwen slammed the window shut again, 'So, how did you get on at the White House?'

The Professor sank into a chair, 'It was strange. The President didn't seem to be taking me seriously at first, but as soon as I mentioned the date of the holocaust, he almost turned green. But he still needs proof.'

'Hell, Frank, what sort of proof? This isn't a laboratory experiment where we double check the results. There's only one world, and when it's gone, that's it!'

'The President does want to help but he won't dismiss the other option.'

Bronwen tossed her cigar into the trash can, 'What other option?'

'Simply that the whole affair's an elaborate Russian plot.'

The woman threw up her hands in despair, 'With geniuses like that running the world, no wonder everything's going bang in August. Surely you don't believe this crap about a Russian plot, Frank?'

The Professor shook his head, 'But it's what the President believes that's important, Bron. He wants the programme to prove itself by predicting a catastrophe.'

The sound of the front door closing interrupted the discussion. 'How did things go with the President?' asked Mary as she entered the study.

Bronwen glared at the Professor, 'Go on, tell her Frank. All we've got to do is predict an earthquake in Peru killing thousands, then the President might just believe our story!'

Mary sat down, 'I've been doing some thinking. Seeing the President may not have been such a good idea.'

'How so?' asked Ian.

'You're a nice lad, Ian,' said Bronwen condescendingly, 'but you ask some stupid questions. Mary's frightened that if we convince the President that war's inevitable, the man might strike first before August.'

Ian looked blank, 'If it wasn't so smart to see the President, then who should we have seen, the Russian Chairman?'

'Go back to sleep!' declared Bronwen dryly, 'The President may have been a bad idea but the Chairman would be suicide!'

'Who then?' repeated Ian.

'The Pope,' answered Mary softly.

The room went silent as the others tried to think of a reply to Mary's suggestion, then Ian said, 'No disrespect, Mary, but why the Pope?'

Mary lifted her face, 'Well I could say that if the world's going to end in August, the Pope should be told, but it goes deeper than that. My church teaches that the Holy Father is God's representative on Earth, so if anyone can stop the holocaust it's him.'

To her surprise, Mary found an unexpected ally in Bronwen, 'I used to be dragged screaming to the Chapel as a kid; the sermons just washed over me,' declared the Welsh woman. 'Yet Mary's right, you should see the Pope, Frank. Not because of any religious claptrap but because he might be the one man who can mediate between East and West when the time comes.'

The Professor raised his hands in protest, 'It was difficult enough to see the President, so without claiming to be an archangel, how do I get an audience with the Pope?'

Bronwen smiled, 'That side of it should be easy. While you were away, I raised a loan in your name for some extra equipment, but don't worry, Frank, it's not repayable until September! Anyway, after your problems with the President, I've taken the precaution of punching in details of people who might be 'needed'. For the last two days I've been amusing myself by running a few famous names through the computer. Believe me, Frank, you wouldn't credit the results, but I'll tell you this, if the holocaust doesn't happen, we can make a fortune in blackmail.'

Bronwen looked at the confused faces of her colleagues, 'The point I'm making is that the Pope's on my list, it'll be easy to run a chart on him.' Then, noticing the expression on Mary's face, Bronwen added diplomatically, 'Not that I'd expect to turn up anything underhand, mind you. Just something to make the Pope wonder which Bishop tipped us the information.'

The others looked on in silent fascination as Bronwen punched the Pope's code number into the Nostradamus file. In less than a minute, everyone was crouched over the print-out. 'No wonder he became Pope,' said the Professor, 'he sure has led a sin-free life.'

'If you can call that a life,' joked Ian, 'no wonder I never came across him at any party I've been to!' Mary frowned, but didn't say anything.

Bronwen jabbed out her finger, 'That little item should get you in, Frank.' The others looked halfway down the print-out, where the Welsh woman's finger was pointing, 'It isn't much by normal standards,' admitted Bronwen, 'but with your skill, Frank, Sistine Chapel here you come!'

CHAPTER 7

'While stands the Coliseum, Rome shall stand. When falls the Coliseum, Rome shall fall. And when Rome—the World.' The words of Lord Byron sprang unbidden into Professor Cooper's mind as he stared up at the magnificent building in front of him. Unless the Pope could help him, the edifice that had stood for over twenty centuries might indeed fall, and with it the rest of civilisation.

Around him, hundreds of tourists were taking photographs, some still using their flash guns even though the city was bathed in brilliant sunlight. Such people, with their loud clothes and voices, cheap souvenirs and indifference were anathema to an archeologist, as out of place in the Coliseum as a hot dog stall would be on the Buckingham Palace lawns. He shook his head sadly and walked on through the busy streets.

As he approached the Vatican, he had to push his way through all the loyal believers thronging St. Peter's Square. Some must have come thousands of miles; he wondered what their reaction would be to the knowledge he carried. Would they still be praying dutifully or might their response be to curse God for the horrors that were approaching? But time had run out for such distractions, already the open gates of the Vatican were in sight. And beyond the gates stood a white stone arch; the entrance to the Vatican itself.

A soldier, attired in what Nostradamus himself would have recognised as the uniform of the Swiss guard, stood sentry at the gates. Two other soldiers were quietly yet efficiently searching priests and nuns as they shuffled silently through the archway. When the Professor's brisk stride showed no sign of slackening, one of the guards stepped forward and barred his path. 'Vietato l'ingresso!' declared the man.

'I'm an American,' replied Professor Cooper.

The guard smiled, 'I not ask where you come from. Vietato l'ingresso means "No Entry".' The guard's tone mellowed a little, 'You have business here?'

The Professor nodded, 'I wish to see the Pope.'

The guard shrugged heavily, 'Everybody wish to see Pope. But fortune smile, you shall see Pope!' This statement took the Professor by surprise. 'You go to Pontifical Prefect's office,' continued the guard in broken but understandable English, 'Go through bronze gates of St. Peter's Square. If everything okay, you be invited for Audience on Wednesday.'

It all sounded too easy so the Professor asked, 'Will it be a private Audience?'

The guard laughed loudly, 'Private with seven hundred people!'

'I need a private Audience,' insisted the Professor.

'Private Audience arranged through own Bishop,' replied the guard patiently. 'Have you spoken with Bishop?' When the Professor answered, 'I'm not a Catholic!' an amused grin spread across the soldier's face, 'You happen to be in Rome so you thought drop in on Pope. You Americans are fantastic!'

At this point, the Professor decided that the conversation had run its course, so he thanked the guard for his patience. As the Professor made his way across the cobbled courtyard, the guard was already recounting the story of the 'funny American' to the other soldiers.

* * *

Back in Omaha, a noise from downstairs woke Ian. He turned over and tried to get back to sleep but then he heard it again. It sounded like glass breaking. 'Better check it out,' he thought as he climbed out of bed and put on his robe.

As Ian approached the study, the low hum of electronic equipment could just be made out. 'It's probably Bron,' Ian thought to himself, 'I wonder if all Welsh women don't sleep? Better make sure she's okay, anyway.' He opened the door and entered the study, everything was in darkness, then the moon edged from behind a cloud. The side window was open, with its glass smashed near the catch. A long-dormant survival instinct told him that he was not alone.

He glanced round the room, staring at one shadowy object after another, until he came to the computer terminal, the power-light was glowing; someone else was in the room! He edged back towards the door, suddenly a long, bony arm locked round his neck, hoisting him off the floor.

Ian's jaw muscles started to buckle as the grip tightened beyond endurance. Frantically, he tried to break free, to get a hold on his attacker but it was no use, he was held rigid by a professional stranglehold. His eyes swirled red from oxygen starvation as his windpipe started its inevitable collapse.

With his life ebbing away, he caught the moon's glint on Bronwen's glass ashtray. In blind desperation he thrust out his hand, clutching, groping, but the ashtray was beyond reach. Then his grasp closed on something standing vertical on the desk. It was his father's antique Egyptian pen.

Using every ounce of his remaining strength, he plunged the pen deep into the wrist that gripped his throat. The blow was of such ferocity that the iron nib ripped clean through the man's flesh as if it was nothing more than a decaying papyrus, severing an artery as it jutted out the far side.

With a wild yell, the man released his grip. Ian slumped to the floor, his lungs fighting for air. As he lay there, he felt something dripping on his face, like water form a warm tap. In revulsion he scraped his attacker's blood from where it was falling in his eyes and looked up.

The man still towered over him, with the moon lighting up his grotesquely distorted face as he tried to get the iron nib out of his wrist. He let out a low moan when the nib snapped, then after flinging the pen butt at the wall, he jabbed his good hand inside his jacket pocket.

'For Christ's sake, the bastard's going for his gun,' thought Ian, and launched himself at the towering legs. The impact broke the man's grip on his gun, jolting it to the floor.

A door banged noisily upstairs then Bronwen yelled, 'Ian, hang on for God's sake, the police are on their way!' The hall light went on, revealing the gun's position under the desk. Ian grabbed the gun but as he turned to settle accounts, a thunderous blow knocked him unconscious.

* * *

The events in Omaha remained unknown to the Professor, but he had finalised his plans to see the Pope. The conversation with the guard hadn't been wasted, now he knew precisely what had to be done to obtain a private Audience. Soon he was in the office of the Pontifical Prefect, where a long line waited patiently for their chance to get onto Wednesday's 'list'.

Acting out of character, the Professor pushed his way to the front of the queue and loudly declared, 'My name is Professor Frank Cooper. I am a personal envoy from the President of the United States, with a private letter for his Holiness.'

The official looked stunned, then he said, 'We have no record of any official appointment being made to see the Pontiff.'

With an exasperated smile, the Professor said 'Bureaucracy! The bureaucracy at the White House always fouls things up. The President himself sent me on this mission with the message for His Holiness.'

The official gave a non-committal smile, 'Of course, we shall have to verify your story.'

'Of course. Phone the President, when everything's been checked out, take this letter to the Pope, personally.'

A porcelain clock was delicately chiming seven, when the Professor was politely ushered into the Papal Audience Chamber. The Pope had been standing near a door opening on to a terrace but now he crossed to where an onyx table and two wrought iron chairs stood. After telling the official he could retire for the evening, the Pope directed his hand at one of the chairs, 'Please be seated, Professor,' he said in slow but good English. 'Since my little mishap, I always prefer to talk sitting down.'

Both men sat down. 'Now this letter of yours, Professor, most intriguing. How did you know of my confidential memorandum on women priests?'

'It's a long story Your Holiness, so with your permission, I'll start at the beginning.'

The Pope smiled, 'That's is usually a sound place.'

As the story unfolded, the Pope's initial tranquility progressively evolved to concern. When the account was complete, the man asked but a single question, 'When is this terrible holocaust to take place?'

'August.'

On hearing this date, the Pope buried his head in his hands. Eventually, he lifted his face and said, 'Forgive me, Professor but by specifying the date as August, your story has acquired a terrible authenticity.'

The Pope walked to the door and asked his secretary to prepare some refreshments. While they sipped their coffee, the Pope remained silent, until finally he said, 'Are you of the faith?'

The question took Professor Cooper by surprise. 'Another person asked me that recently.'

'The President?'

The Professor sat upright in his chair, 'How did you know?'

'Just an informed guess,' said the Pope with a smile, 'and are you of the faith?'

'I hope so, your Holiness, but a different branch. I was raised a Methodist.'

The Pope nodded, 'A different branch but the same tree.' The Pope looked directly into the Professor's eyes, 'Since hearing your terrible story, I have been praying for guidance. Now I know that a secret must be revealed to you, perhaps the most important secret ever entrusted to a human being. Are you the man to keep such a secret?'

'All I can do is give you my word.'

The Pope clasped Professor Cooper's hand, 'Your word is sufficient. Now tell me what you know about Fatima.'

At first, Fatima meant nothing to the Professor, then he remembered the book that a Catholic friend had lent him years before. 'Wasn't that the place in Portugal where three prophecies were told to some children?'

The Pope nodded, 'But the story of Fatima is much more remarkable and awesome then that. Our Lady appeared before one hundred thousand people on October 17th, 1917, near the village of Fatima. She told the shepherd girl, Lucia, that Jesus wept for mankind and it was her task to convey three prophecies.

The first was that a bloody revolution would begin in Russia that very day, October 17th, 1917. And even though the revolution was evil, it would flourish and spread like a cancer until half of Europe was infested; with the very existance of the Church being threatened in the lands under the sickle.

'The second prophecy was that another great war, even more horrendous than that which was then raging, would commence at the death of Pius XI.' The Pope paused, 'You may recall that as Pius the XI lay on his deathbed, Germany occupied Austria?'

The Professor nodded before asking, 'And the third prophecy, your Holiness?'

The Pope looked down at the onyx table as he said, 'The third prophecy was conveyed directly to Pope Benedict by the girl, Lucia. That prophecy has become the most important secret ever held by the Church. Each new Pope, on the day of his consecration, is entrusted with a key which opens a vault deep in the heart of the Vatican. The third prophecy is contained within that vault. I too went through this ritual.' The Pope leaned back in his chair, 'Do you know what the third prophecy is, Professor?'

Although the Professor shook his head, he had little doubt what the Pope was going to say next.

'The third prophecy, Professor, declares that unless mankind repents its sins and returns to the path of Christ, then a third war, more horrendous than even the human mind could envisage, will be unleashed. And the date of that war, Professor, is this August.'

For the first time since this horror began, the Professor sensed the jigsaw slotting into position, 'Does the President know this date, your Holiness?'

The Pope nodded, 'He will preside over your country during the time of the prophecy, so I personally revealed the secret to him.'

'How did he take it?'

The Pope gave a non-committal wave, 'I don't think he believed me, but he did say that he would, what was his exact phrase...launch some boats? But with a politician, who knows what that might mean?'

The Professor walked to the marble mantlepiece, turned round and looked at the Pope, 'In America, we have an expression, "the sixty-four thousand dollar question".'

The Pope nodded, 'I am familiar with the saying.'

'Then the sixty-four thousand dollar question is would God allow the good to become extinct with the bad?'

The Pope pondered on his words before saying, 'That question is not easily answered, but the scriptures reveal that it has happened before. Only Noah and a selected handful of relatives were saved from the Great Flood, while the multitude drowned. And at Sodom and Gomorrah, except for Lot, the whole community perished.'

The Professor held up his hands in protest, 'B...but the extinction of humanity! How could a loving, merciful God sanction such slaughter?'

From the expression on the Pope's face, the Professor sensed that there was an answer to his question but the man wasn't sure whether to give it.

Finally, the Pope asked, 'Have you ever wondered why the word GOOD resembles GOD, and that EVIL and DEVIL sound alike?' When the Professor shook his head, the Pope asked, 'Do you believe in the Devil? Not just as an abstract concept but as an entity whose existence is as absolute as that of God himself?'

The Professor just stood there with his jaw open, not knowing how to reply. Sure, he could go along with the existence of God, but the Devil? That was something to frighten people into churches.

'There's no need to search for an answer, Professor, your silence reveals all. Although this is developing into a seminar on theology, an innermost conviction tells me that God is working through you to save humanity; I shall answer your question.'

The Pope raised himself a little higher in his chair as he assumed the role of teacher, 'It is difficult to show God to those who do not wish to see, yet this is simplicity compared to proving that the Devil exists; for it suits the Devil's purpose to remain a myth. Take my word, Professor, the children at Fatima bore testimony to the Devil's existence. I have read the reports; their poor young minds saw such visions of Hell and Damnation that they were not free of nightmares for the rest of their lives.

Therefore the answer to your question, Professor, is that the balance between good and evil rests on a sharpened knife edge. If the end does come, it will be the Devil's triumph made strong by the wickedness of man.'

When the Pope had regained his composure, the Professor asked, 'And when the balance is taken in August, which way will the scales tip?'

The Pope's eyes again glazed with tears, 'Have you not seen the world, Professor? It is awash with war, famine, abortion, greed; has evil ever been more prevalent? I sorrow for mankind on the Day of Judgement but we must retain out faith, perhaps God will still have sufficient strength to ensure that some, maybe only a handful, survive...'

As the Professor left the Audience Chamber, the Pope's words needed no interpretation, the day of Judgement was fast approaching, and when it arrived, mankind would be found wanting. Yet he took some comfort from the Pope's promise to continue praying for deliverance until the very end.

These thoughts were uppermost in the Professor's mind as he passed beneath the white arch at the exit to the Vatican courtyard. Suddenly, a large hand fell heavily on his shoulder. 'Well, American,' laughed the same Swiss guard he'd spoken to earlier, 'did you have your private Audience with the Holy Father?'

'Why yes', answered the Professor innocently, 'I've just left him.'

'Fantastic!' declared the guard, 'You Americans are bloody

fantastic!'

During the flight home from Rome, the Professor pondered on the Pope's words, 'Perhaps God will have sufficient strength to ensure that some, maybe only a handful, survive?' But where on Earth could they survive? It was one thing to let a wooden ark float on the waters for forty days, but surviving on an Earth pulsating with radiation for centuries, that was in a different league!

The Professor was met at the airport by Ian, 'There's been more excitement while you were in Rome, Dad. Bron's found a catastrophe for the President, and we've had a break-in.'

'You mean the house was robbed?'

Ian shook his head, 'It was like the hotel, he didn't take anything so it was no ordinary rip-off. Bronwen's convinced that he was after the programme. I almost had him, but then he slugged me cold with Bronwen's old rugby trophy...' Noticing the concern on his father's face, Ian added, 'I'm okay Dad, it's like you always warned, all that soccer has turned my skull into granite.' Then with a grin Ian added, 'Can't say the same for Bron's ball though.'

'To hell with Bronwen's trophy,' snapped the Professor, 'it's your head that's important.'

Ian grinned even more, 'That's exactly the reverse of what Bronwen said.'

When they were on the freeway, the Professor said, 'You and Bron get on real well together.'

Ian nodded, 'I guess we do at that. Okay, she's bad-tempered and yells a lot, but the woman's honest and believes in something, y'know? I've never met anyone with such cast-iron convictions, she sure is a contrast to me. For the last few years, I haven't thought about anything beyond the latest girl, or what my next gag was going to be. God knows, I wish I could believe in something like Bron does.'

As father and son glanced at each other across the gulf of a generation, the Professor glimpsed a long forgotten reflection of himself, desperately searching for some peg to hang his life on; then he'd met Ann. 'Yes, Bronwen is quite a woman,' he said, breaking the silence, 'but God help anyone who gets between her and her convictions!' While Ian was garaging the car, the Professor went straight into the study where, as always, Bronwen was crouched over the computer terminal. 'Ian tells me someone's been after the Nostradamus tape?'

Without looking up, Bronwen answered, 'Reckon so, but they

didn't know it needed one of our voices to access the TITAN library.'

Seating himself, the Professor said, 'If the President's theory is right, the thief must have been working for the Russians.'

Bronwen laughed, 'He's more likely to have been the President's man,' she said contemptuously. 'And don't argue Frank, unless you can tell me who else knows about the programme? Anyway, I don't want to talk about the break-in, it brings back memories of what Ian did to my father's trophy! Tell me how you got on in Rome?' Having asked the question, Bronwen caught the expression which crossed the Professor's face. 'That bad?'

The Professor nodded, 'I've given my word to the Pope not to reveal any details, but things don't get any better.'

Bronwen shrugged, 'Somehow, Frank, that's what I guessed you'd say.'

The Professor changed the subject, 'Ian says that you've been successful in finding the President's disaster.'

Bronwen looked upset, 'Yes, Frank, if predicting seven thousand deaths in an earthquake is called success these days.'

Apologetically, the Professor held up his hands, 'Sorry, Bron, success was a bad word. Anyway, when's it going to happen?'

Bronwen pointed to a big cross scrawled on the wall calender, 'Six weeks from now, in a town in Yugoslavia.'

'Any chance of error?'

Bronwen shrugged, 'I wouldn't be much of a scientist if I said no, but I've done a lot of runs while you were in Rome. Once you remove people from the data, the errors go with them. What I'm saying, Frank, is that the programme's damn near infallible when it comes to predicting natural disasters.'

Bronwen picked up a sheet of paper, walked to where the Professor was seated and stuffed it into his top pocket, 'I've written down the details of the quake, so the sooner you speak to the President the better. That way you may save some lives.' Then, as an afterthought, she added, 'That is if saving lives makes much difference with August coming up.'

The Professor's reception at the White House contrasted with his earlier visit. First there was the subtle shift in Clive Glenn's manner, as if he'd been instructed to wear his best kid gloves.

'Hi there Professor. Good to see you,' declared the man. 'The President's left instructions that you're to be taken to him immediately and be spared the hassel of the "search".'

With the minimum of formalities the Professor found himself

being rapidly propelled towards the Oval Office. 'Good afternoon, Professor,' greeted the President from his swivel chair, 'How'd you get on in Rome?'

'Rome? I guess you could say that I had an interesting talk with the Pope.'

The President smiled, 'Good. But next time you want to be my special envoy, how about letting me in on the act? I was pulled out of a Cabinet meeting for the call from the Vatican. I backed your story this time but it makes me look kind of dumb if I don't know what's going on. If you want to jet off somewhere again, check it out with me first, who knows, I might even be able to help.'

The President motioned for the Professor to sit down, 'You said on the phone that a quake's going to hit Yugoslavia. When?'

'March 3rd, Mr. President.'

The President made a note in his diary, 'So we sweat it out for another six weeks, then we know what ball game we're playing.'

'You can't plan to just sit on the information, Mr. President, not with seven thousand lives at stake?'

The President shuffled uneasily in his chair, 'Hmmm. . . I never said that was my intention, but what do you suggest we do, Professor?'

'Why not tell the Yugoslavs our seismology experts have picked up tremors of an earthquake for early March?'

The President stroked his chin, 'If there isn't an earthquake, we're going to look mighty foolish, Professor.'

'And if seven thousand innocent people die? Would any God-fearing man want that on his conscience?'

The President reflected for a few seconds then he smiled, 'You're right, of course. I'll instruct our Ambassador to contact the Yugoslavs tomorrow.'

Politely, the Professor said, 'If you don't mind me asking, Mr. President, why the smile?'

The President's smile increased, 'It always makes me feel good when I play the odds, Professor.'

'I'm afraid that I still don't follow you?'

With a wink, the President said, 'That's because you're a scientist and not a politician. Let me spell it out for you, we kill two birds by warning the Yugoslavs.'

'Two birds?'

'Well, we do the decent thing but we also find out if destiny can be manipulated.'

The Professor stared blankly at the President, 'Destiny ...manipulated?'

'Don't you get it, Professor? If the Yugoslav deaths are below seven thousand, it means that the Nostradamus programme can be moulded any damn way I choose!

'Now, let's get back to the matter of your house being burgled. I don't like it, Professor, not for one damn second.' The President noticed the questioning expression on the Professor's face, 'And just in case you think I was behind it, don't! The first I knew about the break-in was when you told me over the phone. Do you believe me?'

'If you say you weren't involved, Mr. President, then I accept it.'

The President smiled, 'You're starting to sound like a politician, Professor, but let's not kid around, the break-in does confirm the need for security. That's why I insisted you fly here, rather than discuss matters over the telephone.'

The President started toying with an ivory paperweight of an elephant's head, then he put it down and looked at the Professor, 'I propose that your team moves into a top security research base near here. You'll still be civilians but at least the programme will be safe. What do you say?'

After a pause, the Professor asked, 'What are the facilities like?'

Proudly, the President answered, 'Best in the world. What's your reason for asking?'

'Well, Bron...I mean Dr. Jones, would never admit it but she could use some help in fitting the outer planets.'

The President thrust out his hand, 'At Southwood, I'll guarantee that she'll get it. Have we got ourselves a deal?'

The Professor shook the President's hand, 'We'll go to Southwood.'

Thinking that the meeting was over, the Professor started to rise but the President motioned him to remain seated. 'There's something else I want to discuss, Professor.' The President leaned forward before speaking. 'Frank, I hope I can call you Frank?' The Professor nodded politely. 'Now, Frank just supposing there is an earthquake in Yugoslavia, where do we go from there?'

Blankly, the Professor said, 'I'm not following you again, Mr. President.'

The President leaned even closer, 'What I'm saying, Frank, is that if the earthquake happens then, come August...'

The Professor shook his head, 'It isn't as simple as that, Mr. President. The programme's not perfect, it could get the quake right but be wrong about the holocaust.'

The President toyed with the paperweight again, 'Okay, keep your team working on the outer planets, but I'll tell you this, Frank. If the Yugoslav quake happens then my scenario assumes the programme's correct.'

The President beckoned the Professor to move even closer, almost as if he thought that the Oval Office was bugged and he didn't want to be overheard making a treasonable proposition. When he spoke, the man's voice was barely more than a whisper, 'What I'm saying, Frank, is that I've always been a fighter and now, sure as hell, isn't the time to change. So if the programme's right, we need a plan for survival. Should the quake happen, you come and see me again, Frank. That will be the time to discuss options.'

As the Professor approached the door, try as he might, he couldn't think of a single option that was open. When he turned round to ask, the words stuck rigid in his throat; the President was again looking at the photograph of his daughters, and this time the man's eyes were filled with tears. This wasn't the moment to discuss options, March 3rd would be soon enough for that.

'I bet it was that damn President of yours who burgled us in the first place,' stormed Bronwen, 'just so he could step in and offer protection!'

The Professor shook his head, 'Unless the man's a mighty good actor, he really was concerned about the break-in.'

Bronwen strode across to the study window, knocking a chair over in the process, 'I don't like it Frank. Wasn't it Eisenhower, one of your own presidents, who warned about the Military-Industrial Complex, now you want me to work for it.'

Patiently, the Professor said, 'You've got to face facts. We're custodians of the most important secret in the world and we haven't even a gun between us.'

Bronwen threw up her arms in desperation, 'I'm a pacifist, Frank,' she snapped, 'we don't carry guns or didn't you know?'

The Professor picked up the chair which Bronwen had knocked over. 'How's the work going with the outer planets?'

'It's going, Frank, but not fast.'

With a look of concern, the Professor asked, 'Can you include the other planets in the time we've got left?'

Bronwen ran her fingers through her wiry hair, 'I've got to, Frank, but it's one hell of a job. Even with TITAN's regression package, it'll take weeks to fit Uranus.'

The Professor placed his hand on Bronwen's shoulder, 'That'll still leave Pluto unaccounted for. Let's face it, Bron, without help you'll never get a fit on all the planets before August.'

Bronwen kicked the chair over again, 'I know you're right, damn you! But I'll tell you this, if the facilities at Southwood aren't as good as you paint them, I'm coming straight back here.'

Four armed men unobtrusively protected the Cooper house for the next three days. On the morning of the fourth day, an army truck screeched up and out jumped a sergeant who was the size of a gorilla. After bounding up to the door, he hammered the knocker. 'You Professor Cooper?' he growled.

'Yes.'

'I've orders to take your equipment to Southwood, say what you want and I'll have it loaded on the truck.'

Less than an hour after the truck had pulled away from the Cooper house, the Nostradamus team was speeding along the freeway in the back of a White House limousine towards the airport. Although Ian and Mary were no longer essential to the project, the Professor sensed that everyone's survival chances increased by staying together. After the flight in an executive jet, all was blackness when the driver went through the security check at Southwood. Then they were inside and soldiers were helping unload their personal luggage.

Somehow, each member of the team had expected the accommodation to be basic, simple furniture in wooden huts. But it wasn't. The scientists' quarters would have done credit to a five-star Hilton, with Bronwen's face saying it all, 'If the living accommodation's this good, what are the laboratories like?'

At nine the next morning, the team was ceremoniously taken on a tour of the base. Their impressions of the previous night proved to be a gross underestimation of what existed. The facilities at Southwood were in line with the President's boast, 'the best in the world'; even Bronwen grudgingly conceded that the project stood an infinitely better chance of success in its new surroundings than at the Cooper house. 'I must admit it, Frank,' she confessed over lunch, 'Nostradamus didn't have a set-up like this. If the outer planets can't be cracked here, they won't be cracked anywhere.'

Dryly the Professor replied, 'That's for sure.'

Within hours, Bronwen had set about organising the Southwood complex to a single objective, to render perfect the theories of Nostradamus. Although the three hundred scientists found it hard to believe that their total research effort was based on the work of a man who died over four hundred years ago, there was no questioning the directive, signed by the President himself:—

> By virtue of my office as President of the United States of America, I direct that the facilities at Southwood be placed under the joint command of Professor Frank Cooper and Dr. Bronwen Jones. Professor Cooper's team is engaged on a project of the greatest national importance and I urge each scientist to co-operate to the maximum. The need for security cannot be stressed too strongly, therefore all leave is inoperative and in no circumstances should the nature of your work be discussed with anyone outside Southwood.

The work at Southwood had been proceeding three days, when the Professor entered Bronwen's laboratory, nervously fingering a letter, 'You look like you've seen a ghost, Frank.'

The man slumped into a chair, 'I recognise the writing, it's the same as the first one,' he muttered, pushing the letter across to Bronwen.

'You've not opened it.'

The Professor shook his head. 'I'm frightened to.'

Bronwen examined the envelope, 'It's addressed to you here at Southwood; the President's "watertight" security must have sprung a leak!' Something about the envelope caught Bronwen's attention. 'Look at the postmark.'

The Professor nodded, 'Yeah, I noticed it was sent from Cyprus.'

Bronwen thrust the letter under the Professor's nose, 'I didn't mean that, I meant the date, January 10th. This letter was posted before *anyone* knew we were coming here!'

The Professor shrugged his shoulders. 'Ever since this nightmare started, one impossible event has followed another. So why be surprised if some clairvoyant sends a letter before an event happens?'

'Do you want me to open it?'

The Professor shook his head, 'It's my duty to read it first, no matter what it might say,' Having picked up a thin metal rule from the table, he slit the envelope open and withdrew the letter. Now he forced his eyes to focus on its wording.

'Well, what does it say?' asked Bronwen impatiently.

'It's an invitation.'

Bronwen raised her eyebrows, 'An invitation?'

The Professor nodded, 'The last letter told Ian and me to go to Paris, now we've been invited to Cyprus. Here, see for yourself.'

> 'Dear Professor Cooper,
>
> Events have progressed since my first letter. Please believe that I appreciate your torment now you also share the burden of knowledge. Even though it is not wise to entrust many words to the medium of a letter, it is imperative that we meet, for you have a pivotal role to play if humanity is to survive. Therefore I invite you and your son to break bread with a humble shepherd at his home on February 8th. The chemical I employed to write my address at the base of this letter, will now be reacting with the air in your laboratory and becoming visible. Take note of this address, for in three minutes the reaction will be complete and it will disappear!
>
> Until we meet,
> Stavros Kara,
> Farm of the Four Winds
> Troodos Mountains
> Cyprus.

When Bronwen had finished the letter, she placed it face upwards on the desk, 'The address is fading, Frank, but it's easy to remember.' She glanced at the Professor, he was smiling. 'I can guess why you're smiling,' she joked, 'you've just worked out that Stavros Kara is running a bucket shop and he's found a sure-fire way of getting rid of two spare seats to Cyprus!'

Reading the letter a second time, the Professor said, 'I guess the smile comes from the letter turning out to be okay. You know Bron, for the first time since this horror began, we might just be getting somewhere.'

Bronwen placed her hand on the Professor's shoulder, 'Don't fly too high, Frank, but I guess it is another straw to clutch at.'

'Surely it's more than that. The letter implies that war can be prevented.'

Bronwen shook her head, 'That's not what it said, Frank. The letter didn't say the holocaust could be stopped, only that humanity might survive.'

The Professor looked up at the woman, 'Isn't that the same thing?'

With a shake of her head, Bronwen said, 'Not necessarily, Frank, not necessarily at all.'

CHAPTER 8

With few incoming flights being scheduled for Sunday, February 8th, the taxiing airbus was the only plane in sight as it approached the terminal building. 'Sure is a beautiful day,' said Ian to his father.

The Professor nodded, 'But it's too hot for walking, let's hope we can get transport.'

The men needn't have worried, three battered old taxi cabs stood empty outside the airport. As they approached the leading cab, the strains of a Greek dance could be heard from its half-open window. The Professor peered inside; the cab's occupant was a man in a string vest, with an old trilby covering his face. Oblivious to the world outside, the man was slumped in front of the wheel, lazily drumming his fingers to the music. The Professor tapped lightly on the window; there was no response from the driver. Now he gave the glass a hearty knock. In a single movement, the driver flicked the radio off, pushed the trilby back onto his head and smiled affectionately at his customers.

'Are you open for business?', asked the Professor.

The man's bronzed, middle-aged face wrinkled into a grin, 'I been sat here two hours waiting for someone to say what you just say.'

The Professor held out a slip of paper, 'Can you take us to this address?'

The driver fumbled under the seat for his spectacles then, after dutifully giving them a polish, he read the address, 'It far away!' he declared gleefully. The man gave the glove compartment a sharp rap, it sprang open, releasing a random collection of oddments, including an oil-stained map of the island. The driver gazed thoughtfully at the map for several minutes, before marking a big black cross, 'You English?'

'American,' answered Ian.

'Same thing but opposite side of road. This address you give me. It in middle of nowhere, over the Troodos mountains. It take hours to get there and more hours to get back. You got plenty of money for fare?'

The traditional London cab, which by some miracle had survived since Cyprus was a British Colony, was soon clear of the airport. At first, the journey was easy and they encountered no problems in the sleepy streets of Larnaca. Then the scent of pine trees came in through the open windows; the road was beginning its climb into the foothills of the Troodos mountains. 'Do you know anything about where we're going?' asked the Professor.

The driver nodded, 'It a holy place. Before Christianity come to Cyprus, men talk with Gods in mountains.'

Taking a sharp right turn, the taxi deserted the road and began bouncing along a track riddled with potholes. 'D...do you trust this g...guy, Dad?' stuttered Ian. 'He...he's been h...hogging the wr...wrong side since the...the airport.'

'Don't w...worry, th...they drive on the left in Cyprus.'

As he and his father were being violently jerked in all directions, Ian managed to stammer a question to the driver, 'Is...is the road this b...bad for the r...rest of the journey?'

The driver gave Ian a confused glance, 'This good road, we meet bad roads in hills.'

To Ian's surprise, the driver had been telling the truth. As the taxi rattled along on its journey, the cinder track became a dirt track then the dirt track degenerated into little more than a path. Yet the breakneck pace never slackened, it was as if the vehicle only had one gear, top! Any sheep foolish enough to be grazing in the cab's path, had the choice of leaping for its life or suffering the consequences. To the obvious amusement of the driver, one unfortunate animal jumped the wrong way and was swallowed by a ravenous chasm.

The Professor found the hairpin bends horrific, with vertical drops patiently waiting to engulf the vehicle, while on the other side, craggy rock faces encroached onto the track until there seemed no space left for the cab to travel. After the first hour, the Professor lost count of the times the wheels beneath him had seemed to be solely supported by some unseen hand. And just when he was managing to convince himself that the driver didn't have kamikaze blood, he glanced down into a gaping ravine and saw the remains of a rusting car! Beyond a doubt, it was the most frightening journey either traveller had ever undertaken.

Without warning, the driver slammed on his brakes, bringing the cab screeching to a halt only inches away from a huge boulder. The passengers were instantly jolted into a sweaty heap on the floor. 'This is far as cab go safely,' said the driver without emotion. 'The road not good after here. You follow path for two miles then you come to farm.'

Trying to retain some semblance of dignity, the Professor lifted himself off the cab floor and thanked the driver for getting them so far. Then he told the man that if he'd wait there until 6.00 p.m., he'd get a whole week's wages.

'I not sure,' said the driver, 'these roads dangerous at night.'

'Two weeks' wages?'

'I wait.'

To the sounds of yet another Greek dance from the cab's radio, the two men set off on their trek. It was a good day for walking in the mountains, with the air intoxicatingly fresh and warm. Soon they were making steady progress along the winding paths cut into the hillside by generations of sheep. With the sun continuing to blaze down, Ian peeled off his shirt and tied it round his waist before sprinting several yards up the hillside. The sight made the Professor realise how the island was a natural habitat for his son, 'Hey, Tarzan, slow down!'

With a big grin, Ian turned round and began beating his chest, then after letting out the traditional, ape-man scream, he said, 'What's with the Tarzan, Dad, it's light years since the guys on the soccer team christened me that.'

The Professor laughed, 'I've changed my mind anyway, it was Cheetah who had the hairy chest!'

After they had been walking for a couple of hours, Ian said, 'How do you rate the driver's story?'

'About what?' asked the Professor.

'You know, about Pathos being the place where men used to talk to Gods?'

The Professor shook his head, 'Every island has its collection of ancient myths.' Then, almost as an afterthought, he added, 'Although it's surprising how many myths have their foundations in some kind of reality.'

The driver's estimate of distance proved to be optimistic; by the time they reached the first man-made structure, it was already early afternoon. The structure was little more than a hut, built from field stones and sheltering in a hollow between four small hillocks. The only clue of habitation came from a telltale wisp of smoke, drifting vertically from the chimney.

'Could it be that heap of rubble over there?' joked Ian.

The Professor shook his head, 'That looks more like a Scottish crofter's cottage than a farmhouse.' But the Professor was wrong, an old wooden sign was hanging from a post, with the words, 'Farm of the Four Winds' burnt deep into it.

While the men were gazing down at the hut, not knowing what to do next, the door creaked open. Some seconds elapsed then out stepped an old man with a rampant white beard and clothes which would have seemed appropriate for a shepherd from biblical times. The man shielded his eyes from the sun and motioned the travellers to come closer. When they were standing directly in front of him, the old man held out his hand, 'Professor Cooper, I presume?' he said with a smile, 'and this must be Ian. I am Stavros Kara, the sender of the letters. You will be tired after the walk; come inside my simple home where we can talk.'

When the men followed Stavros Kara into the hut, Ian felt as if the building was even smaller from the inside than it had seemed from the hillside. Just in time, the Professor avoided hitting his head on a ceiling beam but his son wasn't so lucky, collecting a glancing blow from a blackened timber. 'Sorry about that,' said the old man, 'the farmhouse wasn't built for giant Americans.'

In the scant light which managed to penetrate the dirty window, Stavros Kara smiled at his crouching guests, 'I know what you're thinking. How could a man who can foretell the future, live in such surroundings? Have patience, when we've taken tea, all your questions will be answered, but first I suggest that to avoid looking like a scene from "Alice in Wonderland", you both sit down!'

Stavros Kara shuffled across to the fire and poured the steaming contents of a kettle into a earthenware teapot, 'This is quite an occasion for me, having tea with visitors. I acquired the habit of tea drinking as a student in England before the war.' The old man scratched his head and smiled, 'How absent-minded of me, I've forgotten to put the tea in the teapot.' He reached up and took an unopened packet off the shelf, 'This is a very expensive brand,' he said proudly, 'I bought it seven years ago in London, especially for this occasion. Unfortunately, there's only goat's milk to go with it but I can guarantee that it was fresh this morning.'

The man turned to a small cupboard and took out four china cups, ceremoniously he filled them with tea, 'You don't mind if someone joins us?' he asked politely.

'Up here?' exclaimed Ian.

With a boyish grin, Stavros Kara dragged a sheepskin rug from the centre of the floor, revealing a small trapdoor. He lifted the door and peered inside, 'You can come out, Demetri. Our guests have arrived.'

After a brief interval, a black-haired young man, still rubbing his eyes, emerged into the relative light of the room. Stavros Kara indicated that the new-comer be seated, then he handed each person a cup of tea. 'Now we talk,' declared the old man, delicately dropping two sugar lumps into his cup, 'but if you are to be at the car by six, time is already short.' As Ian opened his mouth, Stavros raised his hand, 'Don't waste time, Ian, by asking how I know about the car; the moment has arrived to tell you everything.'

Taking a sip of tea, the old man began his tale, 'When Nostradamus died, Chavigny became the first Guardian of the theorems of which you now hold a duplicate. I am the 13th Guardian, through my French grandmother, and, God willing, my grandson, Demetri, will be the 14th. On his deathbed, Nostradamus imposed three laws on Chavigny. The first was that only the Guardian and his successor should view the manuscripts. The second law required that no gain came from the Guardian's knowledge of the future; hence my humble surroundings.'

While the old man replenished his empty teacup, silence prevailed inside the small hut in the Troodos mountains, then he resumed his story, 'The third law forbids a Guardian to view more than seven years ahead.'

Ian put his cup onto the wooden table, 'Sure, I follow what you've told us but I still can't figure out my Dad's role.'

Stavros held up his hand, 'Patience, Ian, everything will be all too clear when the tale is complete. Nostradamus foresaw a terrible holocaust following the death of the 13th Guardian. He therefore left precise instructions on the action to be followed when the 13th Guardian also viewed the holocaust, by then only seven years away. Finally, we come to you, Professor. *You survive the holocaust*.'

For several seconds, the words seemed to echo inside the tiny room, then the Professor gasped, 'I. . . I'm going to survive the holocaust?'

The old man nodded

'Alone?'

Stavros shook his head, 'There are others.'

'How many?'

'Two hundred.'

The china cup slipped from the Professor's limp fingers and shattered on the floor, 'You. . . you're saying that four billion die and only two hundred survive?'

'Yes.'

'Why?'

The old man looked confused, 'Why? Mortal man cannot say why, Professor, other than "it is written".'

In despair, the Professor said, 'Okay, then how do you know that I survive?'

Stavros pointed at a pile of manuscripts in the corner of the room, 'Those foretell that your chart continues beyond the holocaust.'

In blind desperation, the Professor asked, 'And my son, does Ian survive?'

When Stavros remained ominously silent, the Professor lowered his gaze, in case he glimpsed the wrong answer in the old man's eyes.

'Do not misinterpret my silence,' said Stavros soothingly, 'I have not replied because the answer is unknown. It took six long years of calculation to prove that you and Demetri survive, but your son? I have not calculated his chart.' Stavros clasped the Professor's hands, 'Perhaps Ian does escape the holocaust because of his association with you. Remembering the sorrow of losing my own son, Demetri's father, my prayers join yours that Ian survives.'

'Okay,' said Ian calmly, 'if you can only name Demetri and my father as survivors, how come you think that two hundred escape?'

Again Stavros brandished his hand towards the manuscripts, 'Nostradamus wrote of the "two hundred survivors".'

'Swell,' said Ian, 'two down, one hundred and ninety eight to go! Don't you think we should get the war postponed for a while?'

The old man smiled, 'I appreciate humour, even at a time like this, but patience, I have yet to complete the picture. While I cannot name the survivors, your father or more precisely, your father's computer, can!'

The Professor raised his head, 'I'm beginning to make sense of this at last,' he muttered. 'You've singled me out so I can identify the survivors?'

Stavros nodded, 'But more than that, you must also locate the place of sanctuary.'

As if in a trance, the Professor repeated, 'The place?'

'Of course!' declared Stavros, 'your computer showed that life ceases in America, Europe, Africa, apparently everywhere, did it not?'

'That's right,' said the Professor, 'according to TITAN, it's the end of everything.'

The old man nodded, 'Yet if two hundred are to survive, a sanctuary must exist somewhere, which only you can find.'

The Professor held up his hands in desperation, 'You haven't a single clue where the sanctuary is?'

Stavros shook his head, 'Every Guardian has devoted his life to searching for the location but always without success.' He scratched his head, 'If all life on Earth ceases, perhaps the sanctuary is elsewhere? But that is for you to determine.'

After a pause, the Professor said, 'Okay, if you can't tell me where the sanctuary is, then explain how I'm supposed to identify the survivors?'

The old man put down his teacup, 'That's simple, Professor. The survivors are those whose charts continue into September; therefore run the Nostradamus programme for every person on Earth.'

The Professor opened his eyes wide, 'Everyone? Impossible!' he gasped.

'Why impossible? You control the largest computer in the world; the President has placed every resource at your disposal and the theories can cross-reference raw data.'

'Hey Stavros,' interrupted Ian, 'how come you sound more like Bronwen Jones than Bronwen Jones does? What mountain goat taught you about computers?'

With an amused smile, the old man said, 'Forgive my pride but there is not time left in the world for me to tell you all I know. And Demetri, he knows much more than I.'

Almost as if he'd nearly said something he shouldn't, the old man looked at Ian, 'If humanity is to survive, the two hundred must be found, what more is to be discussed?'

Ian shrugged, 'Then speaking on behalf of the silent majority who aren't going to see September, can the war be stopped?'

Stavros glanced at the manuscripts, 'Who knows? Nostradamus wasn't God. Sometimes the equations are wrong, perhaps they're wrong about the holocaust.'

Ian nodded, 'We picked up a few mistakes ourselves so we're working on including Uranus and Neptune.'

The old man placed his hand on Ian's knee, 'Every Guardian has tried to perfect the theories but always without success.'

Boastfully, Ian said, 'Sure, but TITAN can do more calculations than a million Guardians.'

Stavros leaned back in his chair, 'Then perhaps you will be successful. But take care, for with success goes the danger of certainty.'

The Professor asked, 'Is that the same as completing the circle?'

'Yes.'

'In that case, if it's so bad, tell us what it means.'

Although the old man seemed reluctant to speak, finally he said, 'If the circle is completed, a prophecy becomes self-fulfilling. The event does not occur because it should occur but because the knowledge that it might occur makes it unavoidable.'

Ian peered at the old man, 'If I read you correct, humans are relegated into mindless puppets who jump when God pulls the strings.'

Stavros strongly shook his head, 'There are two sets of hands holding the strings and you jump which way you choose.' Noticing the questioning expressions on the faces of his guests, Stavros said, 'Because of your contributions to this work, I will reveal what none but the Guardians have known. Nostradamus wrote that before God existed, there existed nothing, and nothing existed for an eternity of eternities. Then a unique event occurred. If we assume that good and evil are analogous to matter and anti-matter, at the beginning of the beginning, good and evil spontaneously burst into existence.'

The old man looked at Ian, 'Do you follow the analogy so far?' After Ian had nodded that he did, Stavros Kara continued, 'So, out of nothing came forth Good and Evil, or God and the Devil. And these entities were of opposite intent but of equal, infinite power. What do you think would happen now?'

Ian though for a few seconds, then he said, 'They would knock hell out of each other because absolute evil would flip at knowing that perfect goodness was around.'

Stavros Kara smiled, 'Although your phraseology is amusing, what you say is almost right, the problem is, how could they fight? At least, how could they fight directly? If God and the Devil were of equal, infinite strength, neither could triumph over the other. What were they to do? Nostradamus believed that they agreed to combine their energies to create an entire Universe, just to bring a single Earth into existence where they could do battle. And on

Earth was cast a race of beings, a race who was given intelligence, a conscience and free will.'

The old man paused as he noted the diminishing light through the dust covered window, 'Now, we come to the rules of the battle for the souls of humanity. Each time an evil act is freely committed, the relative power of the Devil is increased; when a good act is performed, God is strengthened.' In the dim light, Ian glimpsed the emotion in the old man's eyes as he said, 'In any contest, there must exist a balance sheet, and this can only be counted when neither protagonist can predict the outcome.'

'You mean when the planets are in conjunction?' interrupted Ian.

Stavros raised his hands, 'That's what the planets are, Ian, nothing more than oversize counters. But do not misunderstand me, Nostradamus taught that we are not governed by the planets, they simply reflect our actions.'

The 13th Guardian looked out of the window at the setting sun, 'It grows dark and soon you must return to the car. We shall not meet again; it is written that my days are even less than those of civilisation. Therefore, when the time is right, Demetri will be placed in your trust. Now return to America and make haste in identifying the survivors and locating the sanctuary. When you have achieved these tasks, guard the information with your life, for the very existence of humanity depends on it. May God walk with you both, it is truly a crushing burden that you carry.'

Somewhat shakily, the old man stood up and held the wooden door open while the Americans crouched their way out of the hut. When they were all outside, Stavros Kara held out his hand, 'Goodbye, Professor, and you too Ian, my prayers go with you both.'

The journey back to the car proved more perilous than either man had anticipated. In the darkening gloom, the relative safety of the path was lost and soon the Professor and Ian were helplessly roaming the mountainside. For one terrible instant, if Ian's reactions had been anything less than lightening fast, his father would have disappeared into a black ravine. After both men had recovered from their shock, Ian said, 'You're the explorer, do we try to get back to Stavros or keep looking for the car?'

Hesitantly, the Professor said, 'We're past the point of no return, keep looking for the car.'

The men groped blindly round the mountainside for another half hour, then Ian said, 'Try this on for a heavy thought, maybe the car's already left without us?'

To Ian's surprise, his father said confidently, 'You can be certain that the car's still there, all we've got to do is find it.'

When they were on the point of giving up the search, Ian and the Professor were suddenly held in awe by two shafts of blinding light, beaming high into the night sky. Then the men realised what it was and soon they were thankfully slipping and sliding down the hillside, towards the comparative safety of the car. The driver saw the Americans approaching and turned the beam down to dipped.

'Thanks for waiting,' panted Ian.

'It's okay. I wait till morning if needed, but why you worry? You not late, it only six now.' Ian placed his wrist in front of the cab's headlight, the watch was reading 6:00.

'I guess it was bound to be exactly six,' said the Professor.

Ian nodded, 'We seem to be the lead actors in a film that's had every scene planned in meticulous detail.'

On the journey back to Larnaca, the Professor took some perverse comfort from the blackness; it prevented him seeing the razor width tracks, the hairpin bends and the gaping precipices. At the airport, he awarded the driver a whole month's wages; gratefully, the man pocketed the money and then told the Americans that if they ever wanted to go to the farm again, to ask for 'Theo' personally.

Later, as the plane was preparing to take off, Ian said, 'I've got to hold my hands up. You must be some expert on human nature to have been so certain that the cab would still be waiting.'

The Professor smiled, 'I've spent my life studying people, but that's not why Theo was there. You see, I "forgot" to pay the fare for the outward journey.'

CHAPTER 9

When Mary and Bronwen had been updated on the events in Cyprus, Bronwen said, 'This man Stavros knows his computers, I'll have census files mounted on TITAN today and start the search for the survivors.'

'What about countries that don't keep records?'

Bronwen waved Ian silent, 'No problem, we can get round that by cross-referencing the survivors after the holocaust. It'll take time but I'll winkle out most of the two hundred.' Now Bronwen looked at the Professor, 'With me tied up with the survivors, you inherit the job of finding the sanctuary. People have been asking what Ian and Mary are doing here at Southwood, so draft them as assistants.'

The Professor scratched his head, 'I'm not questioning your allocation of duties but where in tarnation do we start looking for a sanctuary?'

Bronwen thought hard then she said, 'If you've got the stomach for it, use TITAN to simulate a war and then see what happens.'

The President's directive gave the Professor an 'unrestricted access' security rating, equal to his own. With this clearance, the Professor's team of analysts interrogated countless files over the next three weeks. Only now did the true horror of a war between the super powers become horrifyingly clear. Yet for all the sophistication of the computerised data files, with their cross-referenced calculations to three places of decimals, the most chilling document was a simple note, written to the then-President, years before, by a distinguished academic.

Harvard University
October 28th, 1962

Mr. President,

A source, previously found to be reliable, informs me that two days ago, Chairman Khrushchev threatened a twenty megaton strike on your home city of Boston if a single Russian ship were attacked approaching Cuba. You, in turn, replied that if Boston were attacked, we would counter-attack Kiev. I congratulate you, Mr. President, that sanity prevailed on this occasion, with the understanding that two of our missile bases in Turkey would be 'rendered obsolete' if the Soviet fleet returned to the Black Sea. However, my source says that the strike and counterstrike were less than twelve minutes away before an agreement was reached. After our private discussions over recent years, my own views on the hideous insanity of the arms race do not need to be restated. However, I did spend last night analysing what would have happened to Boston if the strike had taken place. My account deliberately avoids the use of emotive language; the horror would be so immense that mere words would have lost their meaning.

* At ground zero, a crater two miles wide, five hundred feet deep, with a rim dwarfing a twenty-storey building would instantaneously be created.

* A second after detonation, an unimaginably bright fireball, with a temperature five times higher than the centre of the sun, would melt the retinas of everyone still alive within a twenty mile radius.

* Everything above ground level for a hundred square miles of the blast would be vapourised and consumed within the radio-active mushroom.

* The water in Boston harbour would be transformed into superheated steam, 'cooking' all life for miles in every direction.

* A raging firestorm would incinerate all combustible material within a twenty mile radius (humans are combustible).

* A lethal, radio-active cloud, with a diameter exceeding a hundred miles, would destroy all life as it passed over the length of our continent.

* In summary, Boston would have ceased to exist.

Knowing how you share my views on the 'the ultimate madness', I urge you to devote the remainder of this term of office, and the whole of your assured second term, to bringing about a lasting disarmament treaty.

Your Good Friend,
Theodore Mills,
Professor of Nuclear Physics

At first, it had seemed impossible to imagine anything exceeding the obscenity of a nuclear strike. As he continued to review top secret files, however, the Professor began to rank the vile effects of bacteriological weapons above the 'clean' death of a multimegaton fireball. And the military euphemisms, used to describe the arsenal of germs, only added a further twist to the nightmare: 'Born on the Wind', 'Silent Spring', 'From Here to Eternity'. But the sickening task had to continue, until all the information was amassed on a master disc, codenamed 'Armageddon'.

On the morning of February 24th, the Professor phoned for Bronwen to join him. 'It's finished.', he declared as she entered the room, 'You name the level of war and I'll simulate it.'

Bronwen slumped into a chair, 'There's only one level to cover, Frank. That's when the crazy bastards throw everything they've got at each other.'

Putting down his pen, the Professor said, 'You know something I don't. What?'

Bronwen looked up, 'We're included the next planet in the programme, Frank. This time De Gaulle doesn't get assassinated.'

Bronwen paused ominously, so the Professor said, 'And?'

'And the holocaust still happens.'

To raise Bronwen's spirits, the Professor said, 'We can't be certain of anything until all nine planets are in the programme.'

Bronwen gave a defeated shrug, 'Technically, that may be true, Frank. But it is going to happen and no power on Earth can stop it.'

Placing his hand on Bronwen's shoulder, the Professor said, 'If you're right, all the more reason to find the sanctuary, if it exists.'

Bronwen nodded, 'I guess you're right Frank, we must keep fighting. Is Armageddon loaded?' The Professor gave the thumbs up sign. 'Okay.' said Bronwen, flicking a switch, 'let's preview the holocaust.'

As the go switch was flicked at Southwood, hundreds of miles distant TITAN began its task. Waiting apprehensively for the printout, Bronwen said, 'Think what's happening in that soulless machine, Frank. As far as TITAN's concerned, it's only manipulating numbers but each digit's a human life. Delete New York, that's eight million digits gone. But we know that eight million people have just been incinerated in a five megaton blast.'

Bronwen's face showed her despair as she said, 'If the programme assumes a westerly breeze over England, a million will die in Sheffield from fallout after the strike on Manchester. Oh don't worry, Frank, the other side's getting it worse. Scratch Moscow, delete Leningrad! Yes, now it's just numbers but in seven months time, each digit deleted will be the death of a human being. I only hope that I'm not alive to see it.'

The Professor had never seen Bronwen in such a state, yet he knew that she was right. What sort of species would allow a computer to clinically calculate the mega-deaths it was going to inflict on its own kind in Paris and Budapest? And would such a species have any moral claim to survival anyway?

'How did we come to this, Frank? Has humanity got a death wish programmed into its genes?' Somehow, the Professor had always assumed that Bronwen was incapable of tears but she wasn't.

Putting his arms around her, he gave what comfort he could as she said, 'That first monkey which clubbed another to get to the top of the heap, he was the one which set us off on the road that ends here. But we're too damn sophisticated for clubs anymore, now it's poison gas, napalm and multimegaton warheads. That's five million years of progress! The Earth could have been transformed into a paradise, with plenty for everybody but greed, pride and hate are going to turn it into a desert.'

While Bronwen found some relief in the Professor's arms, TITAN continued to simulate the effects of an all-out war between the super powers. Bronwen's relief was short-lived as the printer hummed into life and outputted the findings.

Regaining her normal manner, Bronwen said, 'May as well rip off the results, Frank, nothing's going to change by letting them hang there.'

The Professor spread the printout on a bench and scrutinised the data. Then he walked to the waste bin and with all the force at his disposal, threw everything into it.

'What did it say, Frank?' There was no reply. 'I asked what was on the printout, Frank?'

In a scarcely audible voice, the Professor answered, 'Everyone in the whole damn world is going to die. No point in bothering you with the details, I'll just give the bottom line—number of survivors 0 (ZERO).'

Bronwen retrieved the printout from the waste basket, 'Either Nostradamus got it wrong and no one survives, or this programme's crap!' Then she thought for a while before saying, 'Scratch that last sentence, both programmes might be right.'

The Professor scratched his head, 'Both right? How?'

'Okay, so I'm clutching at straws, but what else is left? Does your programme give a breakdown of deaths?'

The Professor took the printout, 'Direct blast from nuclear warhead, eight percent. Nuclear fallout, seventeen percent. Death from chemical, germ or bacteriological weapons, seventy-five percent.'

Bronwen nodded, 'That's what I guessed, Frank. The wind's going to carry the germs to every country on Earth. And if someone's immune to one virus, they'll get caught with another because the planners will have made sure that there's plenty for everybody.'

The Professor gave Bronwen a puzzled look, 'If the computer says that everyone dies, what makes you think that there's any survivors?'

Bronwen raised her hand, 'Just one more question before I tell you the straw that we've got to clutch at. Did your programme list the populations of every country after the holocaust?'

The Professor jabbed his finger at a string of zeros on the printout, 'If you add a lot of zeros together, you get a great big zero for the answer. So where's the straw?'

Bronwen ran her gaze down the programme listing, 'The output records that no one survives where people live now but there may be places where people don't live, yet they'd survive if they did.'

Sceptically, the Professor said, 'Such as where? On a space station or at the North Pole?'

Bronwen shook her head, 'Those would only be temporary refuges. We're looking for a home for generations.'

Bronwen shrugged her shoulders, 'No point in waiting, Frank, let's test that straw. Ask TITAN to calculate where life could survive the holocaust.'

Although an eternity seemed to pass while TITAN evaluated if mankind had a continuing existence, in reality, the laboratory clock only progressed twenty-seven seconds before the printer outputted a single sheet. Nervously, the Professor glanced at it, 'There are three sets of co-ordinates, nothing else.'

Bronwen took the printout to a giant display screen on the wall and keyed in some instructions. A projection of the world appeared. Bronwen looked at the co-ordinates and then at the world, 'It's as I expected, Frank. Each location is surrounded by ocean to avoid fallout.' Running her fingers through her hair, Bronwen added 'What I didn't expect is that there's no land, only water!'

The Professor hung his head in dismay, 'Even Noah couldn't anchor the Ark for a thousand years! There's just got to be land. . .'

Bronwen shook her head, 'See for yourself, Frank, there's only clear blue ocean.'

The two scientists looked dejectedly at the map; this was finally it, the end of everything. Yet even now, Bronwen's battling instincts reasserted themselves. 'What did Sherlock Holmes say when he was faced with an impossible situation?'

The Professor shrugged, 'This is another fine mess you've got me into, Watson?'

Bronwen grinned, 'Glad to see you've not lost your sense of humour. However, what Holmes said was something like, "when you have eliminated the impossible, you're stuck with what's left." So if two hundred survive, and there are only three places where they could survive, let's look at those places.'

'And how do you propose we do that?' asked the Professor.

Bronwen managed a smile, 'Think big, Frank. Every U.S. weather and spy satellite can be accessed from this room, so let's feed in the co-ordinates and see what happens.'

While Bronwen was calling up the operating instructions for satellite control, the Professor said, 'I've heard of longshots but even Sherlock Holmes wouldn't expect to stumble across an island.'

'Why not?' asked Bronwen. 'Dozens are discovered every year and I remember reading that 99% of known islands are uninhabited. Oceans are big places, Frank. The Pacific covers half the world's surface, all we need is a tiny dot of land.'

Bronwen typed a set of commands, making the wall scanner acquire a grid of coloured lights. 'They're satellites, Frank.' After Bronwen had keyed another command, the screen displayed the South Atlantic, with a light flashing the code 'WS173'. When more keys were pressed, the screen filled with the view of Earth seen by weather satellite 173. Finally, the co-ordinates of the first area of safety were inputted and the camera zoomed in to reveal. . .sea.

'Try a close-up.'

‘Bronwen nodded. The close-up revealed...sea. ‘Go to maximum magnification.’

Bronwen keyed in the command. Now individual waves could be identified but no land existed.

‘One down, two to go,’ said Bronwen in a voice lacking conviction, I’ll try the Indian Ocean next.’ The same procedure was followed, locating the area, selecting an appropriate satellite and then locking in the co-ordinates. This time, a military satellite was used whose powers of resolution were prodigious. The playing cards of a sailor playing solitaire on a cargo ship were magnified to the size of oil paintings but no land was seen.

‘That leaves one place left,’ said the Professor, ‘unless Stavros was right and the sanctuary really is in space?’

This time, when Bronwen started the search procedure, no satellite could be found over the target area. ‘That’s strange, Frank. If every inch of ocean is supposed to be under U.S. surveillance, why create a blind zone, exactly beneath the third co-ordinates?’

Instead of answering the question, the Professor asked, ‘Can another satellite be tilted to point at the spot?’

‘Good thinking, Frank, it’s worth a try.’ Bronwen locked onto the satellite nearest the blind zone; a glistening view of the Pacific was instantly cast onto the screen. ‘These high satellites observe one location, Frank, but if there’s gas in the canisters, maybe I can tilt the camera.’

Bronwen interrogated the computer files until the procedure for rectifying satellite deviations flashed onto the screen. After studying the instructions, she said, ‘Well here goes everything.’ As the instructions to aim the satellite at the blind zone were transmitted, high above the Earth, impulse jets started to coerce the camera into its new role. But the woman’s skill was insufficient for the manoeuvre and the satellite started to slowly revolve on its axis. ‘Shit,’ yelled Bronwen, ‘I’ve lost it, and there’s no way of getting it back!’

The scientists watched helplessly as the camera swept across the ocean then, just before the horizon came into view, they saw it! An island, covered in lush vegetation, with waves breaking on a protective coral reef. ‘That’s it, that’s just got to be it!’

As the satellite continued to rotate, the black void of space momentarily filled the screen, before the shimmering ocean returned into view. ‘There’s the island again, Bron!’

The satellite was now rotating at an ever increasing speed and on each revolution, the green blur of the island flashed across the screen. 'Can't you stop it spinning?'

'Fraid not,' said Bronwen without concern, 'The cannister which jammed open was the only one with gas in it.' The Professor thought he detected a school-girlish grin on Bronwen's face as she added, 'Sit back and enjoy it, we've got ourselves a great big pinwheel.'

By this stage, the swirl of rotation had rendered the transient images into nothing more than a psychedelic rainbow. Suddenly, the screen went blank. 'It's exploded, Frank, the centrifugal force tore it apart.' Bronwen laughed at the expression on the Professor's face. 'I wouldn't worry about the satellite, Frank. It's served its purpose and we're better off if no one else sees the island.'

The Professor remained silent. 'Christ, Frank! What's a little satellite when the whole damn world's about to end. Anyway, there's something macabre about what those satellites will be doing soon. For decades after the holocaust, they'll be sending back their scrambled messages to a burnt planet, with no human eyes or ears to understand their transmissions.'

The scientists left the control room and walked to the rest area. After getting two coffees from the vending machine, they sank into easy chairs. 'Well,' said the Professor, 'that's another piece of the jigsaw in position.'

Bronwen nodded, 'But it's still true that for every piece we find, two more go missing. Why isn't the island on any map? And what's the reason for U.S. satellites avoiding it like the plague? There's more to that place than either of us can guess at.'

The Professor dialled himself a second coffee before saying, 'At least we have found the island, how's the work going naming the two hundred?'

Bronwen put down her cup, 'I've got to hold my hands up, there's some bright people at Southwood. If only their normal efforts were for peace.'

The Professor shrugged, 'It sounds cynical but they're working for a paycheck like everybody else, with no questions asked. You still haven't said when the names start coming out?'

Avoiding the Professor's eyes, Bronwen said, 'The survivors in the industrial countries could be named now but we want to run some checks first.' She placed her hand on top of the Professor's, 'I appreciate your worry, Frank. It can't be easy working with Ian each day and wondering...'

Nervously the Professor repeated, 'How long before the run?'

'One week. We need to be sure.'

Security was absolute as the final preparations were made for running the 'September' file. 'It's like picking numbers out of a hat,' said Bronwen, 'with the odds on a winning ticket standing at twenty million to one and the prize being "life".' After saying this, Bronwen felt like biting her tongue off, 'I'm sorry, Frank. It was a thoughtless thing to say.'

Ignoring Bronwen's words, the Professor said, 'If we wait any longer, I won't be able to go through with it. Start the damn programme.'

Both scientists paced the floor while TITAN determined the first survivor; then a name was outputted. 'You read it, Bron, I couldn't.'

Bronwen tore off the printout, 'It's you, Frank. Stavros Kara got that one right.' Another nerve sapping interval elapsed while the programme selected the next person whose life entered September. Bronwen looked at the name, 'It's a French woman, called Lille Duval.'

Now, at regular intervals, Bronwen declared each new name as it appeared. The list stood at twelve when the woman looked at the next survivor. 'It's Ian!' she yelled, flinging her arms around the Professor, 'Ian makes it!'

The Professor hadn't cried since Ann's death, 'Each night I've prayed that Ian. . . that all of us, would make it but I never let my hopes be raised too high.' The Professor went silent for a few seconds then he wiped his eyes and said, 'What fool said that thirteen was unlucky?'

The scene was interrupted by the printer rapidly outputting three names from the same family. Bronwen showed them to the Professor who said, 'I can guess why they survive.'

Bronwen nodded, 'Okay, but at least it isn't our decision.'

For the next half hour, the printer continued its task of issuing details of the chosen few. When it finally fell silent, seventy-three people had been earmarked for survival. Mary Molina was also on the list but Bronwen wasn't! 'Three out of four isn't bad,' said Bronwen philosophically, 'besides, I'd look out of place with a flower in my hair and wearing a sarong on a desert island.'

The Professor drew Bronwen close to him, 'Maybe your name will come out in the next run but if it doesn't, I swear to God that we're taking you with us.'

Bronwen smiled bravely, 'Let's not argue with the computer, Frank. I'll not see September and that's the end of it. Anyway, we've got other things to worry about. Do you know what date tomorrow is?'

'Tomorrow?'

'It's March 3rd, Frank, the day for the President's earthquake in Yugoslavia.'

* * *

Outwardly, March 3rd started like any other day, but for the few who knew, it was the acid test for the programme. If March 4th appeared without the quake, the whole Nostradamus affair could be relegated to the trash can. The clock at Southwood was reading 11:37 when news of the earthquake broke. Less than four minutes later, the telephonist was excitedly telling Professor Cooper that the President himself was on the line, 'I guess you've heard the news, Frank. It's just like your damn programme predicted. There's a car on its way. We need to discuss options.'

When the Professor entered the Oval Office, he didn't at first recognise the slumped figure, in a crumpled suit, his bald patch glistening moistly under the brightness of an angle-poise lamp. Sensing that he was not alone, the President looked up and saw the Professor. He pointed towards a chair, 'Sit down, Frank, let's talk about this nightmare we've got ourselves into.' The President's voice and manner testified that he was a man on the edge of a breakdown, 'I keep expecting to wake up, Frank, but I don't. For the first time since I was seven, last night I got down on my knees in this office and prayed, but it didn't stop the earthquake.'

Clumsily, the President poured two glasses of water and pushed one towards the Professor. 'I keep asking myself one question, Frank, where in God's name do we go from here?'

'You need updating on the last month.'

The President shrugged, 'Then update me. Nothing can be worse than the shit we're standing in now.'

Sipping his water, the Professor said, 'I'll leave out the details but stick to the facts. First, we've included another planet in the programme.'

The President raised one eye, 'And?'

'The holocaust still happens.'

The man attempted a sick smile, 'It doesn't surprise me, Frank. You don't get good news in a nightmare. What else has happened?'

'Well, I met the man who sent the letter. He's Greek and he told me that Nostradamus saw the holocaust coming.'

The President hesitated before asking, 'Did he say if it could be avoided?'

The Professor shook his head, 'He guessed it couldn't and if anyone knows, he does.'

The President poured himself another glass of water, 'I'm not enjoying this updating, Frank. Everything you tell me sinks us deeper in it.'

'I'm telling it the way it is, Mr. President, but now we come to something new. Not everyone dies!'

The contents on the President's glass spilled over the table, 'You. . .you're saying there are survivors?'

The Professor nodded, 'But only a few.'

'How few?'

'Two hundred.'

'Two hundred million?'

'No, just two hundred.'

The President stared blankly ahead as he said, 'In the whole damn world, just two hundred survivors?' He sat there speechless for several minutes then he asked, 'Are the survivors scattered round the globe or in one place?'

'One place.'

This answer seemed to lift the President, 'Where's the place, Frank?' When there was no immediate reply, the question was repeated, but louder. 'I asked "*where*" Frank?'

'On an island in the Pacific. It doesn't appear on any map, even our satellites won't look at it, but it exists, Mr. President, and we've got the co-ordinates.'

Leaning forward, the President said, 'What are the co-ordinates, Frank?'

The Professor handed over a folded sheet of paper. The President snatched the paper and stared at the co-ordinates, then he pressed a button. Two minutes later, a high ranking officer entered the room. 'Interrogate our files, Major, and find out what exists at this location.' The officer noted the co-ordinates, saluted and left.

The President seemed less agitated when he next spoke, 'While we're waiting for details of the island, I'll update you on the quake. I took your advice and warned the Yugoslavs. Their Government acted fast and broadcast warnings, children were evacuated and relief centres set up. What I'm saying, Frank, is that they did the best they could. Yet over six thousand are reported killed and the final figure's going to top seven thousand.'

The President pulled out a tissue, wiped up some spilled water, and dropped it into the waste basket. 'What I keep asking myself, Frank, is what would the toll have been if we hadn't warned them? At least ten thousand? That would have bust the prophecy!'

The Professor shook his head, 'The programme took account of you telling the Yugoslavs. If we'd kept the quake a secret, the programme would have predicted ten thousand dead in the first place.'

The President thought for a while then he murmured, 'Either way, it doesn't seem as if your programme can be beaten.'

As the Professor was about to speak, the officer returned, carrying a file marked, FOR THE PRESIDENT'S EYES ONLY. The President waited until the officer had left before breaking the seal; inside was a photograph and a report. Flashing the photo, the President asked. 'Is this the place, Frank?'

The Professor shrugged, 'One island looks like any other when you glimpse it from a satellite.'

Patiently he waited for the President to open the report, but he didn't. Instead he just nervously turned it over in his hands. After this had gone on for some seconds, the President said, 'You know what, Frank? I'm not usually a coward but now I'm frightened to read this report. If the island's our last hope, where do we go if we've already done something stupid to destroy that hope?'

The President clasped Professor Cooper's hands, 'Before I read this report, will you join me in a prayer?' Although the Professor found the act distinctly embarrassing, the men knelt in silence for over a minute before the President stood up, opened the report and held his breath as he began to read the summary page.

As time elapsed, the expression that was forming on the man's face told the Professor that things were good. This was confirmed when the President said, 'Either I must try praying more often or luck's on our side, Frank. If there's such as thing as luck anymore. Anyway, you call the island "Sanctum", this report calls it "Apocalypse". I'll tell you something else, Frank, we should have guessed the mystery surrounding the island.'

When the Professor looked blankly at the President, he smiled, 'It makes a change to be one up on you, Frank. But it seems that during the war in the Pacific, hundreds of islands were discovered, catalogued and then forgotten. One of our destroyers was steaming on a secret mission, a thousand miles from any shipping lane, when it came across Apocalypse and logged its location. Then someone put two and two together in the fifties when the need came up for a secret island to test weapons of mass destruction.'

The President placed the report back in its folder, 'Now the story takes another twist, Frank. Along comes the test ban treaty before Apocalypse could be used, so the island gets evacuated but its top security rating stayed on the files.'

After the President had finished speaking, Professor Cooper said, 'The place seems perfect but why should I have guessed its use?'

The President sat a little higher in his chair as he answered, 'What you wanted, Frank, was an island immune from fallout and germs, now that's exactly what...'

'Okay, now I get it,' interrupted the Professor, 'that's what the military also wanted but in reverse. A place where they could test anything without destroying the rest of the globe.'

The President nodded, 'That's where the name came from. The military wanted to try out one apocalypse after another.'

When the Professor said, 'So the U.S. still owns the island?', the President managed his first genuine grin in weeks, 'Owns is the wrong word, Frank. No one knows it exists except us. Sure, there's a small military presence, just in case someone else stumbles across it, but that's very unlikely because of one thing I forgot to tell you. We've left four surveillance jammers on Apocalypse.'

'Surveillance jammers?'

The President smiled, 'Sorry about the jargon, Frank. They're devices for blocking out surveillance from satellites directly overhead, you only picked up the island because of the angle. The Russians haven't any satellites in the area anyway, but if they had, they'd only see ocean.'

'With no one else knowing that Apocalypse exists, things become a whole lot simpler, Mr. President.'

The President nodded, 'We were due a break, Frank. And I want you to know that I'll keep Ian and yourself high on my list when selecting the other one hundred and ninety-five people to go to that little island with me, Amy and the girls!'

Professor Cooper jolted upright, the President thought that the inhabitants of Apocalypse were his for the choosing! Looking the President square in the eye, the Professor said, 'The survivors have already been chosen, Mr. President.'

The President's face became crimson, 'Chosen? Chosen by whom?'

The Professor paused before saying, 'Strictly speaking, by the Nostradamus programme. However, you're a religious man so I'd say "chosen by a higher power".'

Angrily, the President knocked his glass flying, 'And did God send you a memo saying that nobody else gets a shout except those on your goddam printout?'

Professor Cooper deliberately remained calm as he said, 'It's a long story, Mr. President.'

Easing himself back in his chair, the President said, 'Then tell me your story, Professor, but this time don't miss out the details.'

When the Professor had finished explaining how the Nostradamus tape was identifying survivors from every nation on Earth, the President stated bluntly, 'Apocalypse belongs to the United States. So what's to stop me putting two hundred people of my choosing on it and to hell with those Nostradamus picked?'

The Professor shook his head, 'There are three reasons why you won't do that.'

The President opened his desk drawer and pulled out the bag of candy. After taking a piece, he said, 'So there are three reasons why I'll go along with the choice of survivors. Tell me them, Professor, but before you start, let me tell you something, they'd better be damned good.'

The President leaned back and closed his eyes as the Professor said, 'First, it would be suicide to ignore the selection of the computer. If we did, the result could be no survivors at all.'

The President waved his hand dismissively, 'With what's at stake here, that's a chance I'll take every day of the week. What's the second reason?'

The Professor delayed his answer a few seconds, while the noise from a routine guard change outside the office died away, then he said, 'Apocalypse is only safe because it's not a target and can't be contaminated by anywhere that is. This would change if the Russians knew it existed.'

The President shrugged, 'I accept the need for security, but I could make darn sure that anybody who knew about Apocalypse disappeared until September. You still haven't given me any reason for going along with your plan, Professor, so your third argument had better be a good one.'

The Professor paused, looked directly at the President and said, 'It is a good one; your daughters are among the survivors.'

The President's jaw visibly dropped open, 'Y...you say my daughters survive?'

'Yes.'

'All...all three?'

'Yes.'

'You're not lying?'

'No, Mr. President, you have my word that your daughters' names were on the printout from the Nostradamus programme.

The President drank Professor Cooper's water, 'B...but the odds must be billions to one.'

The Professor nodded, 'They're even greater than that, Mr. President. The probability of all your daughters being saved is ten, raised to the power twenty-two.'

The President sat back in his chair, 'I'll take your word for the odds, Frank, but how then?'

Looking at the picture of the President's daughters, the Professor said, 'In your case, the programme wasn't playing the odds. You play a critical role in saving humanity—take it that the deliverance of your daughters is payment for that role.'

Having regained his composure, the President found a word jarring in his brain, 'Just what role do I play, Frank?'

'Well, first we need your help in gaining custody of the island.'

The President sat back in his chair and smiled, 'No sweat there.'

The Professor leaned forward and lowered his voice, 'The next task isn't as easy.'

Apprehensively, the President said, 'I can see that from your face, Frank. So tell me straight out what it is.'

'The Nostradamus tape is identifying survivors from every nation on Earth. How do you think we get them to the island without them knowing what's happening?'

'Now wait a damn minute, Frank. I don't like what I'm hearing.'

The Professor held up his hands, 'Do we have a choice, Mr. President? Unless the C.I.A. goes in and kidnaps every person on the list, there's no way to get them to Apocalypse. And if they're not on the island, the prophecy can't be fulfilled. In which case no one survives, not my son, not your daughters.'

'Let's get this straight, Frank. You want the C.I.A. to kidnap Russians so they won't get blasted by our missiles?'

The Professor nodded, 'I guess that sums it up.'

The President opened the desk drawer and pulled out the candy then, without taking a piece, dropped the bag back in the drawer and slammed it shut. 'If I were to go along with your fool plan, Frank, and something went wrong, Watergate would look like a church squabble!'

To add weight to his words, the Professor picked up the photo of the President's daughters before saying, 'Forget Watergate, Mr.

President. Forget the history books, forget about running for a second term, forget everything but the survival of humanity and your daughters.'

The President went silent, then he asked, 'How long before you need a decision?'

'The list of names should be complete by April. If we don't start collecting the survivors then, it will be too late.'

The President frowned, 'It doesn't give much time to come up with an alternative plan, Frank.'

The Professor placed the photo back on the desk, 'There isn't an alternative, Mr. President.'

The President managed a smile as he said, 'A lifetime in politics has taught me that there's *always* an alternative, Frank. But let's not talk about alternatives, let's talk about practicalities. Your team should visit the island, check it out and see if it's as good as it sounds. Now the last thing we want to do is arouse interest, so here's your cover story. You're an archaeologist, I'll give you permission to do some digging to find out if Apocalypse was once inhabited. What do you think?'

The Professor nodded, 'Sounds as good a cover as any. How do we get to the island?'

The President raised his hand, 'No problem, Frank. Be ready at nine in the morning, I'll organise the rest.'

As the Professor was leaving, the President said, 'Treat that little island with respect. If this horror can't be side-stepped, Apocalypse is the most valuable piece of real estate in the whole damn world!'

The Professor shook his head, 'It's much more than that, Mr. President. Six months from now, Apocalypse will be the only piece of real estate in the whole damn world!'

CHAPTER 10

Ian, Mary and the Professor were waiting when the black limousine drew up at Southwood, but Bronwen had snapped that fitting the last planet was more important that swanning off on a package tour of an island that she wouldn't get to live on anyway. A big man got out of the car. The Professor could see he had once been quite powerful, but now looked like a wrestler gone to fat.

Having slammed the car door shut, the man absorbed the characteristics of each person on the porch before asking, 'You Professor Cooper?' The Professor nodded. 'You got identification?' The Professor pulled out three sets of papers, and the man scrutinised their contents. 'They look okay,' he conceded, thrusting them back at the Professor. Then his manner mellowed a fraction, 'I'm Gradham Harris from the Central Intelligence Agency. You can call me Graham. I'm wet-nursing you people on your South Seas trip so hop in the car for the airport.'

On the private jet, Graham insisted on sitting next to the Professor, 'You a personal friend of the President?' The Professor nodded. 'Thought so. How else could you get Government funds to see if natives once built mud huts on an island?' The Professor eased back in his chair but said nothing. 'And why is the island's location sealed in an envelope which can't be opened till we're three hundred miles out of Hawaii?'

'I guess it's the President's sense of melodrama,' answered the Professor with a non-committal shrug.

After an overnight stay at a military base in Hawaii, the party boarded a motor launch for the trip out to the flying boat. 'It doesn't look like anything that I've ever seen,' said Ian, as the launch neared the plane.

'That doesn't surprise me,' laughed Graham, 'you were in diapers when this crate was built. It's the last Martin Sea Master still flying, which means that we're going some distance if we need this powerful old bastard to get us there.'

Now that they were at the plane, the pilot became visible in the doorway behind the wings. He was black, in his middle forties and smartly dressed in a blue tunic and slacks. The Professor guessed that he might be a veteran of the Vietnam War. As the launch bobbed awkwardly, the pilot threw Graham a line. When everyone was strapped in the flying boat, the pilot shouted over the intercom. 'Hold tight back there, this might prove a little rough.'

Any possibility of conversation was killed by the whine from the Sea Master's four turbo-jets as they forced the flying boat forward. Within seconds, the aircraft was bouncing across the waves, buffeting the passengers in all directions. This went on for some minutes before the C.I.A. man joked, 'This must be a new way to beat radar survillance—we're going to skid on our ass to wherever we're going.' At this instant, the Sea Master hit a patch of rough water and it climbed steeply into the air.

The flight was thirty minutes old when the cabin door jerked open and the pilot said, 'We're three hundred miles into the wide blue yonder and looking for some place to go.'

Graham pulled out the mission orders from inside his jacket. He flashed the envelope to verify that the Presidential seal was unbroken, and ripped open the envelope. Out dropped a map, which Graham passed to the pilot, 'Check out these co-ordinates.'

After examining the map, the pilot grinned, 'This must be a swimming trip, because there's nothing within a thousand miles of the cross except a whole lot of ocean. And get a load of this crazy route!'

'Well, you've got your orders anyway,' Graham said. 'Whether they make sense or not is anybody's guess.' He slumped back in his seat.

With the pilot audibly mouthing an oath at each course correction, the Professor reflected on his travelling companions. First there was Graham, wheezing heavily at his side. Discounting Stroud, he'd never met a real C.I.A. operative, but a person affected by altitude in a pressurised cabin, just didn't fit the image. The man would have been better off in a sanitorium than flying half-way round the world on a critical mission. If this was the best agent the President could find, no wonder international relations were in such a state.

His thoughts turned to the two young people and he thanked heaven that they were listed amongst the survivors. Yet there was no island oasis for the countless Ians and Marys not on the list, only the prospect of a quick death on a scorched planet.

With the last course correction having been made, the flying boat headed directly for the cross on the map. No ships had been sighted for over two hours and the pilot had joked, 'who needs radar when you've got the skies to yourself?'

Graham's voice broke the Professor's trance, 'You know why even albatrosses give this place a miss? Because where we're going hasn't been discovered yet.' He took hold of the Professor's arm, 'Now you're a smart guy, so tell me how some natives paddled out here, even if there was some place to paddle to, which there isn't?'

While the Professor tried to come up with a half plausible answer, the pilot shouted back into the cabin, 'Land ho! Island dead ahead, six miles distant.'

As they jostled to get onto the flight deck, the pilot said, 'For Christ's sake, this isn't a 747! Use the starboard portholes.'

By the time everyone's face was pressed tight up against the glass, the island was already displaying the outline of a starfish, protected by a double coral reef. The clear blue waters of a lake glistened at the island's centre, with the lake's pronounced rim testifying that somewhere in the mists of time, Apocalypse owed its creation to a gigantic volcanic eruption. The lake was surrounded by a broad collar of green foliage, which in turn gave way to sandy beaches trailing down to the water's edge. In contrast, each of the five arms of the starfish was dominated by cliff ridges.

'Well I'll be damned,' said Graham, 'the last thing I expected to see was an island. . . Does it fit the co-ordinates?'

The pilot answered, 'Right on the nose.'

As the plane circled low over the island, the pilot said, 'That's the stars and stripes down there but it sure wasn't raised this morning.'

Graham jammed his face against the porthole, 'Yeah, it's the "banner" all right and those are army shacks. This is some kind of military base, so much for that "natives" story. But why isn't this island on the map?'

In the most dominant voice he could muster, the Professor said, 'Your superiors told you all you need to know, let's leave it at that, okay?'

After the plane had passed low over the island for the third time,

Mary asked, 'Why does the camp look so dead, we should have woken everybody up?'

'That's what's been worrying me,' agreed the Professor.' Where are the soldiers that the President told me about?'

The question was interrupted by the pilot, 'This isn't a carousel, either we land now or there won't be enough fuel to get back to Hawaii. What's it to be?'

Graham made the decision, 'Take her down.'

The pilot pointed to the water in the inner reef near the camp, 'That looks as smooth as ice so fasten your belts, we're going down.'

The pilot had no trouble landing and soon the flying boat had been manoeuvered to within fifty yards of the beach. Looking at the camp through the open hatchway, Ian joked, 'This could be the movie lot where John Wayne beat the Japs!'

Mary touched Ian's arm, 'This is creepy, where is everybody?'

Trying to sound unconcerned, Ian answered, 'Judging by the state of that flag, we're not going to get a twenty-one gun salute and that's for sure.'

'Hey!' yelled the pilot, 'somebody help me with the dinghy.'

Ian assisted the pilot in launching the dinghy; then everyone climbed in it, including the pilot. Mary looked nervously at the man, 'Is it safe to leave the plane unguarded?'

The pilot laughed, 'If it isn't safe here, where would it be safe?'

Once the dinghy had been secured to shore, the group drifted over the sand dunes and into the camp. Everything about the place suggested it had been hastily vacated years before. 'Where the hell is everyone?' demanded Graham, pulling a hefty Smith and Wesson from its shoulder holster.

Looking fixedly at the man, the Professor said, 'Put it away. It's obvious that the island's deserted.'

'I wouldn't bet on that,' shouted Ian from one of the huts, 'you'd better look at what I've found.'

The group picked its way through the food cans littering the ground. Inside the hut, Ian was down some steps, with only his head visible, 'It's a massive underground food store. Some crates have been forced open, but there's no telling how long ago.' Graham followed Ian down the steps, shining his torch along the rows of canned food. 'You name it, we've got it,' declared Ian, 'there's enough food down here to feed an army.'

'Okay,' agreed Graham, 'but where's the army it's supposed to feed?'

When Ian and Graham climbed back into the hut, the Professor was holding a dented can in his hand, 'I've been examining the cans outside. Only half are empty, the rest have been mauled like this one.' He tossed the can to Graham, who examined it before saying, 'Whatever tried to get into this didn't know about can openers!'

Ian stared at the man, 'Don't you mean "whoever"?'

Graham handed Ian the can, 'I mean whatever. You didn't read the label.'

Turning the can over in his hands, Ian read, 'Cooking Fat.'

Mary moved nearer Ian, 'Or maybe whoever tried to open the can couldn't read.'

Ian gave Mary a hug, 'Don't go all scared on us. Next you'll say that whatever it was that failed to get into the can, ate the soldiers instead.'

'Whatever happened here took place a long time ago,' insisted the Professor, 'and my guess is that it was peaceful because there's nothing to suggest a fight. As for something still being here, I guess it's possible but the island's too big to search.'

'But what about the empty food cans?' protested Mary.

'Maybe a ship came across the island and the sailors helped themselves to the food,' suggested Ian.

'It doesn't sound very likely,' anwered Mary, 'ships don't come this way, and why would they leave the other crates?'

Graham joined in the argument, 'The lady's got a point, that passing ship theory doesn't explain the missing soldiers, unless it was a Russian ship and the garrison was shanghaied?'

With a shrug, the Professor said, 'It's like Bronwen keeps saying, each time we find a piece of the jigsaw, two more go missing.'

'One thing's for sure,' Graham said, 'this isn't an expedition to dig up relics so why don't you level with me?'

The Professor stayed silent.

'Okay this is one of those days that start bad and then get worse. If you're not going to talk, I've no choice but to radio base and tell them that the army's missing.'

Politely but forcefully, the pilot said, 'You can't do that.'

The C.I.A. man glared at him, 'Oh yeah?'

Raising his hands in mock defence, the pilot said, 'They made me take the radio out yesterday.'

Looking towards heaven, the C.I.A. man exclaimed, 'What kind of idiot would send us on a mission without a radio?'

Calmly the pilot answered, 'Direct orders of the President.'

Graham's face reddened, 'Guess the White House doesn't want anybody to get a fix on us, but it's easy to give orders when your ass isn't on the line.'

With a shrug, the pilot said, 'One way or the other, we're on our own.'

'We're wasting time,' insisted the Professor, 'unless somebody wants to spend the night here, let's do what we came for, and get back on that flying boat.'

Graham agreed, 'Okay Professor, you're still calling the tune, what do we do next?'

The Professor answered, 'I'll go with you to the central lake; Mary, Ian and the pilot can check out the lowlands. We meet back here at four.'

Graham shrugged, 'Sounds okay, but we'd better check our watches.' Then he turned to the pilot, 'You got a gun?'

Shaking his head, the pilot said, 'Who needs a gun, this isn't Central Park.'

The C.I.A. man reached inside his pocket, 'Here, take one of mine.' He tossed a small automatic to the pilot.

The Professor looked concerned, 'I don't think a gun will be necessary.'

With a contemptuous stare, Graham said, 'A lot of dead people have shared your views.'

After a final wave, Ian, Mary and the pilot disappeared into the undergrowth, then the Professor set off for the central lake with Graham. As they made their way across the island, Professor Cooper was awe-struck by its beauty and even Graham came out with a remark that seemed out of character, 'If you believe in God, we've stumbled across Eden.'

Birds of every colour fluttered safely in the warm, fragrant air or rested on trees laden down with fruit, the earth was carpeted with an abundance of exotic flowers; however, the Professor made a pencilled note that no animals seemed to live on the ground.

Some distance away, Ian was also thinking how the beauty of Apocalypse seemed light years removed from the life of Omaha. 'Yeah, a guy could do worse than spend his days with Mary here.'

This daydream was broken by the pilot, 'Okay pretty people, I want you to stay here while I take a look see from that big rock outcrop over the beach.'

Ian scratched his head, 'Why do you want to go up there?'

The pilot smiled, and without answering, handed Ian the gun,

'Here's your protection in case that soldier-eating monster shows up.'

Clumsily, Ian fingered the automatic, 'B. . . but I've never fired a gun.'

The pilot grinned, 'Hey, it's easy, you just point it at something you don't like and squeeze the trigger!'

Once the pilot was out of sight, Ian sat on a flat rock next to a slowly moving stream and took off his shoes. He waded in the shallows, picked up a flat stone and sent it skimming, 'I once read that it's impossible to get more than eleven skims.'

Mary smiled, 'It certainly is beautiful here.'

Ian nodded, 'We could make a fortune selling Apocalypse's location to "Holiday Homes". Trouble is that soon there won't be people out there to buy real estate.' Noticing the tears forming in Mary's eyes, he said, 'I'm sorry Mary, that was dumb, I forgot about your folks.' He moved closer and drew her to him. At first, Mary assumed it was just a gesture to give her comfort; she recoiled like a live wire when she discovered otherwise.

'For heaven's sake, Ian. Just leave me alone!'

Ian flushed guiltily, he hadn't reckoned on the intensity of Mary's reaction, 'I'm sorry, Mary...I guess it's this place...I didn't think what I was doing.'

Mary's eyes flashed angrily, 'Oh sure you didn't, you just thought that this was the Garden of Eden and why waste time with formalities.' Not knowing what to say, Ian turned away and looked for another pebble; this made Mary more angry, 'Don't tell me that you're going to sulk now? I lie awake at nights, praying to God that he'll help you grow up!'

Ian turned round, 'Don't you think you're over-reacting, all I did was touch you.'

'Oh sure, you only touched me, and if I hadn't killed it there and then, that pilot would have come back to find us flattening the daisies! Sometimes you make me sick. The whole world is going to be destroyed and all you can do is try and add me to your list of lays.'

Ian glared at the woman, 'You're really enjoying all this, aren't you? Do you think that I want the world to end? Do you think I'm nuts?'

Mary shook her head, 'No I don't think you're nuts, just a twenty-five year old who behaves like he's seventeen! The way you dress, the way you talk, it's like you were frozen into a teenage cliché the day that your mother died! Can't you face *any* responsibility?'

Ian clenched his fists, then he controlled himself and said, 'I think it might be a good idea if I went and looked for the pilot.'

After he had walked some distance away, Mary called after him, 'I care about you, or I wouldn't talk to you like this, you dumb ox.'

Ian turned round, his face had regained its normal smile, 'I care about you too kid, but we're going to have to put in some work at improving communication.'

When the Professor and Graham reached the rim of the central lake, Graham was panting heavily, 'Let's not kid ourselves,' he wheezed, 'I'm not built for exploring anymore. This lake okay for drinking?'

The Professor scooped some water and tested it, 'It's fine.'

Graham was about to plunge his head into the water when he recoiled in surprise, 'Hey, why's this lake bubbling like crazy?' The water at the lake's centre suddenly swelled up several feet above the surrounding level. 'What in hell's going on?'

The Professor smiled, 'Quit worrying, I've just answered two questions that've been troubling me since we arrived: why there's fresh water in the inner reef and what fuels all those waterfalls we've seen? Now we know that this lake's the outlet to an underground river.'

Graham soaked his handkerchief and wrung it out over his head, 'So the island's got its own water supply?'

'That's how it seems.'

With a wink, Graham said, 'In certain circumstances, having a private tap could be very useful...'

The sound of a twig snapping in the undergrowth made both men swing round; in the same movement, the Smith and Wesson seemed to materialise in the C.I.A. man's hand. 'Can you see anything,' he grunted, holding the gun between both hands and looking fixedly along the barrel. Even though the Professor said, 'No', he still fired two shots into the dense undergrowth, with the gun kicking violently with each detonation.

'What are you doing,' yelled the Professor.

Graham laughed, 'Keep your cool, I'm just sending a message to whatever's out there to stay out there.'

The Professor sank to his knees, 'What sort of man are you? We don't know what snapped the twig and yet you're trying to blast it out of existence!'

The C.I.A. man kept his gaze locked on the undergrowth, 'What sort of man am I? One that's still alive after putting his ass on the line for the last forty years.' Graham stiffened his stance, his ears had picked up another noise, this one was further away and at ninety degrees to the first. 'Stay quiet, Professor, something big's coming this way.'

The Professor grasped Graham's hand, 'There'll be no more shooting!'

The man's finger was already tightening on the trigger when a voice yelled, 'Don't shoot, it's me!'

From out of the undergrowth, about seventy-five yards distant, the pilot stepped into view. The C.I.A. man wiped the cold sweat from his brow, 'Jesus, that was too damn close. Maybe it *is* time to hand in my badge.'

When the pilot reached the two men, the Professor demanded, 'Where are Mary and Ian?'

The pilot pointed towards the undergrowth, 'I was gazing out to sea from the big overhang when suddenly the artillery opened up.'

The Professor stared at the pilot, 'You mean you left Mary and Ian alone?'

The pilot nodded, 'But I left them with the revolver.'

The three men started to run down the hillside but they had only gone two hundred yards when they met Ian and Mary coming towards them. 'What's happening,' demanded Ian, 'we heard shots?'

Graham replaced the gun in its holster, 'Just getting in some target practice. Anyway, unless we want to spend the night here, let's head for the dinghy.'

The sun was already near the horizon when they began rowing out to the seaplane. Mary suddenly straightened on her seat. 'My God.'

'What's wrong?' demanded Ian.

Mary pointed at the island.

'C'mon, spit it out,' insisted Graham, 'what did you see?'

'O. . .on the beach,' stammered Mary, 'over there, something moved, something big!'

Everybody looked where Mary was pointing but the long shadows of the palm trees made seeing difficult. Graham reached inside the flap on the dinghy and pulled out a flare pack. With a muffled explosion, the flare hurtled towards the island, where it bathed the beach in a harsh white light as it gently floated down. But the camp and the beach looked exactly as it had when they landed: utterly deserted.

CHAPTER 11

After spending a day getting back to Southwood, the next morning found the Professor pouring out the virtues of Apocalypse to Bronwen, 'I just wish you could have seen it, Bron. Apocalypse is perfect for our needs. When you're on that island, it's easy to forget the world and its problems.'

Bronwen glanced up from her calculations, 'That's good, Frank, because soon there won't be a world to remember.'

The conversation was halted by a shout from outside the open laboratory door, 'Hey you two. The President wants us at the White House by ten this morning.' Recognising the voice, the Professor glanced apprehensively towards the open doorway, and the unmistakable bulk of Graham.

Bronwen flicked down her pencil, 'Where I come from, we believe in introductions before becoming travelling companions.'

The man walked to where the scientists were standing and thrust his hand at Bronwen, 'I'm Graham Harris and you're Dr. Jones,' he said in an uncharacteristically polite voice, 'that's all the introductions we've got time for. The car's already outside and we don't want to keep the President waiting.'

When they arrived at the White House, the President was in conference with a visiting head of state, but after a brief wait in an anteroom, the Professor, Bronwen and Graham were shown into the Oval Office. The President looked more like his campaign image again, 'Good to see you again, Frank,' he declared, 'and you look better this morning, Graham, the Pacific must suit you.'

The C.I.A. man nodded politely, 'Thank you, Mr. President.'

Now the President offered Bronwen his outstretched hand, 'And this must be Dr. Jones. You're from Wales, I believe?' Bronwen nodded. The President smiled, 'Who knows, we might be related? My grandmother came from Wales, a little place on the coast called Morfa Nefyn. Do you know it?'

Although Bronwen had a lifelong phobia of powerful people, there was something about the President that she liked, 'Yes, I know Morfa Nefyn, it's a fishing village.'

The President nodded, 'When I was a boy, my grandmother told me such detailed stories about Wales that I feel I've been there.'

The President walked to the door, 'We won't sit round the conference table, that's too formal for friends. I've arranged for coffee in the private garden.' The buds on the trees were opening in the mild Spring sunshine, yet the changing of the seasons only brought August that much closer.

'Sorry I couldn't tell you about Graham before, Frank,' said the President. 'Graham Harris is Deputy Director of the C.I.A. and he went to Apocalypse with you to see things first hand.'

'And to check out if we were security risks?' asked the Professor. Although the President didn't answer, Graham Harris nodded, so the Professor queried, 'And how did we come out?'

Graham Harris gave a neutral smile, 'You did just fine, Professor. I gave you a hard time, that's my job but you came through it perfectly.' The man paused, 'But as for Ian, that's another story. I've spent my life analysing people so let me give you some friendly advice. If the going gets tough, that boy could snap and his weak link is spelt, W-O-M-A-N.'

The Professor said nothing for some seconds then he asked, 'And the pilot, was he in on the act?'

Graham Harris nodded, 'Stuart Conway is our best agent, he's due to step into my boots in three weeks time as Deputy Head of the C.I.A. But he knows nothing yet about "Scorched August".'

Bronwen raised an eyebrow, 'Scorched August?'

Graham nodded, 'Yeah, that's the codename for all this.'

Bronwen winced, 'That is one hell of an accurate codename.'

'Now that everybody's got acquainted,' said the President, 'let's get down to business. As you've gathered, Graham knows the whole story, but he's the only one I've told.'

'You weren't supposed to tell anyone,' insisted the Professor.

The President raised his hands, 'I applaud your concern for security, Frank, but how do you expect me to kidnap a couple of hundred people from all over the globe without help? Besides, there isn't an agent in the C.I.A. who wouldn't follow Graham over a cliff edge if he asked them to.'

'I don't like arguing with you, Mr. President,' said the Professor, 'but Graham's only Deputy Director, what about Richard Stroud?'

Graham Harris laughed, 'So you were taken in too, Professor. Sure, Stroud picks up the fat pay cheque for being Director. Why? Because he's got the right "media" image for helping people sleep at night. But take my word, Professor, you're talking to the guy who really runs things.'

'Graham's telling the truth, Frank,' agreed the President, 'Richard makes a good front man, especially when he's fixing things with the Russians, but I never let him in on anything of real importance. That mouth of his makes him a grade one security risk. Believe me, Frank, Richard Stroud won't be in on what's happening when people start to "go missing".'

The Professor shielded his eyes from the sun, 'From the way you're talking, Mr. President, you've decided to start the evacuation?'

The President nodded, 'Yes, Frank, I've finally decided to go ahead.'

After an aide had served coffee, the Professor asked, 'What convinced you to go along with the plan, Mr. President.'

The President shrugged, 'In the end it was simple logic, and talking to Graham since four this morning.'

Bronwen put down her cup. 'Tell me about the logic, Mr. President.'

'It's pretty straight-forward, Doctor. The way we see it, either the holocaust happens or it doesn't.'

There was a distinct note of sarcasm in Bronwen's voice as she said, 'I can't fault your logic so far.' Graham glared at her.

The President began again, 'Let's assume that the holocaust happens, then my part in saving humanity would look good in history books. Assuming that there will still be history books.' The President paused, then he said, 'Now let's assume the opposite scenario, and believe me, Doctor, I'm working my butt off to stop the holocaust. Anyway, if it doesn't happen, what have I lost? If any of this hits the headlines, I'd make a fortune giving T.V. interviews. Now that doesn't sound so bad? And either way, my daughters are alive. So that's the logic, now Graham will fill you in on some details.'

'We've found out what happened to the soldiers on Apocalypse,' said Graham. 'It takes some believing but they were drafted to Vietnam in '68.'

Bronwen laughed, 'And the army forgot to send replacements?'

Graham nodded, 'How'd you know that, Doctor?'

Bronwen waved her hand, 'It just fits my view of bureaucracy!'

'Anyway, what it means is that Apocalypse has guarded itself since '68. You can't get more isolated than that. But rather than take chances, I've despatched eight marines to the island.'

The Professor eased back in his chair, 'Will they be using the same zigzag route we took?'

'The same,' replied Graham Harris, 'it seems to have avoided Soviet surveillance.' He opened his notebook, 'Now for the details, first we can assume that the people on your list will need taking by force.'

'You're dramatising, surely...' Bronwen protested.

Graham sighed, 'I've been through the first list of survivors, Doctor. With the exception of the President's daughters, Ian and the Professor, nobody else is related. Have you stopped to think what that means? Wives without husbands, parents without children, children without parents! What do you think would happen if I had to tell some thirty year old woman that a computer said she could live but her family couldn't?'

Bronwen glared at the man, 'Even if you're right, it's not the best way to start humanity afresh.'

Graham lowered his voice again, 'It may not be the best way, Doctor, but it's the only way.'

The Welsh woman threw what was left of her coffee into the flower bed, 'Since it's "say-what-you-mean" time, will you climb into the dock for one of my questions?'

The C.I.A. man placed his hands on the table, 'Ask your question, Doctor.'

'Okay, you take your job seriously, Graham, and you're good at it. So were you behind the break-in at Frank's house?'

The man shook his head, 'No, Doctor, you can chalk that one up to the opposition. They suspect something is going on, and are doing their best to find out what it is.

'Anyway, here's what we do next. I'll call every morning to collect the list of survivors. No one sees the names except you two and me, okay?'

The Professor and Bronwen nodded.

'Good,' said Graham. 'Once I've got the list, I'll arrange for each survivor to be taken out of circulation and detained separately. Then, on August 1st, they'll be brought together and transported to Apocalypse. It's going to be one hell of an operation.'

Now the President said, 'We've been working on what you'll need for survival on Apocalypse, Frank. We call it the Pilgrim Fathers' Kit.'

The Professor scratched his head, 'I don't follow you, Mr. President?'

'Put it this way, Frank. If the island was equipped with the latest technology, what would you do when it failed? Where could you get generator oil? What would you do when the antibiotics ran out? How'd you make a light bulb? Do you see what I'm saying, Frank? When the Pilgrim Fathers landed here, they had to be self-sufficient. And that's what you've got to aim at, self-sufficiency from day one.'

Graham threw a document wallet onto the table, 'We've a team working on what animals to take. They think it's only an egg-head study but it'll be finished in a month flat because we've given it a priority one rating.' The man frowned 'I've seen some preliminary results, they're weird but I guess Noah had the same problem.'

When the sun went behind a cloud, the Professor noticed how quickly Graham Harris felt the chill. He looked a tired sick old man, yet he was giving his last reserves of energy in the service of his President. Graham looked at the Professor, 'We're trying to tie up all the angles but do you have any questions?'

The Professor nodded, 'It's a personal one. Have you have any family?'

The man shook his head, 'Never got round to marrying and now I'm glad I didn't.' Graham looked squarely at the Professor, 'I can guess why you asked the question so there's something you should know. Two years ago, the doctors gave me a year to live. I'm already on borrowed time so there's no need to worry about me wanting to stay on Apocalypse.'

The President cleared his throat and addressed Bronwen, 'It's time for you to answer the ultimate question, Doctor, can the holocaust be stopped?'

This was exactly the question Bronwen had feared most. The President of the United States had calmly enquired if the world was going to end in August. Worse still, she knew precisely why the question had been asked and the awesome consequences hanging on her reply, 'Sure, there's a chance it won't happen,' she said cautiously, 'but until the final planet's fitted, no one can say for certain.'

The President leaned forward, 'Let's consider a hypothetical situation, Doctor. If I ordered an all-out nuclear strike against the Russians, for tonight, what'd that do to the prophecy?'

Bronwen knew her words had to be right, 'I've been a lifelong pacifist, Mr. President, yet I've also wondered if ninety per cent of the world could be saved by destroying the other 10%.'

The President leaned even further forward, 'And could it, Doctor?'

Bronwen tugged at her yellow hair, 'Something tells me that your question's less hypothetical than you make out, but it doesn't matter because the answer's no.'

The President flopped back, 'Why?'

Hesitantly, Bronwen began her answer, 'Well, Mr. President, you either believe the prophecy, in which case you can't change it, or you don't believe the prophecy, in which case you ignore it.'

'I'm afraid you've confused me, Doctor,' said the President. 'If I decided to send our missiles heading for Russia, what could stop me?'

Bronwen smiled bravely, 'You won't launch your missiles tonight, Mr. President, because the prophecy knows you better than you know yourself.'

The President drummed his fingers, 'I'm still confused, Doctor, give a simple example of what you mean.'

'Okay,' said Bronwen, 'if time is seen as the pages of a book, the prophecy comes from someone who knows the ending. Put it this way, you can read Samson and Delilah a thousand times but the temple always crashes down. The only chance we've got is for the last planet to change the ending.'

The President managed a smile, 'Rest assured, Doctor, there won't be a Pearl Harbour against the Russians. Besides they'd launch their missiles as soon as ours came over the horizon and all I'd do is bring the Apocalypse six months forward.'

Bronwen looked the President in the eye, 'How about a straight answer to one of *my* questions?'

The President forced a smile, 'That's a lot to ask of any politician, but okay, fire away.'

'Well, if the whole damn world is going to go up together in August, what do you lose by giving the hot line a chance and telling Moscow everything?'

The President shook his head dismissively, 'You answered the question yourself when you said that you either believe in the prophecy or you don't. All we gain by letting the Russians in on what's happening is to give them the same chance we had to simulate the holocaust. That might just let them get a fix on Apocalypse and my daughters. No doctor, we keep the lid down tight on this one, our hopes rest with the last planet. So as soon as there's anything to report, I want to know it.'

On their return to Southwood, the Professor and Bronwen had a surprise waiting for them. 'You've a visitor, Dad,' said Ian. They followed Ian into the lounge, where Demetri Kara was seated in an easy chair. 'Security flipped this afternoon, Dad, about a Cypriot getting out of a cab at a top secret base.'

Demetri stood up, bowed slightly and held out his hand. Bronwen grasped it vigorously, 'Hi, I'm Bron.'

The Professor looked at Demetri, 'Do you have any news?'

Although the young Cypriot's English wasn't good, his reply needed no interpretation, 'My grandfather dead. Two days ago he die while two Russians asking him questions.'

Bronwen's voice broke the uneasy silence, 'Did he know the Russians were coming?'

Demetri lowered his head, 'My grandfather know everything.'

Bronwen placed her hand on Demetri's shoulder, 'Then why didn't he skip? Did he want to die?'

Demetri shook his head, 'My grandfather not want to die. He love life but one thing stop him leaving.'

'What thing, Demetri?'

'Grandfather say there was many circles. If he avoid his fate, maybe he complete final circle by mistake. My grandfather say that if man not to be extinct, he must die as written.'

Ian went to the vending machine and dialled a Coke, 'I guess your grandfather was so convinced of the prophecies that he was willing to die for them.'

Having noted the combination, Demetri dialled himself a Coke before saying, 'Not only my grandfather willing to die for prophecies but also my father.'

Politely the Professor said, 'I didn't like raising it before but I've wondered what happened to your father.'

Demetri smiled bravely, 'You have already seen his tomb. He was driver of the car you passed at bottom of ravine in Cyprus. He also know his fate seven years before the accident, and he also go through with it.'

Ian spilt his Coke, 'You mean he knew about the ravine, yet he still got into the car?'

Demetri nodded.

When Bronwen was alone with the Professor, she said, 'The

frightening part of Demetri's story wasn't the torture, it was the old man's fear of inadvertently completing the circle.' She moved uneasily in her chair, 'I had to tell the President that the programme couldn't be beaten, or he'd have launched a first strike to break the prophecy. But what terrifies me, is that we're the idiots completing the final circle.'

Noting the perspiration of Bronwen's forehead, the Professor said, 'Stay put while I fetch some coffee.'

As Bronwen sipped her coffee, the Professor said, 'You'd better explain what the final circle means?'

Bronwen lifted her face, 'Let's start with the letter which triggered off this nightmare. What would have happened if you'd thrown it in the bin?'

The Professor shrugged, 'I nearly did.'

'Say you had, then you wouldn't have found the tomb—Mary wouldn't have translated the manuscripts—I wouldn't have written the programme and we wouldn't be halfway through selecting the survivors. Don't you see what I'm getting at, Frank? We're the cretins completing the circle. Believe me, the holocaust *is* out there, patiently waiting for us to slip the last piece of jigsaw into place!'

The Professor clasped Bronwen's hands, 'Okay, so everything you've said is true, but where's our choice? The President told the Yugoslavs about the quake, yet seven thousand still died as prophesied. If we stopped work now, the holocaust would still happen and the only difference would be that there'd be *no* survivors.'

Bronwen looked a desolate woman as she said, 'I know we haven't a choice, Frank, the project must continue but have you ever stopped to think that Mary might have been right about where the equations originally came from?'

For the next two months, a kind of normality descended over Southwood. Each day, as the computer's new list of survivors relentlessly pushed the total towards two hundred, Bronwen's mathematicians intensified their efforts to include the final planet in the theorems. While in the library, the Professor submerged himself in ecology reports on Apocalypse, until he better understood the island than the plants in his own garden.

To the uninformed observer, this could have been any group of scientists, conscientiously pursuing a routine project. And even outside Southwood, the world seemed to go on as normal, with babies being born, old folk dying and people complaining about prices. It was as if the same long hot summer, that the history books talked about in 1914 and 1939, had emerged again.

However, to the informed eye, a disquieting sequence of events was occurring on the world stage, with a series of 'incidents' along the Sino-Soviet border actually flaring into a small war on May 17th. Although a cease-fire was agreed in less than two days, estimates put the dead at forty thousand.

Then there were reports, coming from the heart of Russia itself, of workers being beaten for forming free trade unions. In the Middle East, seen for decades as the likely trigger for the next war, rumours of revolution were commonplace, with intense great power involvement around the Biblical city of Armageddon. This then was the planet Earth in May, an orbiting powder keg, needing only a spark.

It was Monday, June 1st, when the Professor and Bronwen were summoned to the White House. In the Oval Office, the President gave the impression of a corked volcano about to blow its top. 'They're here, Graham,' he yelled into the intercom, 'you get down and join us.' The President jabbed his hand towards the conference table, 'Sit down, things aren't good.' Although the Professor and Bronwen sat down, the President continued to pace the floor; finally he turned, 'God dammit, Frank, it's bad enough saving Russians but not K.G.B. agents!'

The Professor looked stunned, 'There. . . there's a K.G.B. agent on the list?'

Waving a printout at the Professor, the President snapped, 'That's what I said! His name was smack in the middle of this sheet you gave Graham yesterday.'

The Professor took the list and looked where a bright red hammer and sickle had been scrawled, 'Any chance of error?'

'None!' declared the President, 'we've checked every name you've sent us. Up to yesterday they were all clean but not Victor Poplenko, he's a top K.G.B. man.'

Bronwen stood up, 'I've done some checking on the survivors myself. They're good people, the sort who deserve to live.'

The President glared angrily at Bronwen, 'If these are good people then how did Poplenko get on the list? He's a well-known hit-man.'

When Graham Harris entered the office, the President waved his hand to a seat at the table, 'I've been telling them about Poplenko, you tell them the rest.'

The C.I.A. man twisted his face as he said, 'We've got problems,

Professor. You've been under Russian surveillance since your first visit to the White House. We don't think they know about Apocalypse but they're definitely the guys who broke into your house. They also followed your visit to Cyprus. The Russians found Stavros by trailing you to his farm.'

The Professor shook his head, 'I'd swear that we weren't followed, not along those roads.'

Graham Harris laughed, 'Believe me, Professor, in today's world, you don't follow someone in a cab to keep them under tabs.'

Still pacing the floor, the President interrupted the conversation, 'You're missing the point, Frank. The Russians are on to us, they know it's something big but they don't know what.'

Sensing that the next move had already been determined, the Professor said, 'Bron and I know nothing about espionage, so tell us what you're thinking.'

The President gestured for Graham Harris to answer the question. 'Well it's like this, Professor, as long as your team's at Southwood, the Russians have got you on ice. Sure, the other scientists have been security checked but one of them could still be a Russian agent, it's happened before, sometimes in mighty high places.'

For the first time since the meeting began, the President stopped pacing the office and looked straight at the Professor, 'I want your team to go to Apocalyse tonight!'

After the statement had sunk in, the Professor asked, 'You mean for good?'

The President nodded, 'Yeah, Frank, for good. Once we've got you to the island, there's no coming back, not until September anyway.'

Bronwen stared directly at the President, 'You're holding something back, Mr. President,' she declared bluntly.

The President glanced at Graham Harris, who shrugged his shoulders and said, 'You may as well tell them, Mr. President. If we can't trust these two, who can we trust? Besides, they could find out by asking that damn computer of theirs anyway.'

The President sat down next to the two scientists, 'What I'm going to say doesn't go outside this office, okay?' The Professor and Bronwen nodded their agreement.

This time when he spoke, the President's voice was barely audible. 'It's starting to happen, Frank, the world's slipping towards war. The Russians look set to invade Iran. They'll say that they're trying to stop the civil war but they want the oil.' The President looked at Bronwen, 'You'll have to excuse the language, Doctor, but if the Russians control the Middle East, they've got the rest of the world by the balls!'

Bronwen lit a cigar, 'You still haven't told us everything.'

The President nodded, 'No, Doctor, I've saved the worst for last. I had a Chinese delegation in this office yesterday. They offered to invade Russia if N.A.T.O. would simultaneously attack from the West.' When Bronwen looked up towards heaven for deliverance, the President added, 'Just a conventional war you understand. The Chinese reckon that Russia would be scared shitless of using nuclear weapons because of retaliation. Anyway, the Chiefs of Staff have been at each other's throats most of the night, deciding if we should go along with the plan.'

'And?' asked Bronwen.

The President held up his hands, 'Too damn risky. It could get out of hand in hours, even minutes. All it needs is some fool battle commander to fire off a tactical nuke and that's it. Besides, there's no saying that we'd win a conventional war. Those Russians are armed to the teeth; and remember what they did to Hitler.'

Bronwen breathed a sigh of relief, 'So you told the Chinese no?'

The President nodded, 'But the Chinese hate the Russians even more than we do, so they might go ahead without us.'

Bronwen groaned, 'Hasn't man the wit to avoid war?'

Lowering his eyes, the President answered, 'This job has taught me that "wit" has little to do with decision making. Sure, the band blasts out "Hail to the Chief", whenever I walk into a room, yet ninety-five per cent of the time I'm busting a gut trying to stamp out a bush fire before the whole damn forest burns down.' Looking coldly at Bronwen, he said, 'You think that your hands are clean because you're a pacifist, well let me tell you a little secret, there isn't any bigger pacifist on this planet than the man with his finger on the button, but I've still got to make the big decisions. Truman had it: the buck stops here.'

With a sarcastic laugh, Bronwen asked, 'What sort of pacifist would point thirty thousand warheads at a country, just because he disapproved of their ideology.'

'Like all scientists, you've rammed your nose deep into a test tube to avoid the stench of the real world. Let me tell you something, Doctor. That very day that Frank came to see me, I ordered the Pentagon to simulate every option open to this administration which would guarantee the survival of our great nation. And do you know the result? Anything which disturbs the balance of terror between East and West results in mass devastation.'

Bronwen looked the President square in the eye, 'You said that every option was considered?'

The President nodded, 'Every last one.'

'Even unilateral disarmament by America?'

To Bronwen's surprise, the President answered, 'Yes, Doctor, even that, and do you want to know the result? Three independent studies calculated a ninety-eight per cent probability of the Kremlin wiping us off the map before public opinion voted in a new administration on a re-armament ticket. Now what kind of President would let that happen to his or her country?'

The President started to calm down, 'To complete the study, I had the planners calculate the result if the impossible happened and the Soviets renounced their nuclear weapons; do you want to pull your nose out of the test tube to give us your guess, Doctor?'

Contemptuously, Bronwen answered, 'This time, I suppose it was you who wiped them out?'

The President shook his head, 'No, that isnt so easy in a democracy, but you're still pretty close. For that scenario, it was the Chinese who couldn't resist erasing their "Revisionist Comrades" while their pants were down. What I'm really saying, Doctor, is that the people out there believe I'm the leader of the most powerful nation on God's Earth, yet your programme has turned me into a throwaway pawn on a chessboard.'

The President slumped back in his chair 'Talking of programmes, how's the work going with the last planet?' When Bronwen didn't answer, the President lifted his face, 'I asked how the work was going, Doctor.'

Bronwen stubbed her cigar in an overfilled ashtray, 'We managed an approximate fit on the ninth planet two days ago.'

This reply angered the President, 'I told you to keep me informed of developments.'

Bronwen shrugged, 'It slipped my mind, life's hectic at Southwood.'

'It's damn hectic here too! I need all the help that's going if we're going to pull out of this one.' The President controlled his anger, 'So you've got a fit on the ninth planet?'

Bronwen gave a non-committal nod, 'Only an approximation.'

The President gripped his chair before asking, 'A...and what happens?'

Bronwen glanced sideways, 'You tell him, Frank.'

The Professor looked down at the table as he said, 'Well, the programme now shows that there wasn't an exchange of missiles during the Cuban crisis.'

'The hell with Cuba!' snapped the President, 'What about the holocaust?'

The Professor raised his gaze, 'It still happens, Mr. President. It still happens.'

With the words, 'It still happens' hanging in the air, the President clutched at a straw, 'What did you mean, Doctor, "an approximate fit"?'

Bronwen lit another cigar before saying, 'The equations for the ninth planet are mind blowing, so we used a linear approximation to get a fit on Pluto.'

The President wrote a brief note in his diary before saying, 'So in my language, there's still hope?'

Bronwen nodded, 'Sure, there's hope, we'll not know anything for certain until we get a perfect fit on Pluto.'

Graham Harris asked, 'When will you get a fit, Doctor?'

'Will Apocalypse be in contact with Southwood?' asked Browen.

Graham Harris firmly shook his head, 'No, Doctor. If the Russians get a fix on the island, you're finished; the transmitter must only be used in a real emergency.'

Bronwen gave the man a puzzled glance, 'How's the work supposed to continue without Southwood's facilities?'

There was pride in Graham Harris' voice as he said, 'At this moment, the Programme's being copied onto a top-secret computer, the eggheads label it a bio-processor. And guess who it was who personally okayed the funding five years ago? Anyway, it's got TITAN's capacity even though it stands no bigger than a suitcase.'

'And how do you propose to power it?' asked Bronwen sceptically.

'Solar cells.'

'This discussion is getting off the point,' interrupted the President. 'I asked Dr. Jones how long before Pluto was cracked and in my book, I haven't been given an answer.'

Bronwen twisted the cigar in her mouth, 'How long is a piece of string?'

The answer visibly angered Graham Harris, who snapped, 'Give the President your best guess, Doctor!'

Bronwen went silent, then she said, 'Working on the island...

with the programmes on a portable computer...by about mid-July.

Having scribbled a note, the President said, 'July doesn't leave much time for error.'

Bronwen nodded, 'That's for sure, and something tells me that's how it was planned.'

The President put down his pencil, 'Planned? Who by?'

Glancing at the Professor, Bronwen answered, 'By whoever, or whatever, devised the prophecy in the first place.'

The Professor broke the uneasy silence by asking, 'How's the job going of collecting the survivors?'

Graham Harris smiled positively, 'That's coming along fine, Professor. We've had one or two hitches but we'll near as dammit make it before August.'

Bronwen looked concerned, 'Tell us about the hitches.'

The C.I.A. man pulled a notepad from his pocket and ran his finger down several pages of ticks, until he came to two crosses, 'Yeah, we can handle most of the problems round the world but there's a couple of foulups in our own backyard. Two Americans on the list turned out to be man and daughter.'

'Was that Peter Jeweski off list 3 and Jean Jeweski off list 7?' asked Bronwen.

Graham Harris seemed surprised, 'Yeah, how did you know?'

Bronwen waved her hand dismissively, 'I noticed the names and guessed they might be related. Anyway, what's the problem with the Jeweskis?'

Graham slipped the notepad back into his pocket, 'The problem? Simple, I can't find them. There's not been a trace of either Jeweski since June '71. Jean was only two when she disappeared, that makes her a young woman now, if she's still alive.'

'Do many people just disappear?' asked Bronwen.

Graham nodded, 'Thousands every day but not like the Jeweskis. My best agent can't get a single lead, it's as if they'd vanished off the face of the Earth.' He looked at Bronwen, 'If we don't find the Jeweskis, what does that do to the prophecy?'

'God knows,' said Bronwen.

Graham paused, then he said, 'I'll keep my top men looking for the Jeweskis but if they don't turn up, there's two empty seats for Apocalypse, right? So why not get that computer to output the President's name and Amy's?'

Bronwen shook her head, 'In your language, Graham, that would deal a bum hand for everyone.'

To Bronwen's surprise she found an ally in the President himself, 'Thanks for the thought, Graham, but while there are few things I wouldn't do to save Amy and me, putting the girls in danger is one of them. Anything which might foul up the girls' safety is out.'

Bronwen said 'You mentioned a couple of hitches, Graham, what's the other one?'

The C.I.A. man looked directly at the Welsh woman, 'Just two words, Doctor, Victor Poplenko. I don't want that filth on the same island as the President's daughters.'

Bronwen remained calm, 'You sound like you've met him?'

Graham Harris nodded, 'I have. Our records have lost count of the people Poplenko himself has tortured to death. Why do you want an animal like that on the island?'

Bronwen ran her fingers through her hair, 'Everything you say about Poplenko may be true, perhaps he is vermin, but we're not choosing the list.'

'You know what?' said the President, 'Until Poplenko's name came out, the survivors were falling into a pattern. They were mostly healthy young pacifists from every race on Earth, the sort of people you'd want to save. Only a week ago, I said to Graham that it was the Biblical prophecy coming true. The meek were going to inherit the Earth.'

The President's manner hardened as he said, 'Then you send me Victor Poplenko's name. It just doesn't fit the pattern, Frank. If the other survivors were picked by God, Victor Poplenko is the Devil's nominee.'

The Professor looked across the table at the President, 'You don't want Poplenko on the island, I don't want him on the island. Probably, Victor Poplenko doesn't want Victor Poplenko on the island. But if that's how it's written that's how it's got to be. Besides, what could one man do against two hundred?'

While the President searched for a reply, Bronwen said, 'Frank's right, I don't know Poplenko's role on Apocalypse but he's got to be there to play it.'

'Okay, I won't order you to forget Poplenko, but having that animal on the same island as my little girls makes my flesh creep.' The President leaned across the table, 'Promise me that you'll personally look after my daughters, Frank.'

The Professor nodded, 'You've got my word that I'll protect your daughters with my life.'

Clasping the Professor's hands, the President said, 'Thanks, Frank. That's all a man can ask.'

Graham Harris broke in, 'When you're guarding the President's daughters, forget your allergy to guns, Professor. A bullet is the only language that Poplenko understands. Anyway, you'll all be leaving for Apocalypse tonight, so I'd better brief you about the ship that's waiting at Los Angeles.'

'Ship!' exclaimed the Professor, 'why not a plane?'

Graham Harris shook his head, 'Too damn risky. The Russians are on yellow alert, any plane that showed up on radar would be tracked to its landing.'

'I can see the danger,' conceded the Professor, 'but won't the ship be picked up by satellite?'

Graham shook his head, 'Hold on, Professor, and I'll tell you how we've got round that one.' He wedged open a map of the Pacific, 'The areas shaded red are those under Russian surveillance. You remember our flight out to Apocalypse?'

The Professor smiled, 'Could I ever forget it?'

Graham laughed, 'Well soon you'll be on another zigzag trip through the Russian blind zones, but this time by boat.'

Bronwen looked at the map, 'There's a bug in your plan. This map shows Los Angeles to be under Russian surveillance.' Graham Harris nodded. 'In that case,' said Bronwen, 'aren't the Russians going to get a trifle suspicious if a ship sails into a blind zone and it doesn't come out on the other side?'

Looking like a man who'd put one over on the opposition, Graham Harris answered, 'Nope! And that's because the Russian's don't know about 'Operation Switch.'

Bronwen rolled up the map, 'Go on, Graham, tell us about "Switch" before you burst.'

Smiling proudly, the man said, 'It's a great plan, even if I say so myself. There are two ships, identical to the last rivet, and one of them is already anchored beyond the limit of Russian surveillance. So your ship sails out of Los Angeles under Russian eyes; then when it nears the blind zone, we "persuade" their satellite to go defective. In less than an hour, the "switch" ship has taken your heading and you're sailing sweetly for Apocalypse. When the Russian satellite comes on again, they see a ship, exactly where they expected one!'

'The plan sounds good,' conceded Bronwen, 'but something tells me there's another reason why you want a ship?'

Self-consciously, the C.I.A. man adjusted his tie, 'Well... things need transporting to Apocalypse.'

'Such as?' asked Bronwen pointedly.

Graham Harris looked uneasy as he said, 'All manner of supplies to get you folks started.'

Bronwen stared fixedly at the man, 'Nothing for ''offensive purposes''?'

The President intervened by saying 'With my three daughters on the island, no son of a bitch is going to turn it into an arsenal.' Bronwen still didn't look convinced so the President added, 'You have my word that no offensive weapons will be stationed on Apocalypse.'

The Professor defused the confrontation between Bronwen and the President by saying, 'Your word is good enough for me, Mr. President.'

The President seemed relieved, 'Good. Now you people have a long sea journey ahead, so the sooner you leave the better.'

After Bronwen and the Professor had shaken the hand of the President, Graham Harris said, 'One way or another, I guess that this is the last time we'll meet. So good luck, Professor, and you too, Doctor, there's one hell of a responsiblility on both your shoulders. If it gives you a lift, I'll be in there pitching to the very end.' The C.I.A. man winked at Bronwen, 'You're my kind of lady, one who says what she means. If we'd met thirty years ago, your feet wouldn't have touched the ground.'

Bronwen grinned affectionately, 'That's for sure, I was only twelve!'

When the Professor and Bronwen arrived back at Southwood, most of the packing had already been completed on the orders of the President. All that was left for them to do, was select the few personal belongings that they wanted to save from oblivion.

On seeing his father, Ian said, 'Up to now, everything's seemed part of a movie, where you could get up and walk out but this is for real. We're coolly deserting a ship that's going down with four billion people on board.'

Putting his hand on Ian's shoulder, the Professor said, 'Pretend it's still a movie, if any of us stopped to think what's really happening, we'd go mad.' The Professor's gaze fell on Mary, who was sitting on her trunk, aimlessly looking into space. While it was horrific enough for him to leave the world to its fate, at least Ian was safe. For Mary, leaving her family behind, everything was infinitely worse. Now Bronwen caught the Professor's attention; the woman was neatly placing her things back on the bed, 'What are you doing, Bron?'

Without looking up, Bronwen answered, 'What does it look like

I'm doing? I'm unpacking.'

'In God's name, why?'

'Why? Because I'm not going anywhere.'

'Sure you are,' insisted the Professor, 'you're coming with us.'

Bronwen shook her head, 'No I'm not.'

'Why?'

'You know why, Frank, my name wasn't on the list.'

The Professor picked up a copy of the list, 'There's your name, number 197, Bronwen Jones.'

Still keeping her head bowed, Bronwen said, 'You may have fooled the President by typing my name there but it didn't come out of TITAN.'

The Professor threw the printout into the trash can, 'To hell with the list, you're the backbone of the team and we're not leaving without you!'

There were tears in Bronwen's eyes when she looked up from her unpacking, 'Let's be sensible, Frank. You were the one who argued that Victor Poplenko had to be saved because he was in the prophecy. Well I wasn't! I know I'm expendable, you know I'm expendable, even the damn program knows I'm expendable, so let's leave it at that.'

Mary had been listening to the argument and now she said firmly, 'So you're human after all. For the first time since we met, you're not being logical.'

Bronwen looked at the young woman, 'Prove it.'

Waving her hand dismissively, Mary said, 'Easy. What does the prophecy say about your future?'

Bronwen shrugged, 'It ends in August.'

'And how do you know that?'

'Because my name wasn't with the survivors.'

Mary smiled in triumph, 'So you've not run a personal check on yourself?'

Shaking her head, Bronwen said 'Only a ghoul would want to know if it was going to fry or melt.'

Mary climbed down off her trunk, 'That's what I guessed. And now you can't get a horoscope because the programme's been packed for the island, right?'

Bronwen nodded, 'Everything you've said is correct, but where's the flaw in the logic that says "I stay put"?'

Mary heaved her trunk nearer the door, 'Flaw? You've been standing too close to the problem. Even if we accept that you die in August then we don't know where you die. True?'

Bronwen looked stunned, 'I. . .I guess so.'

'Then why assume you die at Southwood instead of on Apocalypse?'

The Professor punched his case in jubilation, 'Mary's right! You're just as likely to break the prophecy by staying here as by coming to Apocalypse.'

Bronwen didn't looked convinced, 'It's a two-headed coin, Frank. If I go along with the prophecy, I don't like it, if I go against the prophecy, I still don't like it. If ever there was a "no win" scenario, this is it. The final circle is tightening by the second.'

The Professor started to re-pack the woman's case, 'The end is only two months away and there's so much to plan. We need you on the island to help design our new world. Come with us?'

Bronwen hesitated before saying, 'Why not? One place is as good as any other to die.'

'I'm glad you're coming Bron,' said Mary, fighting to hold back her tears, 'now excuse me while I make the most difficult phone call of my life.'

After Mary had left the room, Bronwen said, 'Poor little soul. I guess she's phoning New York, but what can she tell her parents? Goodbye forever? How do you let your whole family die in a five megaton blast without warning them? Thank God I've no close relatives, it must be hell suffering what she's going through.'

The Professor walked across to Bronwen, 'Mary had a little talk with me last night. I told her that those who go quick are the lucky ones, my prayers are for the poor bastards who survive the first strike.'

Bronwen nodded, 'Before you talked me into coming to Apocalypse, my plan was to blow my life savings by renting a room in the Empire State building for the whole of August. To go out in a blaze of glory is better than haemmorrhaging for days from radiation sickness, or having your eyes melt from exposure to some filthy chemical.'

Mary returned a few minutes later. 'Did you make your call?' asked Bronwen softly.

Mary shook her head. 'At the President's orders, all the phones are dead.'

The Professor said, 'I thought that might happen. He wouldn't take a chance of one of us blowing everything by warning someone outside.'

Mary took out her handkerchief, 'I'm glad I can't phone home, somehow it helps clear my conscience. What could I have told Mom and...?'

Mary burst into tears, Bronwen put her arms round the distraught young woman, 'You have a good cry, Mary, and don't blame yourself for anything. You're a good girl who was born into a wretched world.'

CHAPTER 12

At 1:00 a.m. on Tuesday June 2nd, an inconspicuous army truck pulled into Dulles Air Base; there the Professor and his team transferred to a C130 subsonic transport. By the time that dawn broke, the plane was taxiing into a cavernous hangar on the outskirts of Los Angeles. The drone of the engines died away, to be replaced by an unreal echoey silence. 'Please disembark,' said a voice over the plane's intercom. As the travellers stepped onto the elevated platform of a mobile lift, they noted that the hangar was empty except for the C130 and three trucks. The platform started to descend to ground level; Mary touched Ian's arm, 'Those trucks, they've all got the same licence number.'

When the team had transferred to one of the trucks, the sergeant blew a whistle. A growing slit of light testified that the hangar doors were inching open. The whistle sounded a second time and the engines smoked into life. After the trucks had idled for some minutes, the sergeant gave a final blow. Like a well drilled chorus line, the trucks left the hangar, crossed the runway and departed the base in different directions.

Although the truck carrying the Nostradamus team made several, diversionary manoeuvres, it always returned to the heading for the docks. Without warning, the truck turned sharply into an old warehouse. Before anyone could react, the vehicle was engulfed in inky darkness. Mary gripped Ian's arm as a low rumble shook the truck, then the unmistakable sensation of movement was felt. The truck was descending into a deep basement and lights were rising to meet them. The lift jolted to a halt and the driver shouted, 'Stretch your legs. You won't be leaving here for some time.'

Apprehensively, the travellers climbed down, to find themselves in a subterranean hall. The red lamps on the moss-covered walls gave the cavern a hellish aspect. Four passageways bisected the hall, each capable of taking a tank, while a swarm of soldiers had already begun to transfer the luggage from the truck to what looked like a bread delivery van. Not knowing what to expect next, the Nostradamus team stood transfixed in the eerie dampness.

'This must all seem a bit melodramatic but I assure you it isn't.'

When everyone spun round to see who was the owner of the cultured voice, their gaze fell on a neatly groomed man wearing the uniform of a Commander in the Royal Navy. 'You'd be surprised what those Russian satellites can pick out. Not as good as ours, mind you, but still damn good. And if they've had you under surveillance, no point in taking chances now.'

The officer smiled at the confused faces, 'I say, it's bad manners on my part. I know everything about you people, even down to the mole on Bronwen's left buttock, yet none of you know my name. Let's have a coffee while we get properly introduced.' They followed the officer along a passage into a brightly lit room where soldiers were drinking, 'Now you people sit tight while I fetch the drinks.'

The officer returned and handed each person a coffee, then he looked at the young Cypriot. 'I was sorry to hear about your Grandfather but it's our task to ensure that he hasn't died in vain.' He turned to the Professor, 'My name's Commander McGrath, Royal Navy. I'm going to Apocalypse with you.'

Putting down his coffee, the Professor said, 'Just for the voyage?'

The Commander shook his head, 'To stay.'

The Professor frowned, 'I don't think that's possible.'

Bronwen touched his arm, 'It is, Frank. I remember seeing the name, Ken McGrath, on the list of survivors.'

The Professor scratched his head, 'I don't get it? First the program saddles us with a K.G.B. agent, now it's come up with someone in the military.'

Ken McGrath smiled mischievously, 'It's an old cliché, but the Lord does move in mysterious ways.'

The Professor picked up his cup again, 'Okay, Commander, welcome to the team, now tell us how much you know about Apocalypse?'

Putting three lumps of sugar in his coffee, the Commander answered, 'How much? Everything—I was briefed by your President himself.'

'And what was your brief?' asked Bronwen.

The man looked embarrassed. 'I'm in total command on Apocalypse until August, Doctor. Then, if it happens, we see about forming a civilian government.'

Bronwen scowled, 'And what did the President find so wrong with the way that Frank was running things?'

The Commander twiddled his sugar spoon as he said, 'Well Doctor, from what I could gather, the President was upset about the way that information was kept from him. He told me that scientists were unreliable, though his actual words were stronger. I'm the only "military" man among the survivors, therefore he's put me in charge because I'm trained to follow orders.'

'So here we go again,' said Bronwen in disgust, 'we've not even had the holocaust yet and already the island's under martial law.'

The Commander sat back hurt, 'That's not how I saw things. Let's just say that I'll have the casting vote until August.'

This reply pleased Bronwen, 'Okay Ken McGrath, let's find out something about you. Do you have a family?'

'If I had, they would have detained me with the other survivors. Besides, families are not recommended in my line of work.'

Mary had remained silent but now she asked, 'Do you believe the holocaust will happen?'

In a gesture not appreciated by Ian, the Commander placed his hand on top of Mary's, 'No, I don't think it will happen but a serving officer follows orders, and my orders are to get you people to Apocalypse.'

McGrath led the others back towards the eerie redness of the hall. The army truck had gone and only the bread van remained. The Commander pointed towards one of the tunnels, 'That leads to a bakery. What could be more innocent than a baker's van coming out of a bakery?'

'How about a baker's van carrying bread?' answered Bronwen dryly.

Pretending that he hadn't heard Bronwen's remark, the Commander said, 'You people get aboard the van, I'll change out of this uniform to avoid attention.'

The Ken McGrath who re-joined the others looked a very different officer. 'That's a strange way to avoid attention,' commented the Professor.

'Oh, you mean the dog collar. That's for real. Call me Padre McGrath if you like, I'm a serving priest with the Navy.'

As the Professor took his first real look at Padre McGrath, he realised how the man's Navy uniform had produced a dehumanising effect. He hadn't given it much thought before how you always saw the uniform and never the man wearing it. The Padre was about his own age, about four inches shorter and carrying an extra thirty pounds.

The van rumbled along the underground passageway, with its headlights giving the walls a surrealist quality. After watching a rat scurry down a waste pipe, the Professor said, 'I've been to Los Angeles a dozen times without suspecting that a labyrinth existed beneath the city.'

The Padre nodded knowingly, 'Most big cities have a honeycomb like this. They've been dug in secret to act as regional command centres after a nuclear strike.'

'Government must go on,' muttered Bronwen sarcastically, 'even when there are no people left to govern.'

The van continued its lonely journey beneath the automobile jammed streets until it halted in another hall, similar to the first. The driver shouted a command then the van shuddered as hydraulic rams began to lift the vehicle back to ground level. Soon the red glow of the underworld was exchanged for the blackness of another closed space. A gate opened so suddenly that the passengers had to shield their eyes from the Los Angeles sunshine. The bread van kept a straight course for about two miles before veering left through dock gates.

After rattling past ships of all sizes, it halted alongside a grey vessel flying the Liberian flag. 'We're there,' shouted the driver, 'and a crane's blocking out the view from above.'

Padre McGrath held up his hands for attention, 'It's critical that we board the Hudson without being spotted.'

Ian laughed, 'Don't tell us there's a Russian spy in Los Angeles docks?'

Giving Ian a patient smile, the Padre asked, 'Can you think of a better place?' Ian didn't answer.

Padre McGrath crouched across to a tin locker, 'We put on these overalls and hardcaps before walking up the gangplank in twos, at ten minute intervals. Any question?' No questions were forthcoming so he said, 'Okay, the Professor and Dr. Jones can go first then Ian and Mary, finally Demetri and myself. Go straight below deck and whatever you do, don't look up.'

As the Professor and Bronwen walked up the gangplank, she noticed a giant crate which dwarfed the other boxes on the deck. 'That's big enough to hold a tank, I wonder what goodies the

President's packed in it?'

'One thing's for certain, it's coming to Apocalypse with us.'

When they reached the reception cabin, Bronwen asked, 'Have you noticed anything strange?'

'Such as?'

'Such as this cabin not having a porthole.'

'Relax Bron, every cabin can't have a porthole.'

Bronwen lit a cigar, 'You're losing your powers of observation, Frank. None of the cabins have portholes, Which means that those on the outside are fakes. I don't know what kind of ship this is but it's no freighter.'

Ian and Mary entered the cabin. 'What do you reckon is in that big crate?' asked Ian.

The Professor shrugged, 'At least we've got the President's word that no offensive weapons will be stationed on Apocalypse.'

Bronwen laughed contemptuously, 'Will you never learn, Frank? What's a politician's word worth when there's not going to be any more elections?'

Padre McGrath and Demetri entered the room. The Padre said, 'Now the team's complete, would you like a tour of the Hudson, below decks of course?'

Bronwen nodded, 'Sure we'd like to see the ship, and you can begin by explaining why there are no portholes.'

'Shall we say that portholes are inappropriate for this type of vessel.'

'It's a submarine!' gasped Mary.

The Padre held his sides as he laughed, 'The Hudson's an unusual ship but not that unusual. Take my word that I will be extremely concerned if we sink beneath the waves.' Pointing his hand towards the open hatchway, he said, 'Your eyes will answer most of the questions as we walk.'

He led the others through a warren of corridors until they came to a door marked 'cargo'. Bronwen looked quizically at the Padre, 'Have you been on the Hudson before?' The man shook his head. 'Then how come you know your way about?'

'I took the precaution of looking at a blueprint of the layout.' The Padre spun the handwheel and pushed the heavy door open, to reveal a room packed tight with radio equipment.

Ian let out a whistel, 'It's a spy ship.'

The Padre nodded, 'Quite so. Although its official title is "surveillance". Shall I explain what each instrument does?'

Ian laughed, 'A priest explain?'

With a sigh the Padre said, 'People are not born priests. Before the Falklands, I commanded a missile battery.'

When they were relaxing in the wardroom that evening, Ian said, 'I'm the outdoor type. If we've got to spend the day in a ship without portholes, why can't we go on deck at night?'

'Too risky,' said the Padre. 'You might be picked up on "infra–red" and that would be it.'

Mary put down her tomato juice, 'Surely you're not saying that a satellite could identify us in the dark?'

'That's just what could happen,' insisted the Padre.

'He's not exaggerating,' said Bronwen, pouring herself a double, 'When we were scanning the Indian Ocean, Frank and I picked out the cards in a sailor's hand.'

After a mock fight with Bronwen for the ownership of the whisky bottle, the Padre said, 'A couple of years ago, they thought a spy was operating in Downing Street. Counter-espionage tried every trick in the book to catch him, then someone noticed how secrets were only getting out in summer. It turned out that the garden of No. 10 was under surveillance from above, high above!'

For the next four days, the Hudson unobtrusively sailed across the Pacific. On the fifth day, a smiling Padre McGrath entered the Wardroom, 'We've reached the perimeter of surveillance. In three minutes, the Hudson will make the Russian satellite go on the blink. Then after a quick change of crew, we'll be on our way to Apocalypse.'

Ian's eyes remained locked on his watch until a siren wailed. He grinned in relief, 'Why are we still behaving like mushrooms?' With two bounds, he was up the stairs and out into the welcoming sunshine of the equatorial Pacific.

It seemed that the Hudson had the ocean to itself, then Demetri pointed towards a shape converging on them under a full head of steam. When the other Hudson was within hailing distance, the ships held a parallel course before coming to a dead stop. Ian gave Mary a wink, 'It's just like those "identical drawings", where you've got to spot the difference.'

'But this time there isn't any difference, the Hudsons are even identical down to that giant crate.'

Looking up at the blue sky, the Padre said, 'God's smiling on us. In thirty years I've never seen the ocean this calm.'

Brownen stopped watching the lifeboats being lowered over the side, 'Something's smiling on us and wants to make damn certain we get to Apocalypse but whether it's God...'

For a few brief minutes, the Nostradamus team were the only people aboard either Hudson, then amidst a brief burst of cheering, the lifeboats passed each other at mid-point. Soon the crews climbed aboard their new vessels and the manoeuvre was complete. The team gazed over the stern at the decoy Hudson until it had steamed clear over the horizon. 'It'll go at full speed to where we should have been,' said the Padre, 'and when the jamming stops, the same crew will appear on deck.'

Ian looked at the foam coming from the ship's propellers, 'Talking about "full speed", this boat sure is moving.'

The Padre grinned mischievously, 'She's doing about thirty knots, which isn't bad for an old freighter.'

Bronwen scratched her head, 'Not bad? I'd say not possible.'

Ian put down his field glasses. 'Anyway, how come there're two Hudsons in the first place?'

'It's all part of the expensive game that both sides play,' said the Padre sadly, 'like steaming round the world to get to the "blind zone".'

Bronwen shook her head, 'The ship couldn't carry enough fuel for that.'

The Padre shrugged, 'And what if it was nuclear powered and the smoke was a sham...'

'And is it nuclear powered?' asked Bronwen pointedly.

'Both Hudsons are. But don't let's talk about nuclear power, you've all been below decks for days, go and stretch your legs.'

As the others set off to explore the deck, the Padre took hold of Bronwen's arm, 'Could you delay your stroll? I'd appreciate a talk.' Looking over the rail, he said, 'The President said that everything was for real but I can't believe that we're powerless to stop what some fakir predicted centuries ago.'

'That's what I thought as first but not any more. I'm afraid I'm convinced. As a Catholic, you might also be interested to know that the holocaust is the third prophecy from Fatima.'

Padre McGrath started to sway uncontrollably and for one horrific moment he seemed certain to fall into the ship's propellor. Bronwen grabed tight hold of the Padre's jacket and heaved him away from the handrail in a single movement. The only casualty was his cap, which spiralled down into the Hudson's wake. Bronwen helped him back to the crate before saying, 'Sorry about the cap, decent headwear is going to be in short supply on Apocalypse.'

The Padre looked up gratefully, 'Thanks, Bron, that was nearly my last faint.'

Bronwen smiled, 'If you go in for fainting on a regular basis, give me some warning next time. Saving you might get me some brownie points from your Boss. Anyway, what's your problem about Fatima?'

'I've had nightmares about the third prophecy since I was a child.'

Placing her hand on the Padre's shoulder, Bronwen said, 'In that case, grit your teeth because here's the punchline. Frank saw the Pope, and even though he won't say anything straight, from what I can piece together, Nostradamus and the third prophecy are in exact agreement.'

With his gaze fixed where the other Hudson had steamed out of sight, the Padre said, 'Well now I know why the Pope ordered me to Apocalypse.'

'The Pope ordered you?'

'I told the President that the island was a wild goose chase and my work in Belfast was more important. A week later, a private jet arrived at Belfast, carrying Papal orders for me to see the President and then to sail with you people. Now I know why. The third prophecy is starting to happen, and if it's anything like my nightmare, God help the world.'

The Hudson continued its uneventful voyage across the Pacific, always with a compass heading of south-west, until on the morning of the twelfth day, Apcoalypse appeared on the horizon. When the ship was safely at anchor outside the outer reef, Demetri said, 'It look like Cyprus, only more beautiful.'

While the others were admiring Apocalypse, the Professor was noting the razor sharp corals which formed a double protective ring around the island. He walked to where the Padre was looking through fieldglasses, 'The ship can't go inside the reef, so how do we get these heavy crates ashore?'

'No problem, Frank. You'll see why after we open the big crate.'

The Padre gave orders for the crate to be levered open. When the lid was finally prised off, an Augusta Bell, with its back folded, was visible for all to see. 'That's a relief,' whispered Bronwen to Mary, 'who'd have thought it was anything as innocent as a helicopter?'

For the next three hours, the helicopter made repeated flights to the camp. When it looked as if everything was ashore, the Padre gave orders for the ship's hold to be opened. Bronwen touched the Professor's arm, 'I didn't know there was anything else to unload.'

Padre McGrath whispered instructions to the pilot, before

pointing at a mountainous part of Apocalypse. Steel cables were lowered into the hold, then the Augusta Bell whined noisily as it hoisted another giant crate airborne. The Nostradamus team watched as the crate was flown to the island, where it was carefully lowered onto the same flat outcrop of rock that Stuart Conway had climbed.

With the transfer of cargo complete, the team thanked the Hudson's crew for their hospitality, then climbed aboard the helicopter. 'What was in the big crate, Padre?' asked Bronwen bluntly.

He looked embarrassed, 'Believe me, I would tell you if I could.'

Bronwen pressed the point, 'Then tell me.'

The Padre shook his head, 'Nothing's changed, I'm still a serving officer following orders.' When Bronwen's face exhibited what she thought of this answer, the Padre added, 'Let us all pray that the crate rots up there and never needs to be opened.'

The whine of accelerating rotor blades made further talk difficult. Even so, at the mid-point of the short flight, the Padre raised his voice about the engine's noise, 'I would appreciate being the first out of the helicopter,' he shouted, 'there's a small ceremony to be performed.'

Even before the Augusta Bell's blades had stopped revolving, the Padre jumped onto the beach, knelt and began the act of consecrating the island to God. Realising what was happening, the pilot killed the engine and joined the others on the warm sand.

The spectacle presented a strange and moving sight. A golden beach, deserted except for a helicopter, a congregation of six and a priest on his knees in worship. Even the seagulls seemed to respect the occasion by holding their cries in check until the dedication was over. With a tear in his eye, the Padre faced his companions, 'Thank you for your silence. Now apart from Mary, I don't know your beliefs but from this moment onwards, either call me Father or Ken. Military rank and titles have no place on this island.'

CHAPTER 13

The group beside the helicopter were joined by the island's garrison of eight marines. 'Commander McGrath?' asked the sergeant, saluting smartly.

Ken McGrath declined the salute and instead shook the sergeant's hand, 'Father McGrath.'

Momentarily, this reply confused the sergeant, then he remembered being told that when you're not sure of someone's rank, call them sir, nobody complains about being called sir. 'What are your orders, sir?'

'Tell your men to get their kit, sergeant. The garrison's leaving with the ship.' While the other soldiers were packing, Father McGrath asked the sergeant what he thought of the island.

Running his gaze along the gently breaking surf, the man answered, 'Well sir, at first Apocalypse seemed the worst posting in the whole damn world. No women, no bars, no anything, but now we'll be sorry to go. This island must be the most peaceful place on God's Earth.' The sergeant hesitated before adding, 'No disrespect, sir, but I've never had much time for religion, yet now I'm halfway through reading an old Bible I found in one of the huts.'

The garrison was soon seated inside the Augusta Bell, awaiting their return to the outside world. When the helicopter was on the point of lifting off, the sergeant poked his head through the open window and shouted, 'There's something I forgot to tell you, Commander, I mean sir. We think that something big is living on the island.'

This statement brought the terror of her last visit to Apocalypse flooding back to Mary. In the past three months, she'd convinced herself that it was only a shadow on the beach but now she knew better.

Over the noise of the engine, Father McGrath shouted back, 'Don't you mean someone, sergeant?'

The man shook his head, 'Can't be sure, sir. We heard noises in the night, food went missing, that sort of thing. Anyway, whatever it is, we don't think it's dangerous but I reckoned you should know, sir.'

Amidst a flurry of sand, the helicopter began its journey back to the waiting ship beyond the reef. Watching the flight, Mary muttered, 'Poor souls, like everyone else who isn't on Apocalypse, they're doomed.'

The Professor looked at Father McGrath, 'What'll happen to them, Ken?'

Subconsciously, the Priest glanced at the giant crate on the overhang as he answered, 'Too many people know about Apocalypse, so neither Hudson can be allowed to return to Los Angeles. The ship we travelled on will wait in the blind zone for the other Hudson, ferrying in the rest of the survivors.'

'And when is the relief going to take place, Father?' asked Bronwen. Although the term 'Father' would have stuck rigid in Bronwen's throat only a few weeks earlier, now it went unnoticed.

'God willing, Bronwen,' answered Father McGrath, 'Apocalypse will have its allotted two hundred by August.'

While the others were watching the helicopter touch down on the ship, Ian had climbed the sand hill separating the camp from the beach. 'Hey,' he shouted, 'get an eyeful of this.' Scrambling up the hill, the new islanders could hardly believe how the decaying army camp had been transformed into a village, with neat rows of wooden houses forming a series of square streets around a dominating central structure.

There was obvious pleasure in Father McGrath's voice as he said, 'It's modelled on the Pilgrim Fathers' settlement but without the need for perimeter defences.'

Still dazed by the transformation, Ian said, 'It's neat but how's the village been built so quickly?'

The Priest smiled, 'I suppose it's what the President calls, "good old American know-how". It was made in the States and shipped here during the other Hudson's circumnavigation. The Marines only had to assemble it.'

Bronwen asked, 'Why does something tell me that I'm not going to like that big wooden building which thinks it's a fortress?'

Uneasily, Father McGrath answered, 'Eventually it will be a school, a hospital, a church and a meeting hall for the community.'

Bronwen repeated the word, 'Eventually?'

The Priest nodded, 'Unfortunately, it has a less desirable use first.'

Bronwen frowned, 'Such as what?'

'A prison.'

Throwing up her arms in desperation, Bronwen snapped, 'Who needs a prison on Apocalypse?'

Although the Priest's expression showed he agreed with Bronwen's sentiments, he said, 'I'm still following the President's orders and he insists that the other survivors are held under guard until after the holocaust. And, to use the President's words, for some poor Russian named Poplenko, he's got to be locked in a cell that's full of poison spiders!'

As they strolled along 'Main Street', Mary muttered, 'There's something eerie about walking through a ghost town that hasn't even lived yet.'

Ian took hold of Mary's hand, 'You're right, a town's only a collection of buildings until it's been christened. What this place needs is a name.'

The Professor beckoned Father McGrath over, 'Can I have a private word?' The two men engaged in a whispered conversation, before returning to where the others were standing.

With a broad smile, the Priest proclaimed 'By the powers vested in me by the President, I name this town Bronwen.' The Welsh woman's jaw dropped open as she tried to find the right words to decline the honour. Father McGrath held up his hand, 'No need to come up with a speech of thanks, Bronwen, the ceremony's over and the town couldn't have a better name.'

The tour of 'Bronwen' continued, with the survivors noting how the wooden houses were simple yet functional. Windows had shutters but no glass, and the fire-places were designed to burn wood for cooking. Five hundred years of advancing technology had been sacrificed to a single criterion, self-sufficiency. If something couldn't be repaired on the island, it shouldn't be there to start with. The spartan new life on Apocalypse was forcibly brought home to Ian when he decided to wash for dinner. There was no hot water, no soap and no place to plug in his toothbrush. Flinging his electric shaver through the open shutters, Ian grinned as he realised how the men-folk were destined for beards. However, when they gathered at the Priest's house for a simple meal, one piece of advanced technology was being used. Father McGrath was listening to the radio.

The Priest looked up as the others entered, 'It's getting worse. Britain's sent a note, demanding that the Soviet army is withdrawn from Poland. China says that the Russians are conducting 'provocative manoeuvres' on her border. The Saudis have gone on red alert because of the threat from Iran, and the U.S. Sixth Fleet is somewhere off Cyprus, covering the Israeli air reprisals against Syria. The world's sliding towards war.'

Mary burst into tears, 'Do we have to know what's going on out there?'

Switching off the radio, Father McGrath said, 'Bronwen once asked if I had a family, I said no because she meant a wife and kids, but my parents live in London, I've a brother with three children in Cornwall and then there's the Church, the biggest family of all. So if the war does come, just like you, Mary, I'll lose everything, but we must still listen to the news.'

It was midnight when the islanders dispersed to the three houses facing the prison entrance. For security, Bronwen and Mary shared the centre house, the Professor and Ian were on the left, while Father McGrath and Demetri occupied the house to the right. The evening was perfect, with the warm air carrying the fragrance of the countless flowers which grew in profusion everywhere. Even the background chirping of the island's night creatures only added to the charm.

In the women's house, Bronwen stretched her arms and said, 'Stuffy rooms are fine for working but not for sleeping, do you mind if we leave the shutters open?'

Mary hesitated, 'Do you think we should? I still have nightmares about that big black shape on the beach; and the sergeant warned us about something living on the island.'

From out of the darkness, Bronwen replied, 'The sergeant also said it wasn't dangerous. Anyway, I don't know why you're worried? If anyone's taking a chance it's me, your horoscope sails on into the future, but mine?' The shutters were left open.

Once the comforting glow from Bronwen's cigar had died, Mary found the blackness overpowering. Lying there trembling, she kept wondering if it was only blind chance that had made their first night on Apocalypse moonless? Yet the strong contented snores from the bed near the door, showed that Bronwen didn't share her concern. Suddenly, she felt as if an icy hand had gripped her heart. Something *was* in the room, she was sure of it. Over the pounding of her heart, Mary's ear picked up a faint scratching sound. Something was standing at the foot of the bed, staring at her! She shut her eyes tight and pretended to be asleep.

Some minutes elapsed, Mary didn't know how long, then the shuffling seemed to be moving away. She heard a click in the centre of the room, something had stepped on a loose floorboard. When the scratching had retreated to the window, Mary found the courage to force her eyes to open just the narrowest of cracks. For a fleeting second, she thought she picked out a crouching silhouette in the open window but it was too dark to be sure. At least ten minutes passed before Mary's heartbeats started to return to normal. Then she leaped out of bed, grabbed a flashlight, and shook Bronwen from her sleep.

Bronwen wasn't impressed, 'You must have been dreaming,' yawned the Welsh woman, rubbing the sleep from her eyes.

'Dreaming!'

Bronwen nodded, 'It's our first night and you're hell bent on having a nightmare. That's what you get for believing the sergeant's story about something living here.'

Looking Bronwen straight in the face, Mary snapped, 'Something does live here and it visited us a few minutes ago!'

Bronwen shrugged dismissively, 'Is anything missing?'

Mary directed the flashlight at her few belongings, everything seemed to be there, then she looked at the chair near her bed, 'My clothes, they're in a different order to how I left them.'

'Different?'

Mary nodded, 'Ever since I was a girl, I've left my clothes ready for morning.'

Bronwen smiled, 'Why be such a tidy little thing, dump them in a heap like the rest of us.'

Mary started to get annoyed, 'Don't you follow what I'm saying? Whatever came in here examined my clothes. . . maybe even put them on!'

Bronwen grinned, 'And then stacked them again?'

Mary nodded, 'Yes, but in the wrong order.'

'Well, we'll talk about it in the morning.'

The next morning Bronwen had already dismissed Mary's story as melodramatic nonsense, when her gaze fell on the bedside table. What she saw, or, more precisely, what she didn't see, made her shriek in anger, 'There was a box of cigars on that table last night.

Where are they now?'

Flippantly, Mary answered 'My nightmare stole them.'

Bronwen leapt out of bed, 'Don't joke, Mary, this is serious. There isn't a tobacconist's shop on the corner, so where the hell am I going to get more cigars?'

Mary shrugged, 'Why's a box of cigars so important?'

Bronwen looked blankly at the woman, 'Why? Because when that damn fool President of yours ordered us here, he didn't leave me time to get any more. All I had was a box of twenty, so I rationed myself to one every four days until September, didn't reckon I'd need any after that. Now some swine's pinched the last seventeen. I want them back.

After listening to the women's stories, Father McGrath called a meeting on the prison steps. 'I also heard something last night,' he said, 'it was only a dry twig snapping outside the window, but twigs don't snap by themselves. We've got to face the fact that something came out of the jungle last night and entered this camp.'

Father McGrath paused before saying, 'The first rule of warfare is to make your own lines secure; until we've captured whatever's out there, ours won't be.' He looked at Mary, 'You've been closer to the intruder than anyone. What do you think it is?'

Mary shook her head, 'I was too frightened to get a good look, Father.'

Ian flipped a pebble into the air, 'This reminds me of a game I used to play as a kid, spot the killer. What I'm saying is that we already know a lot about the creature, so let's apply some deductive reasoning.'

Breaking off from filling his pipe, the Professor asked, 'What do we know?'

Ian answered, 'Well we know that it's lived on the island for years. It's intelligent enough to fold women's clothes. It's got the agility to get through a bedroom window and it steals things, especially cigars.'

Bronwen laughed, 'That narrows the suspect down to a transvestite gorilla with a smoker's cough.'

The radio in Father McGrath's house was left on that night, while a log fire burned brightly inside the Cooper grate. In the women's house, the beds conveyed the impression of being occupied and, to complete the trap, the floor had been generously littered with dry twigs. It was approaching four in the morning when a twig snapped crisply in the bedroom. Instantly, six beams of light converged on a form that no one expected. There, trapped in the intense glare of the torches was the unmistakable figure of a naked woman!

The woman crouched in the centre of the room, like a cornered animal that had been rendered motionless by the brightness. With a wild yell, she leapt for the open window and seemed certain to achieve her freedom, until her lithe form was caught in mid-flight by the outstretched arms of Demetri Kara.

After a frantic, clawing fight to regain her liberty, which reduced the furniture to little more than firewood, the woman's frenzy subsided. Father McGrath draped a blanket round the young woman's shoulders before asking, 'Do you speak English?'

The woman's blank expression indicated that she was unaccustomed to human speech, then deep in her memory, something stirred and she slowly moved her head up and down.

Father McGrath gave her a warm smile, 'We're not going to harm you, my child, we are your friends. What is your name?'

The woman opened her mouth but no sound emerged. Finally she stammered a single word, 'J...Je...Jean.'

'God be praised,' said Father McGrath, 'She can speak, she'd just forgotten how.'

Bronwen looked closely at the woman, 'Jean Jeweski?'

'J...just Jean,' came the hesitant reply.

Bronwen gave a reassuring smile, 'Are...you...alone, Jean?' The woman nodded. Glancing at the spot where her cigar box had once rested, Bronwen asked, 'Where do you live, Jean?'

The woman pointed through the open window, 'In cave, near mountain.'

Bronwen smiled, 'Tomorrow we'll go to your cave and check it out. Will you stay with us tonight?'

Jean didn't look pleased so Mary said, 'If you stay, you can try on my clothes. Would you like that?' Letting the blanket slip from her shoulders, Jean grabbed one of Mary's jumpers. The act was of such innocence that only Demetri knew how to react, his face filled with a broad grin from ear to ear.

Jean noticed Demetri's grin and smiled back, then she saw that in her frenzy, she'd cut a deep gash in the young Cypriot's cheek. As she gently wiped the blood away, Demetri grinned even more.

Bronwen picked up the blanket and draped it back over the young woman's shoulders, 'Wear that blanket, Jean, at least until the men have left.'

Jean gave Bronwen a blank stare, 'Me...not...cold.'

Bronwen laughed, 'Just do what Auntie Bron tells you, I'll

explain why later.' Then, giving the men a wink, she said, 'Now if everyone will leave the room, I'll declare the show over.'

On the way back to their own house, Ian said to his father, 'Are you sure she's called Jean and not Eve. And did you see Demetri's face when she dropped that blanket?'

In the women's house, Mary and Bronwen spent the night taking turns with the flashlight so that Jean could try on all the clothes. As Jean strutted round the room in the same blouse for the sixth time, Mary smiled patiently and said to Bronwen, 'It reminds me of Christmas when I was a child. Getting up in the night with a flashlight to see what presents were there.'

Bronwen laughed, 'You didn't need a torch in the Rhondda, the presents were always the same, an apple, an orange and a block of carbolic soap.'

It came as a relief when Jean finally let the torch be dimmed; quickly the two women retired to their beds, leaving Jean sleeping on some blankets on the twig covered floor. When Mary awoke the next morning, the blankets had been tossed into a heap and there was no trace of Jean. Mary crossed to Bronwen's bed, giving a painful yelp as she pricked her foot on a thorn. She shook the Welsh woman's shoulder.

Reluctantly, Bronwen opened one eye and muttered, 'Waking up this way is getting to be a bad habit, what does a soul do to get any sleep around here?'

Mary said, 'Jean's gone!'

Bronwen sat up in bed, 'That's a surprise, I thought she was starting to like it round h. . .'

The words died in Bronwen's throat as a long, wet leg looped in through the window. Jean had returned. The woman stood there, dripping wet after her swim. Bronwen climbed out of bed and draped a blanket round Jean's body, 'Here we go again, can't have you making it difficult for Father McGrath to keep his vow of celibacy.' Bronwen winked at Mary, 'if we don't do something, Jean will turn wearing a blanket into a profession. I'm woman enough to admit that she's nearer your shape than mine, so for pity's sake play Oxfam and give her some clothes.'

When the three women joined the men for breakfast, Jean's transformation was little short of miraculous. What, only a day before, had been a rampaging animal was now an attractive teenager, sporting two pigtails and dressed in a cotton blouse and blue jeans. 'Wow!' exclaimed Demetri.

Father McGrath laughed, 'That adequately sums up our feelings, welcome to the family, Jean.'

After breakfast, the islanders set off for Jean's cave. When they had journeyed for about an hour, Jean excitedly waved her arm at a cascading waterfall, 'There cave.' Grinning mischievously at the expressions on her friends' faces, Jean said, 'Cave behind water.' Forgetting that she was wearing clothes, Jean walked into the waterfall and disappeared from view. Without hesitation, Demetri followed her into the falling waters.

The others looked blankly at each other, then Bronwen said 'I could do with a shower,' and she too stepped into the cascade. Soon the whole party had traversed the waterfall.

The cave beyond the water was of good proportions, being about the size of a small church. When the Professor had grown accustomed to the shimmering surroundings, he aimed his torch at the ceiling above, 'Judging by the size of those stalactites, Apocalypse hasn't had a tremor in a million years.'

'That's comforting,' said Bronwen dryly.

When Ian's torch lit up the upper reaches of the cave, he touched his father's arm and whispered, 'There's a mattress up there, and what looks like a grave.'

Jean pointed along the line of Ian's torch, 'That father. And those father's special things.' A Bible and a leather log book rested on top of the grave, while a small wooden box stood against its foot.

Bronwen let out a yelp of delight, 'There's my special things,' she exclaimed, picking up the box.

Jean waved her hands in protest, 'Father like ceegars.'

'Bronwen also like ceegars,' said the Welsh woman, 'And Bronwen can put them to better use than father.'

By the time they returned to camp, the warm air had dried everyone's clothes. Soon Father McGrath was sitting on the prison steps, engrossed in the contents of the log book. With the sun starting to set, he called the others over to hear his report, 'Bronwen was right, Jean's other name is Jeweski, or that's what her father called himself after deserting the army. I guess that if a person changes their name, the programme has no choice but to use the new one?

Anyway, Jean's father was a corporal in the U.S. Army, stationed here to guard Apocalypse. The log covers a fourteen year period in his life. It seems that when Corporal Jeweski was on the island, it affected him the same way that it seems to affect everyone. He read the Bible a lot, marvelled in the beauty of the place and questioned why he was a soldier.'

Father McGrath paused, 'In 1968, what Peter Jeweski feared most happened; his unit was recalled to fight in Vietnam. But by this time, he couldn't even have killed in self-defence. So he deserted, bought some forged documents in the name of Jeweski, took up a new life in California and married. Three years later, when Jean's mother died in childbirth, Peter considered suicide but he'd become too religious to go through with it. Often he'd remember how happy he'd been on Apocalypse, but the island was thousands of miles away, guarded by a garrison of marines, so he concentrated on building a life for baby Jean.

'Then one night, Peter Jeweski had a vision. He woke up to find an angel at the foot of the bed. The angel told him that a terrible war was coming and he had to bring Jean to this island, the only place on Earth where she'd be safe. Next day, he stole a yacht and somehow managed to navigate it here. The yacht sank on the reef but Peter scrambled ashore, holding his two-year-old daughter in his arms.'

The islanders continued to listen in silence as Father McGrath approached the end of the saga. 'Peter Jeweski lived behind the waterfall with Jean until she was ten, then tragedy struck again. He was breaking open a case of food, when he gashed himself and it developed into blood poisoning. Peter's last entry in the log is a plea to God, to care for Jean and spare her from the holocaust.'

The sun had already set when Father McGrath closed the log and the gathering dispersed. Back in their house, Mary said, 'It looks as if God did what Peter asked.'

Bronwen nodded, 'But the poor kid has lived alone since she was ten, no wonder she hid from strangers. Can you picture a ten-year-old girl, digging a grave with her bare hands to bury her father? It's a miracle she's survived.'

Mary smiled, 'That's a perfect description, Bron, a miracle. But unless I'm wrong about the look in Demetri's eyes, she'll get some help surviving in the future.'

CHAPTER 14

While political tensions mounted ever higher in the world outside, life on the island was proving idyllic. When Demetri wasn't helping Bronwen fit the last planet, Jean delighted in showing the young Cypriot every stream, lagoon and valley on the tropical paradise. Although Bronwen still tried to perfect the theorems of Nostradamus, isolated from the troubles of the world, even the Welsh woman's customary urgency started to wane. Mary devoted her time to listing the properties of the plants of the island, while the Professor and Father McGrath passed their days sitting on the prison steps, endlessly debating the best form of government for Apocalypse if the holocaust came.

Ian was the only islander without specialist skills to contribute to the common good, so he became the fisherman, the gatherer of fruit and the maker of maps. Although he had never done any of these tasks before, the abundance of fish within the reef made the job easy. In consequence, Ian found himself with time on his hands and time was something he didn't like because it forced him to think of the world beyond the reef, and its relentless march towards extinction.

Each afternoon, as he strolled the island, trying to find distraction in naming a valley after some half forgotten girlfriend, Ian's thoughts were never far from Omaha. He would picture Brenda, proudly keeping the house tidy for the Professor's return, a return which would never come. Sometimes, he found himself wondering if Brenda would actually be cleaning a carpet when the warhead hit? But it wasn't only Brenda's life that was slipping away; although no-one talked about it, if the programme was right,

Bronwen's days were running out too, and losing Bron would be like losing his mother all over again.

One afternoon in late July, with the other islanders engrossed in their duties, Ian decided to climb to the big rock overhang. Once up there, he could listen to the world news, bask in the sun and not disturb anyone. The climb didn't take Ian long and soon he was viewing the camp from his high vantage point. He could see his father on the prison steps, arguing some point with Father McGrath, while in the distance, he caught a flashing glimpse of Demetri, diving into a lagoon, followed seconds later by Jean, naked as usual.

Ian turned his back to the island and looked at the blue waters of the Pacific, stretching endlessly to the horizon. With eveything so good and peaceful, he felt a sense of revulsion at polluting Apocalypse with the insane news from the radio. Yet Father McGrath had entrusted him with the task of listening to specific broadcasts, to check for a coded message from the President.

Ian placed the radio on top of the crate and turned it on; instantly the shrill voice of a female newsreader shattered the peace of the island, 'Heavy fighting has broken out in the Middle East, with renewed speculation of super power involvement. -----Unconfirmed reports, believed to be coming from Moscow, state that N.A.T.O. battle commanders have been delegated authority to use low-yield nuclear weapons in the event of an attack by Warsaw Pact forces. A White House spokesman said that the President was unable to comment on the rumours and would not be returning from Camp David for three days. -----Reports are coming in of a Chinese force, exceeding three million men, less than ten kilometers from the Sino-Soviet border -----'

The broadcast was free of coded messages; Ian switched off the radio, lay back on the overhang and gazed skyward at three seagulls, effortlessly cutting patterns in the clear air. Having soared high above Apocalypse, the largest gull swooped down, landed on the crate and ran along its length before launching itself back into space. Now the crate, and its mysterious contents, grew large in Ian's thoughts.

Ever since the helicopter had placed the crate on the overhang, there had been endless speculation on what was inside, but only Father McGrath knew and he wouldn't tell. The crate's huge size only added to the mystery, standing ten feet in height, twenty in length and six in width. Ian ran his hand along the plastic cover as an obsessional urge gripped him to find out what was inside.

Ian noticed that the cover was secured by a single zip; all he had to do to get inside was open that zip. With a quick glance to verify he was still alone on the overhang, Ian unzipped the section facing seaward and peered under it. He could see a large wooden crate, with shiny flip catches at each corner, indicating that the assembly had been designed to be opened in seconds.

Ian hesitated, this was the crunch decision, if he flicked those two catches, the mystery would be over! He grasped the first catch and squeezed it open then, as he reached for the remaining catch, Father McGrath's words came flooding back, 'Let us pray that the crate never needs to be opened.'

Ian knelt there for some minutes, fingering the final catch, until a strange compulsion forced him to look out to sea. What he saw removed all interest in the crate. Outside the reef, a torrent of frothy bubbles was making the waters foam, as if some leviathan were forsaking the deep and returning to the surface. Ian gazed spellbound at the waters for some seconds, then he saw it.

At first it was only a periscope but soon a conning-tower broke the surface, until finally the unmistakable profile of a large submarine occupied the waters beyond the reef. Now there were people standing on deck, some seemed taller than the others and they were all pointing towards the island. Within minutes, a dinghy had been manhandled over the outer reef, on a heading directly towards the camp.

Leaving the crate's cover flapping in the breeze, Ian scrambled down from his vantage point and began a frantic dash to warn the others, but when he arrived back in Camp, the place was deserted. After kicking open every door in sight, he scrambled up the sandhill. With a sigh of relief, he saw that the other islanders were standing on the beach, waving to the occupants of the dinghy. Only now did Ian recognise the President, and by his side, waving happily to the islanders, were three young girls.

Even before the dinghy had beached, Father McGrath strode out into the waves and thrust out his hand, 'Welcome to Apocalypse, Mr. President.'

The President grasped the hand, 'It's good to see you people again. After being cooped up in that sub, anywhere would look attractive but this place even beats the image I had of it.'

While Mary was helping the three girls out of the dinghy, the President said, 'I'd like you to meet my daughters. This is Mandy, she's eleven. Theresa's seven--- ' He bounced the smallest girl in his arms, 'and this cute little bundle of fun is Bernadette, she's just three, isn't that right sugar?' The little girl nodded and then buried her head against her father's shoulder. 'She's a mite shy with strangers but when you get to know her, watch out!'

The President looked at the islanders, 'Unless I can't add up straight, you seem to have one woman too many.'

'There's nothing wrong with your arithmetic,' said Father McGrath, 'this is Jean Jeweski.'

Momentarily, the President's face went blank, 'Jean Jeweski?'

'You remember, she was the girl Graham Harris couldn't locate.'

The President smiled, '*That* Jean Jeweski!' Placing his hand on Jean's shoulder, he said, 'You're a bright young lady. I'm glad you made it.' Jean managed a grin but remained silent.

The President turned to his daughters, 'My little girls have volunteered to help you people make the island into a bird sanctuary. Maybe Jean and Demetri could show them some of Apocalypse, before bringing them back in an hour?'

Once the girls were out of earshot, the President said, 'Look, I'm no coward but what father could face saying goodbye to the children he loves? Look after them, they're good kids.' Overcome with emotion, the man turned away and looked out to sea. Father McGrath placed his arm round the President and offered what comfort he could. When the President had regained some composure, he said, 'What makes it worse is that I'm feeling the loss for Amy as well. I told her that story I cooked up about the bird sanctuary, and even then it broke her heart to think that she wouldn't be seeing the girls for six weeks. If I'd told her the truth...?' Trying to inject conviction into his voice the President said, 'But let's think positive, God willing, Amy and I will be standing on this very spot on September 1st, all ready to take a family vacation on Apocalypse.'

After a brief pause, the President raised a questioning eyebrow, 'What I've not figured, is that if all the agents in the C.I.A. couldn't find Jean, how'd you locate her?'

Bronwen laughed, 'You could say that Jean located us, she was already on the island!'

The President wiped a grain of sand from his eye, 'I guess it fits. After "collecting" everybody else on the list, Graham turned America inside out to find the Jeweskis. He even placed ads at peak viewing, saying that they'd inherited a fortune. Apocalypse was about the only place that the C.I.A. didn't sieve. Yes, Graham would have been pleased that Jean turned up.'

Bronwen looked at the President, 'Would have been?'

'Graham Harris died from a heart attack, ten days ago.'

Taking a step up the beach to avoid a breaking wave, Bronwen said, 'I'm sorry to hear of Graham's death, he was a good man.'

The President shrugged, 'When the chips are counted, he hasn't lost much. One month maybe, unless your last planet tells us otherwise.' He looked at Bronwen, willing her to say that she'd fitted the ninth planet and the nightmare was over. But all she answered was, 'We're hoping to get a fit on Pluto within days.'

Grimly, the President paused before continuing, 'We may not have days, it's getting hotter each second out there. Listen, I'm not going to kid around with you people, everything's coming apart. The Chinese are planning to attack Russia any day now. Who knows, maybe they've already done it, communications aren't reliable anymore. And you know what else? The British want N.A.T.O. to back the Chinese, to a "limited" extent. They're crazy.'

The President looked a tired and broken man as he said, 'The top brass at the Pentagon have driven themselves crazy playing wargames on the computer, but the result's always the same. If a conventional war starts, the side that's losing throws a couple of battlefield nukes to stop the advance. The enemy doesn't like it, so they do the same. Within hours, the whole goddam thing escalates and bingo, ICBM's are on their way.' Pointing to a red phone in the dinghy, he said 'One day, and I mean one day soon, that damn thing is going to ring and then I've got four minutes to decide what I'm going to do.'

The President paused, 'As soon as you've fitted the final planet, break radio silence and tell me the result. As long as the transmission is short, the Russians won't be able to trace it.'

Father McGrath broke the awkward silence, 'Pardon my saying so sir, but is that really such a good idea....'

The President smiled wearily, 'I get it, you think I might try to get the drop on the Russians, right? Look, I'm playing it straight, if the programme says the worst, I'm going to try one last gamble. I'm going to tell the Russians everything, except about Apocalypse....'

Bronwen exploded, 'That's the most bloody stupid thing I've heard in my whole life! What do you think they'll do if they believe you?'

The President smiled, 'You're the last person I thought would say that. Let me finish. I've been doing some serious thinking lately...'

'And?,' queried Bronwen.

‘I’ve decided that half a world is better than none. So if the programme says the holocaust happens, I’m going to order our missiles to stand down.’

Bronwen’s mouth fell open, ‘I think you really mean it.’

‘Oh, believe me I do, but don’t think I like it. My first instinct is to go down with all guns blazing, but I’ve never let pride get the better of my humanity or commonsense. Besides, if I’m going to face my maker ten seconds after the holocaust then I don’t want half the world on my conscience.

‘There is a problem though. Contrary to what we tell the public, most of our systems retaliate automatically if Russian warheads hit the mainland. Then there’s the problem of our so-called deterrent missiles away from U.S. soil, like the nuclear subs and the fighter bombers in Europe. The bottom line is that although I’ve “promoted” most of the Pentagon Hawks sideways, where they can’t foul things up, it’ll still take a least twenty-four hours to disarm down to twenty-five per cent strength. But I’m not going to do anything this drastic unless it really is the last resort. So as soon as you know, tell me, d’you hear.’

Father McGrath nodded, ‘You have my word on it sir, and may God bless you for your decision.’

The President gave the priest a grateful smile, ‘Now what’s the situation here?’

‘Everything’s under control sir,’ said Father McGrath. ‘All essential supplies have been unloaded and the construction work is completed.’

The President cleared his throat, ‘I guess you people are wondering what happens next. The Hudson will be here on August 1st with the rest of the survivors and the animals. I’ve seen them and I can tell you, it’s hard to say which is the weirdest collection. You’ll see what I mean when the ship arrives.’

He seemed to be looking at Bronwen when he said, ‘I’ve worked with lots of scientists over the years and it’s been my experience that the only way to make them follow an order is to prod their ass with a bayonet. But I’m going to give you an order anyhow. Lock everyone in the jail I had built.’

Father McGrath began to protest, but the President merely held up his hands, ‘I know you don’t like it, but until this nightmare is over, one way or the other, it’s the only way that you’ll keep order here. Do you still have your gun?’

‘Yes sir, it’s with my uniform.’

‘Good. I respect your beliefs, Father, but use that gun on anyone who puts this island in danger. And as for Victor Poplenko, toss him in solitary and then throw away the key.'

Staring inland, the President asked, 'Is the crate safe?' Father McGrath gestured towards the overhang. The President shaded his eyes and said with a satisfied smile, 'Must be the highest point on the island. The perfect location.'

The Priest hung his head, 'I just pray it's never opened.'

'Amen to that. We've all failed if those two catches ever get flicked. But should it come down to that, flick them fast and I mean like instantly. Okay?'

The President looked at his watch, 'It's time I was getting back to the sub.' After shaking hands warmly with everyone he said, 'If it isn't in God's plan that we meet again, I pray that he watches over Apocalypse until your descendents have built a sane, new world.' He looked at the Professor, 'Will you walk with me, Frank?'

The two men made their way to where the dinghy lay wallowing in the surf. The President motioned for the two marines to move out of earshot before saying, 'The real reason I'm going so soon, Frank, is that I can't bear saying goodbye to my daughters. I'd like to be able to say it's to spare their feelings, but the fact of the matter is, I just haven't got the guts.'

He paused briefly, 'I want you to look after them Frank..... they're good girls and they'll miss their mother. God knows she'll miss them.'

The Professor laid his hand on the President's shoulder, 'They'll be safe here, don't worry.'

It was clear that the President was on the point of tears, 'I know I've been talking a lot about saving the world Frank, and if I can I will, God judge me on that, but as long as they're okay, I still feel ahead of the field. If that makes me a selfish bastard.....' He choked on the words and with that, he climbed into the boat, the marines returned to their positions and the boat pulled away towards the waiting submarine.

As Frank Cooper watched him go, he thought of Ian and said under his breath, 'No, Mr. President, that just makes you a human being.'

As the small group watched the President's dinghy heading back towards the submarine, a worried man was impatiently drumming his fingers in front of a telephone in Washington. Richard Stroud had only managed ten hours sleep in the last three days and his normally immaculate appearance was fraying around the edges. But he had finally made his decision. Purposefully, he picked up the phone, 'Priority call to Piotr Nicholovich, Moscow, please.' He replaced the receiver and activated the scrambler fitted to the phone. 'At least there'll be no spying on this call,' he thought.

For months, Stroud had suspected that something strange was going on. At first it was just small things, juniors not being quite as respectful as they had been, or typists stopping work as he walked past. After ignoring the signs for a time, it eventually became transparently obvious that a major conspiracy was taking place and, to make matters worse, it was Hughes and the President who were behind it! But with Hughes dying from a heart attack, and the President going missing on some hush-hush trip, things had finally come to a head. Now the 'weird reports' were at last finding their way to his desk, yet without anyone to brief him, they didn't make any sense. However, one thing was for sure, the world was smouldering on a powder keg and it was his duty to diffuse it.

At that moment, Stroud's thoughs were interrupted by the phone ringing. He picked up the receiver and a female voice said softly, 'Your call to Moscow, sir.'

There was a moment's pause before he heard the coarse accent of Piotr Nicholovich, the head of the K.G.B. 'Richard my friend, how are you?'

'Fine. And you?'

'I fear I am getting old, but that comes to all of us. How are little Victoria and Elizabeth?'

'Vicky's had to miss school with a cold, but everyone's fine.'

'Good. Tell me Richard, what can I do for you?'

There was a slight pause before Stroud answered, 'To tell the truth Peter, I was wondering if you could give me some information.'

'Information? Of what kind?'

There was another pause, more awkward than the last. 'Well, there have been some crazy rumours flying around.'

'Rumours?'

'That there was a lot of...activity in Europe, even the Soviet Union itself.'

'Well, Richard, it is true that there have been some mysterious disappearances...'

'You don't think that we...'

'Of course not, Richard. If there had been any problems, you know that I would have discussed them with you. With the situation the way it is, I attach great importance to our close liason.'

'Believe me, Peter, I also value our working relationship, especially when the President himself seems to be at the centre of the screw-up.'

'Your President sounds much like my Chairman. Not very informative, eh.'

'You know Peter, often I'm the last person to be told anything.'

The Russian laughed, 'Your President sounds much like my Chairman indeed. We have everything in common, you and I.'

'Sometimes I think you're the only person I can get a straight answer out of.'

'Tell me Richard, what kind of activity has been going on?'

'Meetings with the Chiefs of Staff, a lot of reports being issued, that kind of thing.'

'Exactly what type of reports do you mean, Richard?'

There was a pause, 'Current troop deployments, studies on the minimum time for strategic weapon mobilisation. Jesus, lately we seem to be crowded out with military planners and systems analysts!'

'Really. How long has this been going on?'

'Ever since I let some kind of history professor, called Frank Cooper, get in to see the President.'

'A history professor? That seems rather strange.'

'That's what I thought, but since that first meeting, he's had priority clearance to contact the President, day or night. I just don't understand it.'

'It does seem to be a mystery, Richard. Would you like me to look at it over here?'

Stroud breathed an audible sigh of relief, 'I'd be very grateful, Peter, you don't know what it's been like. . .'

'Of course, Richard, sometimes I find it hard to keep track of events myself. I will call you soon.'

Stroud felt more calm now that he'd acted 'positively' and for a while he just sat there relaxing. But his mood gradually began to change and as the call to Moscow started to play back through his mind, over and over again, a terrible realisation swept over him. He leaned forward on his elbows, both hands covering his face, and muttered, 'Oh, Jesus, I hope I've played this right.'

Unaware of events in Washington, the President gave a final wave of his hand from the conning-tower, before disappearing from view. Soon the vessel had submerged for its voyage back to Hawaii. Ian touched his father's arm, 'That's another prophecy notched up. Do you remember the one?'

The Professor nodded, '"Both weapons and orders are enclosed in a metal fish. The Great One travels far but returns to whence he came." Yes Ian, it's still happening exactly the way that Nostradamus said it would.'

'Where's Daddy?' repeated Mandy, the eldest of the President's daughters. While everyone had been looking out to sea, Jean and Demetri had returned with the three young girls.

Mary kneeled on the sand and said, 'Your father's had to leave for the White House. But before he left, he told us to tell you that he loves you all very much and he will come back with Mommy in September.'

Bernardette, the youngest girl, started to cry, 'I don't like being away from Mommy and Daddy.'

Mary picked up the little girl, 'Do you want to see some baby parrots? I know where there's a nest.' Soon, while the President's submarine was passing unnoticed beneath the waters of the Pacific, his daughters were arguing about which baby parrot had the most colours.

Within days of the President's departure, tranquility re-established itself on the island, with the only disturbing feature being the ominous news bulletins from the outside world. Then July was gone and the first rays of August dawned on Apocalypse. From his lookout point on the overhang, Ian noted a telltale dot on the horizon, which Father McGrath's fieldglasses revealed to be the Hudson, jutting through the water at full speed for the island.

Within an hour, the vessel was swaying at anchor outside the reef and its captain was stepping ashore. Only now did Ian realise how easy it was to lose track of which Hudson, and which crew was where. Unthinkingly Ian had expected their own Hudson's captain, and not one that was now walking up the beach towards Father McGrath.

After exchanging formalities, the captain said, 'We've brought you a hundred and ninety-two prisoners, Father, and one amazing collection of animals. They're so varied that the crew's been arguing like fury about what's happening on Apocalypse. One of my officers reckons that the Hudson's been turned into a Noah's Ark, and so he's waiting for the flood. My bet is that a new weapon's ready for testing, to find out exactly what it does to people and anim...'

The words died in the captain's throat, he had caught sight of the President's daughters, playing on the beach. The man's weatherbeaten face twisted in thought, then he said, 'That rules out the weapon theory, which only leaves the flood....'

Having vainly searched the faces of the islanders for a clue to the real purpose of Apocalypse, the captain shrugged and said, 'Anyway, my orders are to high-tail it away from the island at maximum speed by noon, so I'd better start briefing you. First, the humans. They're the strangest people I've ever seen, half of them spend the day reading the Bible or reciting the Koran, the other half just sit there crying. God knows what crimes these people committed but the President has ordered maximum security.'

The captain paused and stroked his chin, 'Pardon the language, Father, but I guess I should warn you that there is one evil bastard on board, a Russian named Poplenko. He broke out of his cell three nights ago and tried to strangle the radio operator. Luckily for everyone except Poplenko, an officer heard the scuffle and clubbed him from behind!'

After prisoners of every race had been imprisoned in the stockade, the Hudson's crew began ferrying the animals ashore. 'That is one weird collection of wildlife,' said Ian to his father as a pygmy hippo dragged a distraught sailor across the wet sand, 'who selected *them* for survival?'

'It wasn't a who.' Ian looked confused so his father said, 'How were we selected for survival?'

'Now I get it, TITAN again?'

The Professor nodded, 'TITAN kept on adding animals to Apocalypse's existing population until a viable eco-system was created.'

Once everything was secure, Father McGrath signed the transfer document and soon the ship was nothing more than a receding dot on the horizon. Mary asked, 'What'll happen to the Hudson, Father?'

The Priest took Mary's hand, 'It's heading for the anchorage inside the blind zone, to wait further orders.'

Looking down at the sand, Mary said, 'It's all so futile, a ship and its crew, waiting for orders that will never come.'

Bronwen tossed the fieldglasses to Ian, 'I'll tell you what'll happen to the Hudson,' she snapped, 'the crew won't know what hit them or where it came from! Anything in the water will be some fool's target, with the subs being the first to get blasted by missiles from land, sea and air, but not before they've fired their own missiles at other poor bastards. But at least the ships which are incinerated quickly will have the lucky crews, because the stinking fallout from the land war will drift thousands of miles out into the ocean. And any crew that's dumb enough to escape the missiles and the fallout, will still get their share when they put into some bacteria infested port!'

That very afternoon, the islanders began releasing the animals at places where they could thrive and multiply. Riding behind Mary on the largest zebra of a herd they were escorting to the central planes, Ian said, 'I've never seen animals as tame as these.'

Mary squeezed his hand, 'Maybe they've been hand-picked too?'

However, Demetri and Jean found greater difficulty in shepherding an unruly collection of anteaters to their computer designated habitat.

It was early evening when the process of freeing the animals entered its final phase; sitting on the steps, Father McGrath confided to the Professor how he wished that they were also releasing the human prisoners. The Professor shook his head, 'If we were opening the prison gates, it would mean that the holocaust had happened!'

The days on Apocalypse continued to pass uneventfully until Wednesday August 26th. With the sun directly overhead, Bronwen burst into Father McGrath's house, 'Without Demetri's help, I could never have done it! The boy's a genius!'

Apprehensively, the Priest asked, 'Done what?'

Waving a printout in the air, Bronwen shouted, 'Done what? We've fitted Pluto into the equations!'

On hearing this, the blood drained from Father McGrath's face, 'As each day has passed safely, I've thanked God and prayed for September. But now the project is finally complete, it's like a death sentence hanging over mankind.' He paused and said falteringly, 'I'm not sure that we should run the programme.'

Bronwen placed her hand on the Priest's shoulder, 'No disrespect, Father, but bullshit! We've come too far along this road to quit now. It's like the song says "Que sera, sera; whatever will be, will be."

Deep down, Father McGrath marvelled at the woman. Her own fate hung by the same thread as the rest of humanity, yet the mathematical logic that she believed in left her no room for appeal. Father McGrath glanced at the crucifix on the wall, 'I suppose it all comes down to a question of trust. I gave the President my word that we would run the programme; if a man doesn't keep his word, what has he got left?'

'Okay,' said Bronwen, 'it will take me all afternoon to code the programme, therefore I'll expect you at six.'

That evening, when the islanders were gathered round the bio-computer, Bronwen said, 'This machine may be a masterpiece of miniaturisation but it doesn't have TITAN's speed. It'll take six hours to calculate if the holocaust happens.'

'Six hours!' gasped Ian, 'Isn't there some quicker way to test it?'

Bronwen rustled Ian's hair affectionately, 'I can always rely on you to say the right thing. Finding out if I survive only takes thirty minutes.'

Without further discussion, Bronwen typed a brief set of instructions into the computer and then walked towards the door. Ian took hold of her arm, 'Where are you going, for Christ's sake?'

'You don't think I'm going to sit here while that thing calculates my fate? Anyway, it's time to relieve your father at the prison.'

She opened the door, but paused and turned to Father McGrath. 'Dr. Johnson once said "When a man knows he's going to be hanged at dawn, it concentrates his mind wonderfully." That just goes to show how much the bloody English know.'

Bronwen slammed the door and began the short walk to the prison. The Professor had been listening to the radio on the steps but he stood as the woman approached, 'Hi, Bron, it's good of you to come five minutes' early.'

Bronwen smiled, 'I wasn't doing anything important.'

Pointing to a book lying open on the second step, the Professor said, 'I've never known a night as bright as this, it's good enough to read by.'

Glancing at the night sky, Bronwen said, 'It's the inner planets; Venus, Earth, Mars and the Moon are lining up to within a second of arc. But what I can't figure is that the conjunction is scheduled for tomorrow, yet I'd swear it was happening now.'

Picking up his book, the Professor said, 'Forget the conjunction and update me on the situation with the programme?'

Bronwen smiled bravely 'There's a boring trial run taking place now; if it works, we can test for the holocaust tomorrow.'

All the nights on Apocalypse were perfect, with August 26th being no exception. Soothed by a warm comforting breeze, Bronwen sat on the steps listening to the news bulletins from the B.B.C. And between the worsening statements, a New Orleans jazz band filled the air. Although the music brought some comfort to most of the detainees inside the prison, it did nothing for Victor Poplenko.

The Russian was still confused by the events that had started when he was asleep in his Moscow flat. Two men had burst in and clamped a chloroform pad over his face. The next thing he remembered was waking up in a damp cellar, before being rattled across Russia in the back of an old truck. Although he'd vomited every day on the first sea voyage, this had been nothing compared to the stifling heat of a week, with little water, in a Singapore basement. If that American hadn't clubbed him from behind on the second ship, he'd have killed the operator and radioed Moscow what was happening.

But he hadn't warned Moscow and now he was rotting in some kind of asylum with two hundred religious fanatics. Maybe the sheer illogicality of the events was all part of an American plan to send him insane, or make him think that everything was a dream?

When the jazz faded to make way for a news bulletin, Victor Poplenko's command of English made him forget his own plight. 'This is the B.B.C. World Service. There is increasing tension in Europe, with workers' riots being reported in Warsaw and Budapest. ----Eyewitness statements say that Russian soldiers have fired on civilians in Czechoslovakia. ---Washington reports that satellite surveillance of the Sino-Soviet border reveals massive troop movements on both sides. ---The Indian Premier dismissed claims of an invasion of Pakistan's border as propaganda. ---Full-scale hostilities are reported between Iran and Saudi Arabia...' As the announcer continued to describe a world on the verge of war, Victor Poplenko resolved that his duty was to warn Moscow about the American base where he was being held prisoner.

While the K.G.B. man was pursuing his thoughts of freedom, a short distance away, the islanders were silently gazing at a sheet jutting out of the printer. 'What's wrong?' asked the Professor entering the room.

Father McGrath placed his hand on the man's shoulder, 'Do you know what that paper contains?'

'Sure, Bronwen told me it was a "boring trial run.".'

'Wrong,' said Ian in a low voice, 'it's Bron's future.'

The seconds continued to tick away then Father McGrath said, 'Someone's got to look at it sometime.'

The Priest tore off the printout and read its message, then he passed it to the Professor. Praying for a miracle, the Professor made his eyes focus on the bottom line.

'What does it say?' asked Ian apprehensively. 'Bronwen doesn't survive,' answered his father in a barely audible voice.

Engulfed by an overpowering despondency, Ian stammered, 'Who...what do we do now?'

Mary placed her hand on Ian's, 'Bronwen would expect to be told.'

Looking at Ian, Father McGrath said, 'You and Bronwen are close friends, go to the prison and ask her to come to the house.'

With tears clouding his eyes, Ian stepped into the night. With each successive step on that short journey, Ian's emotions grew ever more contorted. The sound of jazz became louder as Ian approached the prison, yet when he reached the steps, the radio was lying on its side and there was no sign of Bronwen. At first sight, the big wooden door seemed secure but when he pushed it, the door swung open. His mind suddenly clear, Ian shone his torch along the corridors which converged at the point where he was standing. The light lit up an open door, halfway along the central corridor. Cautiously, he approached the cell and pointed his torch inside. It was empty. Now he aimed the beam at the name on the door, 'Victor Poplenko'.

Ian ran down the prison steps, then some instinct made him tear at the nearby ferns. At first he found nothing, then his foot struck something large and soft, lying passively near a tree stump. Ripping away the ferns, he reeled back in horror at the mutilated face which gazed up at him in the bright moonlight.

Although the face was brutally disfigured, there was no mistaking who had been the owner of the wiry yellow hair that was now so heavily matted with congealing blood. By the woman's head lay a jagged blood-stained rock. Ian was engulfed by sorrow but this rapidly evolved into a furious rage.

His thoughts focused for a moment, and then stealthily, he crossed the clearing to Father McGrath's house where the radio transmitter was, and like a cat stalking its prey, squeezed up close to the window.

Hearing sounds through the shutter, Ian edged along to the next room and climbed in through the window. In Father McGrath's bedroom, the room which contained the Air Force uniform and the revolver, Ian felt around until he located the wardrobe, then he opened it. Only now did he use his torch to light up the revolver; quickly he checked its condition, the gun was fully loaded.

With the revolver clutched firmly in his hand, Ian moved towards the transmitter room. Outside the door, he paused, took a deep breath and then in a single movement, kicked the door open and shone his torch inside. Victor Poplenko was seated at the transmitter, a candle burning by his hand. As the Russian spun round to confront his assailant, Ian fired point-blank at the man's face.

The bullet hit Poplenko's forehead and passed cleanly through his brain before exploding his skull on exit.

It was only after his Father had burst into the room, quickly followed by Mary, that Ian allowed the revolver to slip from his grasp. Finally, he slumped down onto the floor and wept.

CHAPTER 15

The morning of August 27th witnessed Apocalypse's first official burials, with Bronwen Jones being laid to rest near her killer, on land consecrated by Father McGrath at the island's cemetery. After Victor Poplenko's service was completed, the small congregation moved to where the Welsh woman gazed skyward from the soft soil at the bottom of her grave. Although Bronwen's face was badly mutilated, it somehow conveyed an expression of peace which had been lacking in life. This allowed the mourners to find some solace in the knowledge that the woman's labours were finally over and she would rest for eternity on the tropical paradise which her efforts had helped secure.

Mary was crying as she walked down from the hillside with Father McGrath, 'I still can't believe that Bronwen's gone. She seemed indestructible.'

Father McGrath took hold of Mary's hand, 'Bronwen's at peace with her maker, and in the final analysis, what more can any soul achieve?'

To reduce their personal sorrow, Ian and the Professor had agreed not to talk of Bronwen, therefore, they led the small procession in silence, back towards the township. At the door of what had been Bronwen's house the Professor hesitated, as if some non-human force were urging him not to enter. Yet the latch had to be lifted if the future was to be revealed, for even while the service had been taking place, the Nostradamus programme was passing judgement on humanity. Now it was ready to output the results.

Demetri brushed forward past the Professor, lifted the latch and entered the house. With less certainty, the other islanders followed Demetri inside. Now, as they stood in a circle round the console, each person was overwhelmed by a sense of helplessness in the face of mighty forces. They were merely puppets, and the final act of the play had now been written for them to act out. 'Are you sure the programme works?' asked Father McGrath.

'Certain,' replied Demetri.

Mary took a step back, 'Do you mean it's now "infallible"?' she asked softly.

Demetri shook his head violently, 'Infallible is a word my grandfather would not use!'

Raising his hand, Father McGrath said, 'We're wasting time, I'm as frightened as anyone, but the President needs to know.'

Demetri pointed to a small green light, 'That mean the Nostradamus programme stored in memory and we can now ask any questions.'

For a few lingering seconds, the islanders gazed at the green light, finally Mary's nerves could stand it no longer, 'In the name of mercy, output the damn programme and see if the holocaust happens!'

Ian took hold of her hand, it was trembling, 'Mary's right, we don't gain by waiting.'

After checking that there was no dissent, Father McGrath nodded to Demetri to type the fateful instructions. Within seconds, the programme began to output its clinical evaluation of humanity's fate beyond the reef. Fearfully awaiting the result, Mary took a step back from the console, her foot knocked the table bearing Bronwen's cigar box. The box came to rest at the Professor's feet. As a reflex action, he picked it up and opened it. Out dropped a single last cigar.

Momentarily, the islanders' attention was diverted to the cigar, then its importance was lost as the room assumed an eerie silence, the run was complete. Demetri passed the printout to Father McGrath. With the fate of the world held between his finger and thumb, the Priest mouthed a prayer. And in the few seconds that the prayer lasted, Mary's mind projected a vision of the family photograph, hanging proudly in the hall at home. This image seemed to burst into flames as Father McGrath made the sign of the crucifix and said just two words, 'It happens.'

With Mary sobbing uncontrollably in Ian's arms, the Professor studied the printout, 'Everything was in balance until last night, then the scales tipped to destruction for August 28th. It seems that as the holocaust approaches, two events make the equations go the wrong way. The first was Poplenko's death but the printout doesn't say what the second was.'

'Or is.' said Demetri.

'The name Poplenko has just given me an unpleasant thought,' said Ian.

'No point in worrying about Poplenko, now,' said the Professor.

'You're missing the point, Dad. The guy's dead, so how can he be a survivor.'

The Professor slumped down in a chair, 'Now I get it, the list of survivors is out of date.'

Ian nodded, 'So let's cross our fingers and get an update.' Soon, the Professor had the old and new lists spread open. 'Are there any changes?' Ian asked nervously.

The Professor nodded, 'You were right about Poplenko, his name's gone.'

Mary stifled a tear, 'But not soon enough to save Bron.'

Father McGrath placed his arm around Mary, 'The President always said that Poplenko had been placed on Apocalypse by the Devil.'

Ian asked, 'Are there any other changes?'

'Well, Jean's father isn't on the list. I guess the old programme must have calculated that he recovered from the blood poisoning.' The others watched silently as the Professor continued to compare the two printouts. Raising his head, he said, 'Two more names are missing.'

The room went silent then Mary asked bravely, 'Any of us?' The Professor shook his head.

'Who then?' asked Father McGrath.

'One's a father of seven children from Hong Kong, called Bruce Leung.'

'But Bruce Leung is already on Apocalypse,' protested Ian, 'he's the guy in cell thirty-four who refuses to eat.'

Demetri adjusted the solar regulator, 'Leung may be on the island but if he not on list, he not see September.'

Looking over the Professor's shoulder, Father McGrath asked, 'Who's the second person?'

'A Greek woman named Yousterdopolis doesn't make the final selection.'

Ian threw down his pencil, 'Something doesn't add up. I've counted the changes and if I'm right, there's only one hundred and ninty-eight survivors.'

'No,' said the Professor, 'two new names have been added to the list.'

'New names,?' gasped Ian incredulously, 'how can there be new names?'

Shaking his head, the Professor said, 'Don't ask me, but the names of Metcalfe and Regis are now listed with the survivors.'

Noticing that the tall trees were no longer casting shadows, Father McGrath said, 'This isn't the time to discuss Metcalfe and Regis, the President is waiting for my call.'

'That not wise,' insisted Demetri.

Father McGrath opened the door, 'Radioing Washington gives the President the chance to try his final gamble; besides, I gave him my word.'

As the Professor walked with Father McGrath to his house, each step of their journey was watched by the prisoners from their cells. The floor in front of the transmitter displayed a crimson tint, where Victor Poplenko's blood refused to be scrubbed clean. When Father McGrath seated himself at the transmitter, the Professor said, 'Demetri's right, it's insanity to break radio silence. If the Russians get a fix on us, that's the end of Apocalypse.'

Continuing to set the controls, the Priest answered, 'It's like I keep telling you, Frank, the President put me in charge because I'm a serving officer who obeys orders. Anyway, stop worrying about Apocalypse, we won't be located, unless the Russians already know where to look.'

With the transmitter set, Father McGrath spoke in a clear voice, 'Apocalypse calling the White House. Apocalypse calling the White House, come in White House.'

For a few seconds there was only the silence of empty airwaves, then a man answered, 'This is the White House. Come in Apocalypse.'

'We must speak to the President.'

'The President left instructions to put you straight through, Apocalypse.'

After a brief delay, the President's voice said, 'That you, Father McGrath?'

'It is.'

'You've run the programme?'

'Yes.'

There was a momentary pause then the President asked, 'And the result?'

'The holocaust starts tomorrow.'

The President's transmitter went sickeningly silent then he said, 'No chance of error?'

'No sir.'

'Then may God have mercy on us all!'

As the transmission continued, neither the President nor Father McGrath guessed that hostile ears were recording every syllable of their conversation. Victor Poplenko had been in the act of radioing the location of Apocalypse when Ian's bullet shattered his brain. Although the longitude of 175° had been transmitted, the latitude hadn't, but by monitoring all broadcasts along the 175° meridian, the missing latitude had been found. However, the Soviets had discovered much more than just the location of a secret American base, they'd found that a nuclear strike was callously being planned against them for tomorrow.

Pyotr Nicholovich sat thoughtfully under the portrait of Lenin. Although Stalin and Brezhnev had come and gone, with Andropov hardly staying long enough to warm the chair, it was always safe to sit under Lenin, who could argue with the ideology of the father of the revolution?

This day, however Pyotr Nicholovich was not concerned with political ideals, great men or improving his own ranking in the Politburo hierarchy. He was thinking of his grandchildren, of lost innocence and of how little death meant to a seventy-three year old man.

One day previously, his department had received a message from someone claiming to be Victor Poplenko. At first Nicholovich had not believed the communication. Although Poplenko was reputed to be a hard-liner, the best explanation for his disappearance was still defection. Moreover, the sender of the message had given only half a position. Still, standard procedure was to check out anything of conceivable importance, and since it required two forms, in triplicate, to countermand standing orders, he had given instructions to monitor all broadcasts along the 175° meridian.

One hour earlier, this very day, the monitoring had born unexpected fruit, with the source of the transmission being pin-pointed by intercepting a message to the President of the United States, from some obscure location in the Pacific. Incredibly, the message seemed to be that the Americans were about to launch a pre-emptive strike against the Soviet Union. And to complete the nightmare, everything seemed to be authentic, leaving the head of the K.G.B. with the most difficult decision of his life. If he passed the taped message to the Supreme Soviet, together with the dossier in front of him, he did not need to be clairvoyant to predict the result.

Certainly only a reckless fool would plunge the world into war on the basis of a radio message, and Pyotr Nicholovich was neither reckless nor a fool. However, there was more evidence. Nicholovich fingered the reports from his White House spy, Clive Glenn, saying that an obscure archaeology professor had seen the President on a 'matter of National Security'. And when the Professor's house was searched, confusing texts had been found, predicting a nuclear holocaust.

This same professor was next reported in charge of 'The Nostradamus Project' at a top American arms laboratory called Southwood. Then there was the phone call from the head of the C.I.A., no less, saying how this professor had unlimited access to the President and that nuclear strike strategies were being evaluated. Perhaps Stroud had been mistaken or lying, but after surviving for forty years in the Kremlin, Pyotr prided himself on being a judge of character, and he judged Stroud to be weak, naive, but honest.

True, the evidence was insubstantial in itself, with more characters than a Tolstoy novel. And why had the professor made all those journeys, seemingly without purpose? For what conceivable reason should he visit the Pope of all people, or go to Cyprus to see an old shepherd? Yet clearly there was something going on. Perhaps the 'Nostradamus weapon' was some kind of defence against Russian missiles, due to become operational tomorrow?

Certainly the world situation was deteriorating rapidly and the old nightmare of being threatened from three sides was coming true. Over the Arctic, America was bristling with a war-machine that made Hitler look like a pacifist! In the East, China had fifty million men under arms, screaming to attack. While to the West, like a hungry wolf, N.A.T.O. waited to rip out the throat of the wounded bear. No, Pyotr Nickolivich was neither reckless nor a fool, but he was a patriot and Mother Russia's back was against the wall.

Nicholovich crossed to the telephone, dialled his daughter and suggested that she take the children to his mountain cottage for a few days holiday, then with a heavy heart, he wrote his recommendations to the Chairman, placed the letter, the tape and the 'Nostradamus File' inside a big envelope and called for a messenger. Now that he was alone again, for want of anything better to do, he reclined on the sofa and played Tchaikovsky. Certainly Nicholovich appreciated the irony that while for his whole life he had considered religion a western self-indulgence, prayer was now the only course of action left open.

After the tape of the transmission had been played a dozen times within the Kremlin, with its authenticity established beyond question, the Supreme Soviet coldly calculated the options. At home, the people grew hungry, with the great food silos, once brimming with American grain, now echoing empty. On their Eastern border, the Chinese were already attacking with overwhelming conventional forces, and N.A.T.O. was poised to support the attack. Pro-Western revolutions were already succeeding in Poland and Hungary, and now they had discovered that America was planning a devastating holocaust without warning.

As the minutes ticked away, the Russians came to realise that their options numbered only two; they either capitulated or fought for survival with all the weapons in their arsenal. But to succeed, a pre-emptive strike had to be launched against the missile silos of America, N.A.T.O. and China. Only when their enemies' teeth had been drawn, could an honourable peace be negotiated from a position of strength. The strike was ordered for that very hour, at 9 a.m. Moscow time.

The first warheads to hit U.S. silos avoided radar detection by being launched from orbitting Russian satellites, but soon hordes of I.C.B.M.s were picked up, streaking towards the American mainland. These missiles were also targetted on U.S. silos, yet the Americans had no way of knowing if they were zeroed for centres of population; similarly, the Russians were unaware that American micro-technology enabled their own I.C.B.M.s to be automatically launched in less than two minutes flat, which they were.

Within seconds of Moscow detecting the approaching heat trails of the American I.C.B.M.s, a single message was flashed to the Russian submarines, nestling silently beneath the waves on America's eastern seaboard, and the wording of the message was 'FIRE'.

Now the situation that every sane man had feared since the obscenity of Hiroshima was coming to pass. Quivers of missiles, each with their allotted cargoes of mega deaths, were silently passing each other high above the Atlantic. The same grisly exchange was also taking place over the Arctic, Central Europe and East Asia. And as each warhead efficiently annihilated its target, a further wave of 'deterrence' was generated. Across the breadth of America, the blackness of the night was incessently rendered more brilliant than a million suns as each gargantuan explosion extracted its horrendous toll. As Bronwen had foretold, the lucky families were vaporised as they slept!

The war was twenty-three minutes old, and already approaching its insane peak, when the first news bulletin was picked up on Apocalypse, 'It's started!' gasped Father McGrath in despair. 'The cretins have brought the holocaust a day forward!'

With a mixture of horror and revulsion, the islanders clustered round the radio, listening to the reports of carnage. Less than an hour had passed since that first warhead annihilated Omaha Command Centre, yet deaths were already being measured in hundreds of millions. Now the escalation was complete as both sides, in a lemming-like frenzy, unleashed every weapon still in their arsenal.

The initial broadcasts retained some comic, tragic overtones of the Cold War, with countries still trying to gain a meaningless propaganda advantage, but as the full horror of Armageddon became manifest, the programmes evolved through a phase of advising citizens on how to save the unsaveable, to nothing more than the repeated playing of national anthems. On several occasions, the islanders were actually listening to a station when a screech over the airways testified that its city had ceased to exist. The Pope himself was in the act of broadcasting a prayer for sanity, when an uncaring warhead rendered the Eternal City eternal no more. With the remnants of humanity going through their death throes, Father McGrath crouched in front of the radio, tears streaming down his face.

The transmitter bell started to ring, 'It's the President,' said Ian, 'he wants to speak to you, Father.' The Priest slumped down at the controls.

'Is that you, Father?' said the President's voice.

'Yes.'

'It's happening, just like you said it would. I was trying to get Moscow on the hot-line, at one minute past midnight on the 28th, when those insane Russians blasted Omaha Command Centre!'

Father McGrath's palms went wet, 'Wha...what date did you say?'

'The 28th, Father.'

'It...it's only the 27th of August here.'

'So what, you're on the other side of the date line.'

Mary collapsed in tears, 'We caused it' she sobbed, 'We caused the war!'

Taking Mary in his arms, the Professor said, 'The computer's time base must still be set to Southwood. The Russians picked up the transmission and decided to strike a day early, except it was already the 28th!'

Father McGrath looked towards heaven as he said, 'Bronwen's worst nightmare has happened. *We completed the circle*!'

'I don't have time to understand what you people are saying!' yelled the President's voice, 'is the crate opened yet?'

The Priest hesitated, 'Not yet.'

'Then in God's name do it now!' yelled the President. 'The Russians have a fix, so they're certain to send some missiles your way. If you don't want Apocalypse to go the same way as the rest of us, get the damn system operational!'

As Father McGrath ran from the house, the President's voice continued to come over the receiver, 'When Air Force One was taking off, a Russian missile blasted Washington. We managed to get into the air but my aides reckon it was a neutron bomb and the radiation will kill us within the hour. If this is the last message you get from me, take good care of my children, d'ya hear?'

The Professor switched off the set and turned round; only now did he see the President's daughters, and from the expressions on their faces, they had been in the room for some time. The eldest girl was sobbing in Jean's arms; mercifully, the other two hadn't understood what was happening, only that it was something sad and it involved Daddy.

Not knowing what to say to the girls, the Professor blurted, 'Ian and I will run on ahead to the overhang to see if Ken needs help, the rest of you follow with the children.'

When Ian reached the overhang, the Professor was trailing hundreds of yards behind. The crate was already hinged open and Father McGrath was seated at a control panel, intently looking at a screen. Behind the controls, the nose cones of three small missiles pointed skyward from a mobile launcher. Ian was about to speak, when Father McGrath thumped a red button.

Instantly, a missile hurtled into the air, leaving a whispy trail in the early evening sky. Twenty seconds elapsed, then a brilliant fireball rose above the horizon, slowly evolving into a white hot mushroom.

The Priest wiped his forehead, 'The wind's away from us, the fallout won't come this...' Father McGrath didn't finish the sentence, another ominous dot had appeared on the screen. After a momentary hesitation, the Priest brought his fist crashing down on the red button. With a deafening roar, the second missile locked onto its interception trajectory.

This time, only seventeen seconds elapsed before another

blinding flash appeared over the horizon. 'Th...they're multi-megaton warheads, Ian. If one gets through, there won't be any island!'

Ian looked nervously at the remaining missile, 'You've only got one left!'

The Priest nodded, 'Let's pray that we don't need more.'

While they watched the radar screen, the two men were joined by the Professor and the other islanders. Without warning, the thunderous shockwave from the first thermo-nuclear explosion engulfed Apocalypse. Seconds later, the ear-shattering blast from the second fireball traversed the hundred mile gap between the interception point and the island.

This shockwave was of such ferocity that the President's youngest daughter was swept screaming towards the cliff edge. All seemed lost, until the Professor grabbed tight hold of the girl's dress and shielded her from the hurricane with his body.

The people on the overhang were not the only ones terrified by the gargantuan explosions. In the stockade, the passive detainees had been equally awe-struck by the events and now, as a raging mob, they ripped open their cell doors and streamed out of the prison in the direction of the overhang.

For some minutes, Father McGrath's attention was distracted from the screen by the turmoil in the camp below, until a high-pitched screech from the console brought his eyes rivetting back. The priest went rigid at the sight of a large dot on the scope, zeroing in on the island at ferocious speed. Ian waited for the launch of the third missile but Father McGrath remained rooted to the spot.

When Ian leapt forward and banged the red button, the trace was already much closer than the previous two. With a roar, the final rocket streaked from the overhang on an interception path. This time, only ten seconds elapsed before an all-consuming brightness filled the horizon. Although the detonation had taken place over fifty miles away, the onlookers had to shield their eyes from the blinding intensity of the light.

Father McGrath placed a grateful hand on Ian's shoulder, 'That was the first time I've frozen under fire.'

While everyone's attention had been fixed on the missile, the prisoners from the stockade had reached the overhang. 'Don't look now,' said Ian, 'but guess what's coming. If these guys are pacifists, how come I feel like General Custer?'

As the prisoners advanced menacingly towards the small group, the Professor pulled the revolver from the pocket where he had lodged it the previous night. Yet now that he brandished the gun, he wasn't sure what to do with it. In his whole life, he had never considered the possibility of shooting someone; he didn't even know how to release the safety catch.

Father McGrath had no such indecision. 'That's mine, I believe.' he said, taking the revolver. On seeing the weapon, the prisoners hesitated marginally before continuing their advance.

At that moment, the siren screeched into a deafening whine. Thinking that another missile, and its cargo of destruction, was heading for the island, Father McGrath made the sign of the cross. But at the last instant, he realised what was happening and acted without conscious thought. 'Get down!' he yelled, 'flat on your faces!'

The shock wave from the third explosion had been immeasurably reduced during its fifty mile ocean rampage yet it still struck the island like a piledriver. The islanders clung like limpets to the rock face, all except Bruce Leung, who chose to remain standing and take the full impact. The tumult lasted only seconds, yet it was enough time for the trees facing the blast to be wrenched from their roots. Miraculously, all the islanders survived, except for Bruce Leung, who had been swept away like a matchstick in a hurricane.

In a daze, the prisoners rose to their feet and wiped the dust from their eyes. But once their emotions had passed through shock and relief, they became angry and started to jeer their former captors, then someone threw a stone, which struck Mary on the arm.

Father McGrath raised the revolver and fired three shots over the heads of the mob. Then, after holding the weapon high for all to see, he turned and threw it over the cliff, 'Brothers and Sisters,' he yelled loudly, 'there is no place for weapons here. Even now, the world around us is dying. Soon, we few will be the sole survivors of mankind, therefore, the luxury of slaughtering ourselves is a price we can no longer afford. All life is precious and we dare not squander it.

'The war that was dreaded for so long has come to pass and we, like Noah before us, have been chosen to perpetuate mankind and carry on the work of God. You deserve an explanation as to why you are here. My friends, I swear you will have it, but first let us pray together as one. Protestant and Catholic, Hindu and Buddhist, for as the Koran says, "there is only one God".'

Father McGrath sank to his knees. There was a pause although short, it was still long enough for a million to die. Then, one by one, the people began to pray, each according to his custom.

When the prayer was completed, Father McGrath started to recount the events that had led to the holocaust. As everyone listened in stunned silence, not quite believing what they heard, an ear-piercing scream broke the air. Before anyone could stop her, a young woman rushed forward and threw herself over the cliff edge. Five seconds later, Nana Yousterdopolis joined her husband and children in oblivion.

Even amidst four billion deaths, the smashed body of a woman on the rocks below made the people turn away in horror. After saying a prayer for the dead woman, Father McGrath lead the islanders down from the overhang and back to the township. Now, with the radio turned on full, the people wept as they listened to the death throes of civilisation. And to add to the horrific broadcasts from the cities, the long night was incessantly punctuated by pleas from airline pilots, begging to be told a safe place to land.

Slowly a picture emerged of what had happened. The first hundred, multimegaton, explosions had saturated the atmosphere with radiation, thereby destroying the guidance systems of missiles still in flight. The result was that the remaining thirty thousand nuclear warheads fell randomly amongst the nations of the Earth, with no country being spared. Friend, foe or neutral, all received their quota of destruction.

At first, it was only the awesome nuclear explosions that brought the devastation; but now it was the turn of the biological and chemical warheads to reap their harvest. Made worse by each explosion, and gases dispersed over the surface of the land.

When the dawn of August 28th finally came to Apocalypse, only a scattering of islanders emerged from their houses. The rest were locked in private sorrow or valiantly trying to come to terms with their new life. Father McGrath had not slept and now he touched the Professor's arm. 'Come on Frank, we've a job to do.'

The Professor stretched, 'Job?'

Father McGrath nodded, 'It's going to give me immense pleasure to put a hammer through that damn computer.' When they arrived at what had been Bronwen's house, however, the job the had already been done for them. The bio-computer lay smashed in a thousand pieces; with the same bloodstained rock which had been used to kill Bronwen, jutting out of its centre.

Mary had been sitting with her head bowed but now she looked at the two men, 'That evil machine caused the death of my whole family, now the future's back where it should always have been, in God's hands.'

As the days passed, the scattered transmissions from the remnants of humanity grew ever more rare, until on the morning of September 1st, silence prevailed across all the wavebands. Apocalypse and its inhabitants were all that remained. Professor Cooper found Ian seated at the transmitter, randomly trying one setting after another, always with the same result—silence. 'Let's face it, Ian, that transmitter's the most obsolete item on Apocalypse.'

Spinning the dial, Ian said, 'Okay, but I still can't figure out what happened to the last two survivors, Metcalfe and Regis.'

His father shook his head, 'I guess we'll never know but there are only one hundred ninety-eight people on Apocalypse. If those two people really exist, they're someplace else.'

With the real task of survival only just beginning, leaders were elected to write a constitution for Apocalypse and to plan for the centuries which seemed to stretch endlessly ahead. On September 3rd, Father McGrath was chairing a meeting of the 'Elders' when Ian burst into the room, 'You'd better come with me. We're picking up a transmission from somewhere!'

On the short walk to the house, Ian explained how he'd been about to strip down the transmitter, when habit made him give the frequency dial a last spin. That was when he'd heard someone's voice.

The Professor looked up from the transmitter when they entered the room, 'It's weird, I've got their frequency but the source of the signal keeps changing position.' He switched on the mike, 'Come in come in, do you read?'

Over the interference, an American voice exclaimed, 'Jesus Christ, you want your asses kicked blue Houston for keeping quiet so long. What the hell's been happening down there, it seemed like the whole world was blowing up then all we got was one almighty crackle across every waveband. Anyway, thank God you're safe, so for pity's sake jet up here with that goddammed shuttle!'

As these words died away, the islanders' jubilation changed to horror as the real situation became clear. Father McGrath felt a pain in his gut, 'Get that mike switched off, we don't want them to hear this. Because we're using a military transmitter they think that we're Houston. Oh God, how do we tell them the truth?'

Ian slumped down, 'What a bum trick. Those poor guys survived the holocaust and now there's no way to get them down.'

'But. . . but there must be a way,' pleaded Mary, 'they're listed as survivors.'

The Professor shook his head, 'Now that September's arrived, the prophecy has been fulfilled and everybody's on his own.'

Father McGrath turned on the mike, 'You people up there, is it Metcalfe and Regis?'

A worried voice came back, 'Hey, what's the confusion, Houston? This is Ben Metcalfe, Moses Space Lab, now identify yourself and spell out what's going on.'

While Father McGrath searched for the right words, Metcalfe spoke again, 'Don't keep going silent on us, Houston, you're our only link with the world, so for Christ's sake say something!'

Father McGrath said gently, 'Brace yourselves for what I'm going to say. We are the only people left alive on Earth, and we're speaking from a tiny island in the Pacific.'

'For Christ's sake, are you saying that Houston's gone?'

'Not just Houston, everything was destroyed in the holocaust.'

'Then why couldn't we have gone up with the rest of creation?'

Only the crackle of static was heard for some minutes then Metcalfe said, 'I've just drugged Regis. He was acting like a wild man. Lucky they issued us cyanide with the rest of our kit—at least it'll be quick. Anything is better than looking down on a dead planet and waiting for the air to run out...'

Mary grabbed hold of the mike, 'Don't give up, there's still hope...'

'Hope! Listen lady, if you know a way out of this hell then tell us and we'll bust a gut trying it.'

Mary hesitated, 'Well--can't you try for a landing?'

'Are you kidding? We're hundreds of miles high, no engines and no heat shields, the whole world's a stinking mess except for a dot in the Pacific, and you say "try for a landing." Even if some miracle took us out of orbit, remember what happened to the first sky lab when it fell back to Earth, they took the remains home from Canada in a *briefcase*. Let's face it lady, not even Flash Gordon could pull out of this one. I'd accepted death before hearing your fool voice, then your goddamm transmission made me think we stood a prayer, now you turn out to be a bunch of well-meaning amateurs in the Pacific. Listen, do us all a favour and put a hammer through that transmitter, I've got work to do.' As the listeners looked at each other hopelessly, the radio transmitter returned to its customary crackle.

* * *

With the passage of each day, Ian noticed how Mary was growing more silent. On the evening of September 5th, when they were sitting alone on the prison steps, he said, 'Okay, spit it out, what's wrong?'

Mary refused to answer at first but then she said, 'I keep having the same weird dream that nothing's happened out there. New York's still standing and my family's alive.'

Ian shook his head, 'That's crazy and you know it.'

'Why's it crazy? Apart from a few radio broadcasts, what real proof do we have that the holocaust actually happened?'

Ian grasped Mary's hand, 'You've got me real worried, y'know. I've been watching you for days and you haven't eaten a single thing. The only way to make you snap out of this is to prove that Apocalypse is all that's left.'

Mary looked dismissively at Ian, 'Don't use a word like "proof" unless you can back it up.'

'Okay,' said Ian, 'I wanted to spare you this; if you saw New York in ruins, would that be proof?'

Opening her eyes wide, Mary gasped, 'Saw? How?'

Ian hesitated, 'Well, unless I figure it wrong, the screen on the rocket launcher was designed to link in with spy satellites, I saw the control setting when I was up there. So if it's that important, we can go to the overhang before anyone's awake and try it out.'

'It is that important, to me.'

Dawn was approaching Apocalypse when Ian met Mary on the prison steps. Edging their way through the undergrowth, Ian said, 'I quizzed Dad last night on whether the screen could be used to see the world out there.'

'And?'

'He reckoned it could but advised me not to try it. He said that the screen was the last link with the past and it should have been pushed over the cliff edge after the third missile was fired. Destroying the launcher is his number one task for today.'

The sun was already above the horizon when they reached the overhang. Ian switched on the set and turned the dial to 'satellite surveillance'. The screen lit up, with a list of names and control settings. Noting the co-ordinates, Ian set the controls and an image appeared. Looking blankly at the screen, Mary gasped, 'What's that supposed to be?'

'Moscow!'

Mary stared in disbelief, 'I...it looks like the surface of the

Moon. That big crater must be five miles across and a mile deep.'

Ian nodded, 'Targets like Moscow attracted multiple strikes. America, Britain, France and China each sent enough warheads to be certain that some got through, so the crater just got deeper.'

Ian looked at Mary, 'Are you sure that you still want to see New York?' Mary nodded slowly. 'Okay, then brace yourself while I dial the co-ordinates.' When another image came into view, Ian said, 'That's New York, Mary. Or where New York used to be.'

Mary looked incredulously at the screen. By this time, she had resigned herself to seeing extinct skyscrapers but not this sight. 'Th... there isn't even any sign of Coney Island!' she gasped.

'So much for civil defence,' muttered Ian.

Mary wiped her eyes, 'Well, that's my dream gone,' she said bravely, 'don't look at any more cities, they must have been hit like New York and Moscow but a place the size of Africa can't have disappeared.'

After Ian had managed to lock onto another satellite, Africa seemed quite normal. There were no bomb craters or outward signs of devastation; however, when the camera zoomed in for a close-up, death was everywhere. Yet in a contest terminally weighted against success, some life still clung tenaciously to existance. Even as they watched the screen, the last elephant of a once great herd, perhaps the last elephant on Earth, sank onto its hind legs. Then, with its trunk thrashing a final gesture of defiance, its unasked-for struggle ended. A few seconds elapsed, then Mary said, 'Your father simulated the holocaust, is the destruction of life absolute?'

Ian shook his head, 'Not absolute but near as dammit. Dad reckons that the big redwoods will fight for years before they perish, and some of the smaller animals could learn to live with the radiation. Bronwen guessed that the insects stood an even chance of mutating to the new conditions; she even wondered if there might be pockets of sub-humans out there? But one thing's for certain; wherever the wind goes, death goes with it.'

Mary nodded, 'And the wind goes everywhere.'

'Except here, hopefully.'

'Yes.'

Mary sat with her legs over the cliff edge, 'From a place as calm and beautiful as this, it's still hard to believe what has happened. God devoted four billion years to creating the beauty of the Earth, yet we needed only four days to destroy it. Bronwen was right, the world beyond the horizon will soon pass into our legends, like Atlantis.'

Kicking a pebble into the foaming waters far below, Ian said, 'You're right, if our distant descendants ever set foot on the mainland again, only God knows what they'll find. It will be like discovering a whole new planet.' He sat down next to Mary and put his arm around her shoulders, 'Let's pray that they treasure it more then we did.'